"Okay, now you can congratulate me,"
I prompted.

"Congratulations." Connor gave me a hearty pat on the back. "You are officially no longer a hostess. Which brings me to my next point: What are you doing this weekend?"

I stared at him, trying to gauge his intent. Was he asking me out?

"I'll get the new manager to cover Friday night here, and you and I can ditch this hole-in-the-wall and go celebrate your new design career." He looked at me expectantly.

He *was* asking me out. But . . .

"But you're not interested in me that way," I insisted.

"Not when you're engaged and working in my restaurant, no. But now that you're single and quitting, it's a whole other ball game." He waited a few seconds while I considered this. "Or not."

Apparently, today was National Whiplash Karmic Reversal Day and no one had marked my calendar.

FASHIONABLY LATE
is also available as an eBook.

FASHIONABLY LATE

BETH KENDRICK

New York London Toronto Sydney

An *Original* Publication of POCKET BOOKS

 DOWNTOWN PRESS, published by Pocket Books
1230 Avenue of the Americas
New York, NY 10020

Library of Congress Cataloging-in-Publication data is available.

ISBN-13: 978-0-7434-9959-0
ISBN-10: 0-7434-9959-X

This Downtown Press trade paperback edition January 2006

10 9 8 7 6 5 4 3 2 1

DOWNTOWN PRESS and colophon are trademarks of
Simon & Schuster, Inc.

Designed by Jaime Putorti

Manufactured in the United States of America

For information regarding special discounts for bulk purchases,
please contact Simon & Schuster Special Sales at 1-800-456-6798
or business@simonandschuster.com.

*For Barbara,
for everything*

Many thanks to:

Designer Kelly Nishimoto, who explained how to make a corset, where to shop in West Hollywood, and what, exactly, makes haute couture so haute.

All the friends who told me hilarious and horrifying stories about trying to make it in the Industry. You know who you are, *chicas*!

My editor, Amy Pierpont, who believes in me and challenges me and keeps me supplied with scary books about serial killers.

Chandra Years, best RWA roommate ever.

My husband, Larry, who makes a mean eighteen-dollar martini.

Susan Mallery, my fellow crazy dog lady.

Plus Megan McKeever, Irene Goodman, Anne Dowling, Kresley "Party Girl" Cole, Catherine Johnson, Meg Higgins, and the Pocket Books Art Department.

FASHIONABLY
LATE

1

I knew what was coming as soon as he handed me the teddy bear. White and fluffy, clutching a little red satin heart, this was the harbinger of Kevin's marriage proposal. No matter how I wanted to deny it, I knew, deep in the pit of my stomach, that the moment of truth had finally arrived.

"I have a surprise for you," he murmured, sitting down next to me on the inn's lace-canopied bed and pressing the bear into my hands.

"Oh . . ." I conjured up a shaky smile and tried to gaze at the bear with a reasonable facsimile of adoring, childlike whimsy. "It's so . . . cute."

"I'm glad you like it, but there's more," he said, his eyes gleaming with intensity. "This bear has a secret."

Oh no. "Oh yeah?"

"Look closely."

It could not have been more obvious that the red satin heart had been gutted and resewn; from the garish pink thread and large, uneven stitches, I'd say he did the handiwork himself. But in a desperate bid to buy some time, I feigned bewilderment, turning the bear upside down and examining the manufacturer's tag, the back of the head, the red-lined ears.

"Aw, sweetie." My voice came out thin and scratchy. "It's adorable. Listen, do you want to go grab some dinner at that little café we saw down the street?"

"In a minute." He turned the bear back over and placed my fingers on the red heart. "Look at this."

"It . . . it looks like . . ."

"There's something in there." His face lit up as he squeezed my hand. "Something special."

"Let me go grab my nail scissors." I jerked free and dashed into the hotel room's tiny bathroom. After splashing some cold water on my face, I caught my reflection in the mirror above the sink—a wild-eyed, ashen-faced woman who'd just lived through a car crash or a bank robbery. I couldn't let Kevin see me like this. He'd be devastated.

But when I emerged from the bathroom, manicure scissors in hand, he didn't seem to notice my distress. He just smiled and thrust the bear back into my arms. "Open it."

Each severed stitch brought me closer to the inevitable. *Snip. Snip.* Remember to exhale.

I could feel his hot breath in my ear, accelerating each time another stitch gave way.

Snip. Snip. The room started to spin.

Snip. The heart burst open, spilling polyurethane stuffing and a diamond ring into my lap. Before I had time to put together an appropriate response, he dropped to one knee and slipped the ring onto my finger. "Rebecca June Davis, I love you and I'll love you forever. Will you marry me?"

I looked at his face, bathed in hope and pride. I looked at our suitcases by the door, already unpacked since we were going to be at the bed-and-breakfast for three more days. And then I looked at the ring, already on my finger, and said the only thing I could say: "Um. Yes?"

2

"Holy shit." My sister Claire called from Los Angeles the instant she heard the news. "He did *what*?"

"He took me to a bed-and-breakfast in Sedona, sat me down and gave me a teddy bear with a ring hidden in the—"

"Gag. That ain't right. Do you hear me? That ain't right."

"I hear you but, you know, it's Kevin."

My boyfriend—scratch that, my *fiancé*—had given me a stuffed animal for every major celebratory occasion since we'd started dating my junior year of college. Birthdays, anniversaries, Christmases . . . my closet was a veritable menagerie of plush penguins, lions, frogs, and of course, bears. Which would have been winsome had I been the kind of girl whose hobbies involved Disney collectibles or Barbies still sealed in their original boxes. But I wasn't. And I never had been. My interests lay more along the lines of flipping through Australian *Vogue*, fabric shopping, and ransacking flea markets for vintage Dior pajamas. I suppose he kept hoping that, given sufficient exposure to Gund, I would start oohing and ahhing over the sorts of things he thought females *should* ooh and ahh over, but so far, nothing doing.

"Let me tell you a little story," Claire said. "I once dated a guy who had no money but was really fun and good-looking—this was when I was still young enough to have the luxury of dating poor people, you understand. When Valentine's Day rolled around, would you like to know what Mr. Perfect brought over to my apartment?"

I sighed. "A teddy bear?"

"A teddy bear *holding a CD*. And would you like to know what was on this CD?"

I smiled for the first time all day. "Michael Bolton songs?"

"Worse. It was a recording of him. Singing Billy Joel's 'She's Always a Woman.'"

"Wow."

"Yeah. And you know what I did?"

We said it in unison: "Dumped his sorry ass."

Which was what Claire had done to all her boyfriends until Andrew King came along. Because, along with looks, charm, and social connections out the ying yang, he *did* have lots of money.

"Life is short," my sister informed me. "I don't have time to date Cheesy McCheester, mayor of Cheeseville."

"So what are you saying? That I shouldn't have said yes?" Part of me wanted to tell her about the despair that had been welling up inside of me since I saw that ring shoved onto my finger—the crying jags in the shower, the loss of appetite. (The special "celebrity weddings" issue of *People* had induced hyperventilation. I'd had to rummage through the kitchen drawers for an actual brown paper bag.) "Because now that you bring it up, I have to tell you, I'm having a few—"

She cut me off. "I'm willing to let it slide this one time, but only because it's Kevin, a.k.a. Old Faithful."

"Yeah." My shoulders slumped. "I guess."

After years of dithering aimlessly through adolescence and early adulthood and then moving back in with my parents after college (oh, the shame!), I still didn't know exactly what I wanted out of life. But I knew what I did *not* want: to get married to Kevin.

The problem was, I had no concrete reason for this. He didn't cheat on me, didn't beat me, didn't stay out all night gambling away his rent money at the craps table. He was perfect husband material who wanted kids and already had significant retirement savings. He had purpose and direction in life, and everyone agreed I was lucky to have someone like him to steer me along the path toward suburban prosperity.

"But do you really think I'm ready to get married?" I asked.

"Of course you're ready to get married. What else are you going to do with your life?"

"Well . . . what about my design career? Phoenix isn't exactly the next Milan."

"Oh please," she scoffed. "If you were going to do something with your sewing, you would've done it by now."

I set my jaw and reminded myself that Claire could not possibly appreciate the endless hours of research, instruction, and practice I'd endured in order to start making my own design patterns. "It is more than 'sewing.' My cutting and seams are practically up to couture standards."

"I know. That's why I decided to let you make my wedding dress."

"Let me? You begged me!" And she'd been a pain in the ass about it, too, constantly changing her mind and demanding first an empire waist, then an A-line silhouette, before finally settling on a simple strapless sheath.

"Fine. Whatever. I'm just saying, don't blame Kevin because you're too scared to strike out on your own. We had this exact same conversation when you decided to go to Arizona State instead of the Rhode Island School of Design, remember?"

"Okay, that was about scholarship money, but this . . ."

"This is about a ring in a teddy bear. I hear what you're saying, but I still don't see you getting on a plane to New York or Los Angeles. I've told you a million times you should come stay with me out here, but it's one excuse after another. At least now you have someone to take care of you."

"But . . ."

"And as long as we're talking weddings, do me a favor and don't start planning yours until I'm done with mine."

"Don't worry. We haven't even set a date yet." Although Kevin was already poring over the calendar, circling Saturdays in June and July.

"Good. Because in just six short days, I'll be walking down the aisle at the Beverly Hills Hotel and I don't want anyone thinking about anything except how perfectly perfect my wedding is."

"'Perfectly perfect'?"

"That's right. The cake, the flowers, the vows, the canapés—they're all going to be perfect. Everything. All day long. Perfect."

I rolled my eyes. "Don't you think you're setting your expectations a little high?"

"Nope. I just know what I want. You've heard of Bridezilla? I make Bridezilla look like Shirley fucking Temple. And it's not like I'm expecting Mom and Dad to foot the bill—Andrew loves to spoil me and who am I to deny him? So you just make sure my dress looks perfect and don't start worrying about your own wedding till next month. Oh, and congratulations or whatever."

"Thanks a lot," I said dryly.

"Hey, you want warm fuzzies, call Gayle. She got my share of the Care Bear DNA."

Gayle, our oldest sister, now had several fancy degrees and a dark-paneled office to go along with her occupation (psychotherapist), but she had always been the mediator of our family—a good listener, a good communicator, endlessly supportive.

Which was why it was odd that I hadn't heard from her yet about my newly engaged status.

"Maybe I *will* call Gayle," I said.

"Fine, but first put Mom on the phone. She e-mailed me a photo of her dress for the rehearsal dinner and it's mauve. Mauve! If I've told her once, I've told her a million times, mauve is not the same as lavender! Why is it so hard for you people to get your act together? I don't ask for much, but . . ."

I put the phone down and headed off to find my mother. Let her deal with Mauve Watch 2006. I had problems of my own to tackle.

"We're buying a house," Kevin announced.

I choked on my final sip of white wine and signaled the bartender at Park Wines for a refill.

"Becca? Are you all right?" Kevin placed a hand on my shoulder, then turned to the approaching bartender. "She needs a glass of water."

"I'm okay," I croaked. "Really. No water needed." I scanned the list of tonight's offering and decided. "I'll try a glass of the Johannesburg Riesling, please. And keep 'em coming."

Kevin frowned. "I don't think you'll like the Riesling. It's too sweet; you prefer drier wines. Why don't you stick with what you already know you like?" He nodded to the bartender. "She'll have another glass of the Fumé Blanc. Thanks."

I smiled sweetly until the bartender was out of earshot, then whirled back to Kevin. "Darling. I've already had the blanc. I want to try something new."

"But I'm telling you that you won't like something new," he explained patiently. "You'll say it's too sweet and then you'll have wasted seven bucks. Just have the blanc again."

"I don't want the blanc again. *I want to try something new.*"

He stared at me for a long moment. "Why are you being like this?"

"Like what?"

"Difficult. Contrary. Are you upset about something?"

This was it: the perfect lead-in to tell him how I really felt. I could slip free of the paralyzing dread brought on by my new diamond ring. Taking a deep breath, I put down my wineglass. "Yes, actually, I *am* a bit upset."

He sat back on his barstool and stacked his hands under his chin with indulgent, almost paternal concern. "What's going on?"

I glanced down at the ring. "Here's the thing."

"I'm listening."

"I just . . . sometimes I just feel like I'm not . . . ready."

"For what?"

I flung out my arms. "For any of this! A ring, a husband, and now a *house*?"

He nodded. "You're surprised about the house."

"Of course! A house is huge! That's like a thirty-year financial commitment! And that's nothing compared to the commitment of getting mar—"

He jumped right in to solve my problems and, in so doing, cut me off before I could get to the biggest one of all. "Don't worry, I've got everything figured out. You know I wouldn't risk our financial future if we weren't ready. One of the guys in my office is married to a mortgage broker and I've already sat down with her—"

The choking started up again. "You already spoke to a mortgage broker? When?"

"A few months ago. I didn't want to tell you until after I'd given you the ring. I like to do things in the right order. But now that we're engaged . . ." He leaned over and gave me a quick kiss. "Surprise, sweetie. I love you."

"But you . . . you . . ."

"And that's not all."

"It's not? Where the hell is that wine?" I demanded, just a tad louder than I'd intended.

"Your blanc." The bartender materialized right on cue. I snatched the stemmed glass from him and gulped.

"See?" Kevin seemed pleased. "You like it. I told you to stick with the blanc."

I fought the urge to start screeching and tearing my hair out. "Just tell me the rest of your news, okay?"

"Okay. I met with this mortgage broker and she pulled my credit rating—which, of course, was excellent—and she said that, given the disparity in our income, we could probably qualify for a home loan with just my salary."

I flushed. "You know the boutique gig is just temporary. As soon as I can find something better in my field, I'll be making more, but there's not much work in fashion design locally so—"

"I know, sweetie, don't feel bad." He patted my hand. "Besides, we're better off budgeting with just my income because once we have kids . . ." His grin widened.

I chugged the rest of the wine. "Yeah?"

"Well, you'll be home with them, right?" He shifted in his seat, his grin wilting. "We've talked about this. It's part of the ten-year plan."

Oh God. Again with the Kevin Bradley Ten-Year Plan, a plan I'd agreed to three years ago when I was fresh out of college and had even less direction in life than I did now. Wedding, house, kids, careers—he'd plotted it all out in black and white with absolute confidence. He'd made it sound so simple; we'd never have to struggle. I'd always gone along with the idea of staying home to raise our two children (who would be spaced precisely four years apart, as recommended by the child development textbooks Kevin had consulted), but suddenly, the idea of giving up my miserable job—a retail peon at a third-rate boutique where the owner kept reneging on her promise to start stocking my designs—made me want to impale myself on my pinking shears.

And he'd saved the best for last. " . . . so I put a down payment on a plot of land. I want you to come look at it tomorrow."

My kingdom for a brown paper bag. "You already made a down payment? On a piece of land I've never seen?"

"You're going to love it." The grin reappeared. "It's a brand-new development out by Camelback Farms. Great schools, great view, great neighborhood. Our yard is going to back up to a greenbelt, and the floor plan has four bedrooms so we'll—"

"You already picked out a floor plan?" I gasped.

"Well, I didn't think you'd be interested in the construction aspect."

"Yeah, but if I'm gonna *live* there . . ."

"Don't worry—you'll have free rein to decorate."

"Oh my God."

Maybe it was the tone of my voice or the expression on my face, but Kevin finally realized that this surprise was not going over as planned.

"You seem a little shocked."

I nodded.

"But you know I would never do something like this unless I really believed that it was the best thing for us. I want you to be happy, Becca, you know that, right?"

I nodded again, bile rising in my throat.

"So just trust me."

"But, when we started this conversation, you said, 'We're going to buy a house.' Which, I mean, I don't want to be Little Miss Literal, but I didn't realize that meant you'd already picked out a parcel of land, talked to the builders, and arranged for a down payment."

He brushed this off. "I know it's a lot to take in. A wedding, a new house—things are stressful right now. But we can handle it! We're a great team."

I closed my eyes and tried to see this whole thing from his perspective: a grand romantic gesture in the same vein as the surprise engagement ring.

Except even more expensive and permanent.

"We're going to have a great life together." He reached over to rub my lower back. "All I want is to make you happy. Are you happy?"

The left side of my face started twitching uncontrollably.

"We'll go see the land and the plans this weekend," he continued, "and if you don't like it, we'll find something else. Okay?"

"Okay."

"I love you."

"I love you, too," I said.

Then I scurried off to the ladies' room and threw up.

After Kevin drove me home that night my sister Gayle, she of the therapy degrees and the Care Bear DNA, finally called.

"Hi, Becks, I know it's late but we're moving into the new office in Chandler and I've been buried under boxes of files all day."

"No problem," I said, flopping back on the little twin bed I'd had since seventh grade. "What's new?"

"Not too much." She paused. "Mom said Kevin popped the question."

"Yep." I inhaled deeply. "We're getting married."

She cleared her throat. "You sound pretty matter-of-fact about that."

"Well, it's not like it's a big bombshell. We all knew it was coming."

"I see."

There is nothing quite so condescending as a psychotherapist's prim "I see" coming from your oldest sister. But after twenty-five years of hearing it on a daily basis, I'd built up a pretty high tolerance.

She let another long pause stretch out between us. "Is this really what you want?"

"What, with Kevin? Well. Sure." I tried to sound enthusiastic.

"Good, then. If you're happy, if this is really what you want, I'm happy for you. But sometimes I can't help but feel you're a little, shall we say, under assertive. I'm sure I'm partially responsible—the whole family is, really—for patronizing you and drowning out your voice in childhood."

"My childhood was great. My voice is loud and clear," I assured her. "I couldn't have asked for a better family."

"See? This is exactly what I mean. You're saying what you think I want to hear, instead of what you really feel."

I made a face into the phone.

"Becca?"

"Yeah." I gave a theatrical rendition of a yawn. "Sorry—I'm really tired. I just got home and I have to open the boutique tomorrow."

"I thought the boutique was closed on Sundays?"

Busted. "Oh yeah. I got confused, I guess. Too much wine."

"I see."

Okay, *now* it was getting irritating. "Gayle—"

"You don't have to talk to me about this if you don't want to," she said. "Truly. It's fine. And I'm delighted for you and Kevin. I've always liked him."

I kicked off my shoes, which landed on the carpet with two muffled *thunks*. "Yeah, yeah, you and everyone else. I'll never find a better guy, right?"

"Hmm," was her only response to that. "Have you guys set a date yet?"

"No."

This time the "hmm" was much more drawn-out and judgmental.

"But only because Claire made me promise I wouldn't start planning my wedding until she finished hers," I hastened to add.

"Claire is so self-centered she should have her own gravitational field," Gayle said. "She cannot expect you to stop *thinking* about your own wedding. Besides, I'm sure you've already decided what you'll wear to walk down the aisle."

I blinked. "Actually, I haven't."

"What? You've been showing me wedding dress sketches since you could hold a crayon. And you're telling me you haven't even thought about your gown now that the ring is actually on your finger?"

"Well . . ."

"Oh, honey, that is so depressing. Tell you what—meet me at the bridal salon at Macy's in Fashion Square tomorrow. We're going to go try on wedding dresses."

"But Claire said—"

"Claire is not the boss of you." She paused. "*I* am. We are going, understand? And Mom, too, if she wants."

A vision popped into my head—a vision of me, trussed up in tulle and a sturdy polyester undergarment, standing in front of my mother and sister while salesgirls dutifully asked to see the ring . . .

My stomach gurgled.

"Becca? You still there?"

"Yeah, yeah, I'm here." I curled up into the fetal position. "But you know I'm going to make my own gown, so there's no point in looking at off-the-rack stuff I'm never going to buy."

She seemed startled. "But you wouldn't have to buy anything. This would just be for fun. To get in a nuptial frame of mind."

"You know what would be even more fun? The flea market in Paradise Valley. Remember when I found those great green pedal pushers from the sixties? I'm looking for some sandals to go with them, something really retro and off-beat—maybe white espadrilles with big chunky heels—and I thought there'd be good pickings at the flea market. Let's do that instead."

"I guess. If you're really not up for the bridal salon . . ."

"Forget the bridal salon. This will be much better. Meet you there at noon?"

"I worry about you, Becks," she said right before she hung up.

"Don't," I told the dial tone. "Everything's perfect."

3

"You aren't wearing your ring," my mom said as she pulled into a parking space at the flea market.

"I'm not?" I glanced down at my fingers. "Oh. I must have forgotten to put it on this morning."

"You take it off at night?" She sounded scandalized.

"I just feel better knowing it's safe." In the impenetrable vault of my sock drawer.

"Let me tell you something." She gazed down at the small diamond chip on her left hand. "Your father gave me this ring when I was twenty years old and I have never, to this day, taken it off."

"Not even in the shower?"

"Not even in the shower."

"Not even when you were pregnant and bloated?" My mother's third-trimester bloat was the stuff of legends, as she routinely reminded all three of us during our many mother-daughter battles.

"I only took it off to have it resized. And then resized again after you three were born. And when I die, I'll be buried with it on." She smiled fondly at the thought.

Since I couldn't think of any appropriate response to that, I got out of the car and walked around to meet her at the sidewalk, which—this being Paradise Valley—was edged with lush green grass and palm trees, all of identical height.

But Mom wasn't finished. "So you better put that ring back on and keep it on, missy. You'll hurt Kevin's feelings. Men are very sensitive about these things."

"Relax. I just forgot this one time."

"That's my little Beck-Beck. Head in the clouds. So artistic and forgetful." She ruffled my hair. "Now, come on. We're going to be late meeting Gayle and I hardly ever see her as it is." As we hustled toward the smoothie stand, our appointed meeting place, she confided, "I'm glad you asked me along today because I'm on a mission. I'm going to look for one of those old-fashioned back-tie aprons for you to wear at your bridal shower. Like the housewives used to wear on *Leave It to Beaver*. Wouldn't that be hysterical?"

I tried to be tactful. "I appreciate the thought, Mom, but I don't need a bridal shower."

"Of course you do. Every girl needs one. How else are you going to get all the things you need to set up a household?" She wrung her hands. "I can't believe my last little baby is leaving the nest."

"I'm twenty-five years old. Most people my age would be deeply ashamed to still live with their parents, and rightly so. You don't have to worry about setting up my household. I have some savings—I can buy my own toasters and blenders and fancy-schmancy cooking pots." I waved as I caught sight of Gayle.

"Ha. I know you; left to your own devices, you'll wind up with a house full of sewing machines and fabric swatches, with spools of thread in your silverware drawer. Poor Kevin will starve to death."

"But at least he'll be well-dressed. And thin enough to fit into runway samples."

"Don't make this into a joke." She paused long enough to give Gayle a hug and a kiss, then lit right back into me. "You're going to be a wife and that's a big responsibility. It's not just about you and your hobbies anymore."

I exhaled slowly and counted to ten. "I know that, Mom. But sewing is more than a hobby to me, okay? It's my passion. It's going to be my *job* someday."

She let this pass without comment, but I could feel the effort it cost her to hold her tongue.

"Besides, it's not good etiquette for the mother of the bride to throw a shower."

"Says who?" She turned to Gayle. "Have you ever heard that?"

With an air of supreme authority, Gayle said, "No, but regardless, I think it's just another one of Becca's typical self-effacing attempts to shun the limelight."

My mom's head snapped to the left as she spied a rickety card table laden with old vinyl records. "Ooh! LPs! I wonder if they have any Bob Dylan. I've been searching for *Blood on the Tracks* in the original dust jacket."

"I'm going to look for sandals," I huffed. "I'll meet up with you later."

"I'll call your cell when I'm ready." Mom made a beeline for the record bins. "And don't take everything so personally, sweetie." She shook her head at Gayle. "It's beyond me how a youngest child turned out so prickly and introverted. Aren't youngests supposed to be flamboyant little divas?"

"Typically, yes, but Claire had already had that role for five years before Becks was born, and you know Claire—she always has to be the center of attention."

"True. I wonder if things would've been different if she'd been a boy . . ."

I left them to their armchair analysis and headed for the vintage clothing booths. This market was nearly an hour's drive from our house on the west side of Phoenix, but it was worth the trip. Paradise Valley is one of the nation's wealthiest zip codes, nestled up against the affluent neighborhoods of Scottsdale, which meant that some tantalizing pieces could be found if one was not averse to a little digging. Genuine Pucci for pennies. Givenchy scarves—from back when Givenchy *was* Givenchy—for a song. Sometimes I'd refurbish the pieces to their original glory, sometimes I'd use the fabric as part of another, more contemporary design, but the thrill of the hunt always made me happy. Just the sight of the racks of hand-tagged clothing sweetened my mood.

As the blazing Arizona sun crested higher in the sky, I took off my cardigan and tied it around my waist. I pawed through racks of peasant skirts and polyester pantsuits, forgetting all about bridal showers and Kevin's real-estate ambush and the ring stashed deep in the bowels of my dresser . . . and then I saw it.

Sandwiched between a moth-eaten corduroy shirtdress and gold lamé trousers so hideous Liberace would roll over in his grave was a gorgeous peignoir set straight out of the 1920s. Made of peau de soie in the palest shade of dove gray, expertly cut to skim without squeezing the body's contours, the nightgown was trimmed with insets of ivory Schiffli lace at the neckline and hem. Very Ava Gardner. I could practically hear the tenor sax wailing in the background as I slipped the robe off the hanger and focused on the gown.

No holes. No stains. No giant rips, although there were a few loose threads along the side seam. The back fastened up with delicate mother-of-pearl buttons, only one of which was missing. Then I glanced at the price tag and my ecstasy was complete: fifteen bucks.

Someone tapped me on the shoulder. I jumped and

clutched my find to my chest, unwilling to let anyone else even look at my treasure.

"Becca?" Gayle sounded amused. "I'm not mugging you. I just want to know if you're almost ready to move on. I want to go rummage through the used books."

"Almost. Just have to buy this and I'm done."

"Ooh, let me see. You always find the best stuff here. Stuff that makes me jealous even though I've been brainwashed by the cult of Ann Taylor."

I held out the peignoir for inspection.

She eyed the rich folds of silk. "Nice. Fancy."

"I know. I've been thinking about where I'm going to wear this . . ."

"Wedding night, maybe?" She winked.

"Actually, I was thinking more like wedding *day*. I'll take out the lace panels and replace them with something else—maybe a really lustrous silver charmeuse?—hitch up the neckline a couple of inches, put my hair up, and throw in a couple of orchids. What do you think?"

"You know . . ." The Ann Taylor devotee nodded. "That could work. It's a little unconventional for the west Phoenix crowd, but I think you'd look great. Now, would Kevin wear a tux or just—"

The bubble burst. "Oh wait. Forget it. I can't get married in this."

"Why not?"

"Kevin. He'd freak if I wore gray down the aisle."

"He doesn't seem like the type to care about female fashion."

"He's not; that's the problem. He's stuck in the old school, bride-in-a-white-dress mentality. If I show up in this, he'll be crushed."

She tilted her head. "Are you sure?"

"Positive." I sighed. "Damn. I'm gonna have to wear a big poufed ball gown with a train and a veil."

"Now try not to project. You don't know—"

"I do know." My spirits plummeted as I fingered the slippery silk. "He wants to have the ceremony in his parents' backyard and he wants me to consider wearing his mother's wedding dress. From the late seventies."

She grimaced. "How bad is it?"

"Cinderella meets Peter, Paul and Mary. I'll have to come up with a good excuse—maybe I'll wear Claire's gown and cite sentimental value? But I definitely can't wear a revamped nightgown, however stylish, without hurting his feelings."

"That's a shame; that dress could really be a knockout once you get through with it."

"No. I'm buying it, but I can't wear it for the wedding." My mother's words echoed through my head. "His feelings, remember? Men are very sensitive."

"Talk about contrasting ideological visions." Gayle clicked her tongue. "And that's just the wedding. You two are going to have quite a time picking out a house together. How do you compromise between old Victorian flair and new construction practicality?"

"Oh, he already picked out a house for us." I watched her reaction closely, trying to figure out if the whole deal was as crazy and bizarre as I suspected. "As a surprise."

Gayle's expression would suggest that my instincts were right on. "He picked out a house and didn't tell you?"

"Yeah. I'm going to see the lot this afternoon."

"Are you serious?"

"Like a heart attack. He already worked out the mortgage and everything, so . . ."

"*Really.*" She gave a crisp nod and for the rest of the morning restricted her remarks to "hmmm" and "I see."

On the bright side, at least we were no longer talking about wedding gowns and engagement rings.

"Here it is: the site of our future home!" Kevin removed his hands from my eyes and awaited my outpouring of gratitude.

Blinking as my eyes readjusted to the afternoon sunlight, I gazed at the ground in front of me and beheld the spoils purchased with Kevin's down payment: a giant scraggly pit.

"It's . . . beautiful?" The hole was shallow, muddy, and crosshatched with what appeared to be bulldozer tracks. Little green weeds had started to sprout around the edges.

"Don't worry, it won't look like this forever." Trish, the builder's onsite sales rep, swirled her hands over the hole like a fortune-teller. A platinum blonde clad in a magenta blazer, soccer mom jeans, and white cowboy boots, she was the picture of consumer confidence. "Wait until they pour the foundation and start framing the walls. You'll be so excited you'll want to come by every day."

"Yeah, you can pick out colors for the walls and the shutters and the front door," Kevin said. "While I bring by my measuring tape and level to make sure they're building everything properly."

"Oh, you engineers are all the same!" Trish pshawed. Apparently she thought he was kidding. "It's a big responsibility, picking out colors. But I'm sure you'll do fine. Kevin here tells me you're real stylish."

"Well, not at the moment, obviously." At the moment I was wearing the same outfit I'd thrown on for the flea market: an ASU T-shirt, flip-flops, and a loose knee-length skirt I'd made myself out of gray sweatpant material. "But I think I can rise to the challenge of selecting a door color."

She got all serious. "There are a few restrictions, of course. We can't have one flamingo pink house bringing down the property values for the whole neighborhood. So here at Lilac Lakes, we urge all our residents to stick to a palette of neutral earth tones—beige, tan, brown, khaki, and mocha. You *might* be able to use maroon or hunter green accents, but you'll have to get special permission. Next time you come out here, swing by my office and I'll give you a copy of the home owners' association handbook."

"Lilac Lakes?" I glanced around at the acres of brown, bulldozed dirt partitioned into squares by gray concrete walls.

"Yes, that's what the neighborhood will be called when it's

finished," she said. "Sounds homey, don't you think? Homey but gentrified. And that's exactly the image we're going for here. Happy, comfortable families who want the very best west Phoenix has to offer at an affordable price."

"There'll be a lake by the time we move in," Kevin added. "Right down the block."

"That's right. A playground, a park, and a big ol' lake. We might even stock it with perch or sunfish so you can teach the kiddies how to fish." She winked at Kevin. "Are you planning to have children soon?"

I stared at the ground and shrugged while he said, "Yes. At least two. We'll use the loft space on the second floor as a playroom and the office near the master bedroom as a nursery."

"That's a great idea." Trish marveled at my good fortune. "What a guy. You are so lucky to have him."

"That's what everyone says," I murmured.

"And you two just got engaged? How exciting. Let me see the ring!"

I hid both hands behind my back. "I'm sorry to be so abrupt, but do you mind if I have a moment alone with my fiancé? I just need to check something."

"No problemo. I'll dig out the maps in my car so I can show you exactly where the property lines are." She moseyed off toward the mud-spattered SUV she'd parked on the flat patch of land that represented our future driveway.

"What's up?" Kevin furrowed his brow as I grabbed his

sleeve and tugged him toward the far corner of the empty lot. "You're covered in sweat—do you need to get out of the sun?"

I dropped my face into my hands. "I really don't want to have this conversation, but we have to."

He drew me into his arms, rubbing my sweat-drenched back through my T-shirt. "You know you can tell me anything. I love you."

Somehow, between his comforting embrace and my desperate denial of the gulf that had been widening between us for the last few months, I convinced myself that everything would be fine if I just spilled my guts. He'd understand because I *needed* him to understand.

So I lifted my head and plunged in. "Okay. Remember when you said that if I didn't like this house, we could find something else?"

His eyes narrowed. "Yes."

"Well . . . I don't like it. I'm sorry, Kevin, I really am. But I can't—"

"Becca, don't say it."

"I have to say it." My voice caught and broke as my eyes stung with unshed tears. "I'm trying to be a good girlfriend—fiancée, whatever—and a good sport, but I am *freaking out* here. Everyone keeps talking about wedding dresses and mortgages and kids, but all I can see is this *hole* in the ground and I—"

He pulled me closer. "Sweetie, I know it's just a messy patch of dirt right now, but it won't always look this way. I'm talking to the builder about a lot of upgrades—marble countertops, gas fireplace, a big Jacuzzi for you to soak in when your shoulders get sore from hunching over the sewing machine . . ."

If guilt could kill, I'd be flatlining right about now. "I know you're trying to make me happy and I appreciate that. Truly. And I'm not objecting to anything about the actual house. How could I, when it doesn't even exist yet? But I don't want to live in a neighborhood where I have to get special permission to paint my front door red."

"Maroon," he corrected. "I don't think there's any way we could get the go-ahead for bright red."

"Well, that's my point. We're paying the mortgage . . ." I trailed off as I realized my error. "Okay, *you're* paying the mortgage. But I'll have to live here, too, and I want the option of painting pink and purple polka dots on my door if I feel like it."

"Don't get so emotional, Becca." His voice was tinged with impatience. "Everything will be fine."

"I'm not emotional, I'm just saying—"

He held up his palm. "Just so we're clear: do you have your heart set on a polka-dot front door?"

"Well." I scuffed the dirt with my flip-flop, flattening one of the baby dandelions. "No. But if I *did,* I'd want to have the freedom to—"

"So you're starting an argument about an aesthetic problem that doesn't exist?" He looked at me the way preschool teachers look at whiny three-year-olds who won't go down for naptime.

"I'm not trying to start an argument. But I'm not going to decorate my house in eighteen shades of beige because some stupid handbook says I have to. Where will it end? Will we have to get a permission slip signed every time we want to plant a shrub?"

He jammed his hands into his pockets. "Of course not. Although . . ."

"Although what?"

"We can't plant any olive trees or citrus trees because of the pollination issues. They don't allow anything that aggravates people's allergies."

I threw up my hands. "But I *like* olives!"

He finally snapped. "Why are you being so ridiculous? When have you ever in your life showed any interest in landscaping?"

"I might, you never know. Once I have a yard and a garden, who knows what I might want to do?"

"You want olives so damn much, go to the store and buy yourself a jar of kalamatas."

Across the lot, Trish opened her car door, caught a snippet of our conversation, and slammed the door shut again.

I took a step back. "Try to see the olive tree and the red door as a metaphor. Can you do that for one second?"

"No, I cannot." He started pacing in a tight little circle. "And would you like to know why? Because I'm breaking my back to build a life for us and you're throwing it all back in my face."

"How can you say that? I want to help you, but you aren't

letting me be an equal partner. You never ask for input, you just assume—"

"If you didn't want this, you should have spoken up!" His tight, measured pacing sped up.

"You never gave me a chance!" I exploded. "You never asked what I want!"

"You don't *know* what you want, Becca." He stopped pacing. "You never know what you want. And I do. So I'm trying to do what's best for both of us."

I crossed my arms, at which point he noticed my left hand.

"You're not wearing your ring."

"No, I'm not."

"Well, what is that supposed to mean? Is that supposed to mean something?"

"I don't know," I said slowly. "Probably." I turned on my heel and started toward Trish's SUV. "I have to go home now."

"You're just going to walk away?"

And that's exactly what I did. Because he was wrong. Maybe in the past, I'd had no idea what I wanted out of life, but I was starting to figure things out. I had goals and I had dreams, and they didn't include that gaping hole between us.

4

"So the world's most repressed couple finally broke down and duked it out. I knew it was only a matter of time," Claire crowed.

"Yes, well, how sweet of you to care." I glared at the phone.

"Oh, don't be so snitty. Every couple fights, especially engaged couples. Just last night, Andrew and I had a huge blowout over the seating chart at the reception. He wanted to put all his old frat buddies from USC at the *same table*. Can you imagine? We might as well give them all shot glasses and togas and wait for them to do keg stands in front of the string quartet. But it's fine now. I explained that frat party shenanigans have no place in my perfectly perfect day and he saw reason. That's how normal people do it—you fight, you make up, and if you're lucky, he coughs up some flowers in apology. Or in your case, a hokey stuffed koala."

"Well, that's the thing." I prayed that my mother would hurry and pick up the kitchen extension so I could hand the future Mrs. King off to her. "I'm not sure we're going to make up."

"What?" She stopped muttering about frat boys and got serious. "Of course you're going to make up. Must I hold your hand through everything, Becks? Say it with me now: 'I'm sorry, darling.' Follow with blow job and an icy cold Guinness and repeat as necessary. *Finis* fight."

"No, I mean, I don't *want* to make up." I paused, considering the ripple effect my next words would start. "I'm thinking about taking a break from Kevin."

"A break," she repeated. "For how long?"

"For, um, ever."

Apparently, this pushed my sister beyond the point of words because all I heard on the other end of the line was her gasping for air.

I collapsed on my parents' overstuffed, denim-slipcovered sofa and glowered at the carved wooden hearts and teddy bears my mother had crammed onto every available flat surface. "You don't understand."

"What's to understand? He loves you, he treats you well, he makes good money. He wants to marry you and buy you a house, for God's sake."

"But it's all wrong! You should have seen us out there. He was so excited about the house and the neighborhood and our future children fishing in the faux lake and all I could see was this yawning mud pit in the ground like an open grave."

"How Arthur Miller of you."

"He's ready to move up to the next level and I'm not."

"Any why is that? Because you have *so* many more important things to do with your life?"

"I might, actually," I snapped. "I know you don't take my design business seriously, but—"

"You're right about that. No one takes it seriously, and do you know why?"

"Yeah. Because—"

"Still talking! We don't take it seriously because *you* don't take it seriously. And since when are you running a 'business'?"

"I've made a few samples and I'm thinking about shopping them around Scottsdale . . ."

"Child, please. I've heard you say that a zillion times."

"This time I mean it," I vowed.

"Well, decision time has arrived. Fish or cut bait. Scottsdale's a dead end and you know it. Either move out here to L.A. or roll yourself into the open grave. But you're an idiot if you let Kevin slip away over a stupid tiff about olive trees and red doors."

I lowered my voice to a whisper. "But I don't love him."

"What's that?" she trumpeted. "You don't love him?"

"No. I used to, I *want* to, but I don't."

"Listen. You don't always have starbursts and rainbows. Passion waxes and wanes in a long-term relationship. It'll come back, you'll see."

"You say that, but you wouldn't marry Andrew if you weren't head over heels in love with him."

"Sure I would! I'm marrying him because I know what's good for me, not because I have some deluded fantasy about marriage as one long DeBeers commercial."

"Then why didn't you marry any of the other guys who proposed?" I demanded.

"It wasn't the right time. And I still thought I might have a chance of making it as an actress out here. And none of them were rich enough."

"Whatever. You love Andrew and you know it."

"It's none of your business," she huffed.

"Why are you so afraid to admit you're in love?" I grinned.

"We're not talking about me; we're talking about you. And your pigheaded insistence on breaking up with a man who's offering you safety and security for the rest of your life."

"Maybe I want more out of life than safety and security."

"Then you're a grade-A nimrod who's beyond help."

I reverted to my time-honored tactic of peacekeeping via repression and changed the subject. "Where are you guys having the rehearsal dinner, anyway?"

Her tone brightened. "The restaurant is called Rhapsody. Fabulous Northern Italian place near Melrose. Andrew was one of the original investors so he knows the owner. He knows everyone who's anyone; he's so very accomplished and charming."

"See? You do love him."

"You bring that up one more time and you're fired as bridesmaid."

Mom *finally* picked up the phone in the kitchen.

"Claire? Hi, hon. How's the weather out there?"

"Seventy degrees and sunny. Perfect weather for my perfect wedding. You guys are flying in on Thursday, right?"

"Yes, don't worry," my mother and I chorused in unison.

"Good. Because if even one more thing goes wrong, I'm going to have to be institutionalized. The caterer just called and they don't have any ecru napkins, can you *believe* that? Only white! I cried so hard my manicurist had to give me a Xanax."

"I've got to run!" I interjected. "It's been great talking to you, Claire. I'll see you Thursday!"

"Don't forget to bring your sewing stuff," she cried before I could hang up. "One of the flower girls had a growth spurt and I need you to re-hem her dress."

After I extricated myself from Claire's Bridezilla tractor beam, I retrieved my engagement ring from the linty depths of my sock drawer, jammed it on my finger, and tried to convince myself that my sister was right. I would be an idiot to screw up the happily ever after Kevin was offering. My pipe dreams of becoming the next Vivienne Westwood were just that. And I could probably live without olive trees in my yard.

So why did I feel the burning need to get back on the phone and beg Claire to score some extra Xanax for me?

I spent the next few days screening all incoming phone calls, but Kevin had never been one for drama. He left a single perfunctory message on my cell: "When you're ready to talk this out like a rational adult, let me know." At work, I volunteered to help unpack new deliveries in the back room in case he dropped by the boutique, but he didn't. He had a strict set of rules against dragging personal business into the office, and these rules extended to my workplace as well.

It wasn't that I was pouting or trying to exact punishment for the things he'd said in anger. Quite the opposite; I knew he was right and I was wrong.

But I still didn't want to marry him.

And if he managed to corner me into a "rational, adult" discussion, I would be powerless to refute his unerring logic. Then I'd be right back where I started, having panic attacks at the mere mention of something borrowed and something blue.

Due to our silent standoff, Kevin did not accompany me to Claire's wedding in California as originally planned. I told my family he had an emergency at work, which elicited some speculative looks from my parents, but no one asked any awkward questions. During the flight from Phoenix to Los Angeles, I outlined the argument I'd present to him in favor of breaking up. My case needed to be airtight. And my opening line had to be compelling. Something like:

In an attempt to gain fortune and fame in a reality TV series, I'm undergoing radical new surgery to become a man.

Or:

The neurologist tells me that I sustained a heavy blow to the head, but I don't remember a thing. No, you don't look familiar. Who am I? Where am I?

The simple truth—

If I have to spend another five years—let alone the rest of my life—cooped up in a subdivision called Lilac Lakes, cooking combinations of the six foods you will actually eat and making weekly pilgrimages to Home Depot to buy paint in every conceivable shade of beige, I'm going to make that chick in Mr. Rochester's attic look like Marianne Willamson.

—didn't cast me in a very flattering light. Because really, there was nothing wrong with suburban Phoenix. Or with Home Depot. There was something wrong with me.

As the pilot announced our descent into LAX, my mother reached over from the seat across the aisle, grabbed my hand and said, "I just hope my new rehearsal dinner dress passes the lavender test with Claire."

"Mmm," I said.

"You won't be this difficult about your rehearsal dinner, will you?"

"No. You can wear whatever you want," I promised.

"That's what they all say in the beginning." She released my hand long enough to rub her temples and pop an Advil. "But I suppose Kevin will keep you in line. He's always so sensible."

"Mmm," I said again.

By the time we'd collected our bags, piled into a taxi, and rolled up to the terrifyingly chic hotel Claire had recommended, I'd cemented my resolve to sit down with Kevin as soon as I returned home. He was going to be shocked. My parents were going to be worried. *His* mother was going to go critical—she had already announced name choices for her future grandchildren. (Charles Maximillian for a boy, Philippa Rosalind for a girl. We had gently explained to her that we were not pretenders to the English throne, but nothing doing.)

For the first time in my life, I was going to be the "problem child" in the Davis family. Which would give Claire a welcome respite.

Then we headed to the rehearsal dinner, where I got a rude refresher on how Claire had earned that title in the first place—she was leaving *me* at the altar.

5

Claire maintained a Zen-like state of serenity through the mock ceremony, stopping only once to upbraid the wedding planner. And she actually complimented Mom's dress. But when the bridal party reassembled for dinner at the hip West Hollywood restaurant, she pulled me aside, her face grim.

"I have some bad news, Becks."

"What? You're not going to go through with the wedding?" I perked up. She and I could be single girls together! We could find a fabulous apartment on the beach and start exciting new lives, practically the stuff of sitcoms, and—

"Of course I'm going to go through with it, you git. Do you have any idea how hard it is to snare a straight, single, good-looking man with a nice car and a decent stock portfolio in this town?" She gave me a pointed look. "*I* know how to hang on to a good thing."

"So what's the problem? Is this about the flower girl who had the audacity to grow three inches before your perfect day? I told you, I'll fix the hem tonight."

She twisted her fingers together around her 2.88-carat diamond ring. "This isn't about the flower girl's dress, but you're getting warm."

"What's going on?" I asked, the first stirrings of dread creeping into my stomach.

She reached into the crowd and dragged Gayle into our little dance of dysfunction. "I can't say it. You tell her."

Gayle sighed, straightened her prim yellow cardigan, and looked me straight in the eye. "There's no way to put this gently. The wedding dress you made is out. She's decided to go with a Carolina Herrera."

My jaw hit the floor as I turned back to Claire. "You . . . but how did you . . . ?"

"I ordered it six months ago," she confessed, covering her eyes with both hands. "Just in case yours didn't work out. I'm horrible, I know. You're going to hate me forever."

"So you've been planning to wear a different gown since . . ." I did a quick count back. "June? And you wait until the night before the wedding to tell me?"

She shrugged helplessly. "I know you hate confrontation."

Gayle snorted. "*She* hates confrontation?"

"I can't believe this." I gaped at them. "That dress took me months to make. I've been cutting and sewing and scouring the entire Southwest for Venetian lace in just the right shade of ivory and all this time you knew. You *knew* you were going to throw me over for Carolina Herrera?"

"No! I only decided for sure last week. I've been going back and forth about which gown to wear, and I just think that, for the newspapers and everything, the Carolina Herrera would be better."

Ah, yes. The newspapers. Way to grind another shaker of salt into the wound. "The newspapers," which would *not* be photographing the dress that had consumed the greater part of my twenty-fifth year.

"Claire. Do you have any idea how many other design projects I turned down so I could do this gown?"

My sisters exchanged a look.

I put both hands on my hips. "Listen. I *could* have worked on other design projects."

Gayle patted my shoulder. "Oh, Becca, no one's saying your feelings aren't valid . . ."

". . . But seriously, come *on*," Claire finished. "Other design opportunities? Name one."

I set my jaw, but had no reply.

"Besides, the bridesmaids' dresses will still be in the paper. And try not to cry over this, okay? No one wants puffy-eyed bridesmaids in their wedding photos." She gave me a quick hug. "Be strong, Becca. For me."

Gayle took a sip of her Chardonnay. "Claire, could you dial down the narcissism for one second, please?"

"I'm allowed to be a narcissist today. All weekend long, in fact. It's my God-given right as a bride."

"Can't we please focus on Becca for one second? She's very upset."

"And you think *I'm* not? The florist just called and said they ran out of white tulips! I don't have all night to chant healing affirmations, okay? I have a wedding to throw."

"Claire . . ."

"Ugh. *Fine.*"

My sisters turned to me, exasperated.

"Go ahead," Gayle prompted.

I threw up my hands. "What on earth would possess you to buy an extra wedding gown anyway?"

Claire patted my head as she would a fuzzy bunny's. "Babe, this is Los Angeles. Everyone buys at least two gowns. It's the thing to do. Seriously. *Modern Bride* says it's the hot new trend."

"*Modern Bride* says no such thing." I appealed to a higher authority. "Gayle . . ."

But Gayle shook her head, digging her cell phone out of her bag. "I've said my piece and now I have to call Tiffany and Co. to order some platinum-plated hors d'oeuvres forks for the happy couple."

"If that's supposed to be some kind of dig about our registry . . ."

"No, no, I know lots of brides who request eight-hundred-dollar ceramic fruit bowls."

"Choke on my bling, Gayle!" Claire yelled after her.

"Eight hundred dollars for a fruit bowl?" I marveled.

"Totally reasonable." She huffed, smoothed her thick blond hair back behind her ear. "Do you have any idea how much we're spending on this wedding? And ten years down the road, when Andrew leaves me for his personal trainer and I get shafted in the divorce and have to live in . . ." She closed her eyes against the horror of it all " . . .Van Nuys, I'll need something to remind me of my halcyon days."

"That's not a very romantic thing to be thinking about the night before your wedding."

"I'm not a romantic, I'm a realist." Claire paused to wave across the room to her future husband, who had been trapped by our mother and was currently enduring a lengthy monologue on the merits of lapel versus wrist corsages. "You wouldn't understand. It's fine for you—you can design clothes until you drop dead. Even if you never set foot out of Phoenix, you can keep telling yourself that success is right around the corner. But I'm not risking my entire future on some fantasy that's never going to happen. If I haven't made it as an actress by now, it's never gonna happen. I'm thirty. Thirty!" She frowned down at her green bias-cut slip dress. "And look at me!"

She was actually thirty-one, but I sensed that now was not the time to split hairs.

"You look great," I said grudgingly. Better than she deserved to look, considering what she'd just done to me. Tall and willowy, a fanatic disciple of Bikram yoga and Pilates, the undisputed beauty of the Davis family. "And how do you know your acting career won't take off any day now?"

"With a fresh batch of nineteen-year-olds bouncing off the bus every day? I don't think so. I've gotten *three* acting gigs in the past five years. Two beer commercials and a deodorant print ad do not a career make. Even my agent has given up and decided to try screenwriting. You only get so many chances and I missed mine. So down the aisle I go."

"Plus, you love him," I reminded her.

"Maybe I do." She leveled her gaze. "But that's irrelevant. Love and security are very different things, and you have to get your priorities straight."

I didn't argue. As the youngest sister, my role in our family was to tag along with my sisters and be agreeable. Gayle was the level-headed mediator, Claire was the dramaholic glamour gal, and I . . . well, put it this way: when we were little and my sisters decided to play *Annie* in the backyard, I was always assigned the role of Sandy the dog.

"Life is about compromise," she lectured. "You'll see. Speaking of which, where's Kevin?"

I took this as my cue to go find a new conversation partner and an adult beverage.

*　　*　　*

The clink of silverware and the buzz of Friday night conversation spilled out onto the restaurant's patio as I stared up at the white twinkle lights punctuating the cool evening air. Anxiety and bitter disappointment oozed from my every pore as my mood pitched into a downward spiral.

I snapped to attention as a clean-cut stranger approached purposefully from the bar, holding two glasses of champagne.

I glanced over my shoulder, hoping a buxom blond beach bunny behind me had caught his eye. But no. It was just me, about to have my first encounter with an L.A. pick-up artist. Claire had warned me about this unctuous breed of bottom-feeder: "Seriously, Becca, they're toupee-wearing, STD-carrying skeeves who feed on wide-eyed tourists like an entourage on free Cristal. Don't talk to them. Don't even say hi. They'll take the slightest courtesy as a sure sign they'll be bagging you in their jacked-up Camaro by the end of the night. Trust me."

To be fair, this guy didn't look like the toupee-wearing type. On the contrary, he was tall, dark, handsome; a veritable walking cliché. But whatever. I was frustrated, I was depressed, and I was in no mood for this.

The guy got a load of my stormy expression but forged ahead, clearing his throat and leading in with: "Excuse me, miss—"

I dropped the porcupine routine and rolled my eyes. "*That's* your opener?"

"My opener?" He furrowed his brow.

"'Excuse me, miss.' I heard that . . . aren't you supposed to slither up to me and be like, 'Your legs sure must be tired 'cause you've been running through my mind all night'? Or 'Can I look at the tag on your shirt? I want to see if it says "Made in Heaven"'?"

"I'd like to think I'm a little smoother than that. Actually, I'm just wondering if you're a member of the bridal party. For the rehearsal dinner?"

Oops. "Oh. Well. Yes, I am."

"Because they're getting ready to do the toasts, and I'm supposed to be rounding up all the barflies like yourself."

"You're the maître d'?"

He leaned back against the doorframe. I could see amusement gleaming in his eyes. "Yeah, something like that."

"Oh God. I'm sorry." I desperately scanned the patio for a place to hide. "And mortified. I'm usually not so rude. This is my first time in L.A. I thought you were—never mind. I feel awful. I work in retail myself, so believe me when I say that I *know* from rude customers."

"You must, if you hear pickup lines like those."

As I accepted the flute of fizzy booze he offered, I couldn't help noticing that his left hand was free of any matrimonial hardware. "This wouldn't happen to be spiked with Prozac, would it?"

"'Fraid not." He extended his hand. "I'm Connor Sullivan. Anything I can do to help?"

"Becca Davis. Beyond help at this point."

He raised his eyebrows in silent inquiry.

"The bride—" I jerked my head toward Claire, who had curled up next to Andrew and was now gazing at him like a loyal little Pomeranian "—was supposed to debut my line of wedding wear."

He followed my gaze, then nodded. "Operative phrase: 'supposed to.'" He did not seem at all fazed to hear that I was into clothing design. Probably because Southern California was already teeming with aspiring Stella McCartneys, all of them more talented than I.

"That's right. In the grand tradition of rookie designers, I got shoved to the back of the closet." I shook my head and studied the shadows under the brass-rimmed bar. "I know, it's horrible for me to even be thinking about this at my sister's wedding, but I just . . ."

I could almost hear the gears in his head whirr into male-problem-solving mode.

"Does she still have the dress?"

I turned my palms up. "One can only hope so."

He shrugged. "Why don't you wear it?"

"You mean like for *my* wedding?" How had he known I was engaged? My diamond ring was once again interred in my dresser in Phoenix. "Oh, that's a whole other can of worms. I'm supposed to marry this guy, Kevin, but I don't think it's going to work out. He's a good person, but we're just so differ-ent and I really don't know—"

He looked a little taken aback by this barrage of intimate

information. "It doesn't have to be for your wedding. You just said you were a designer. Can't you *design* it into something else?"

My mouth was saying, "Oh, that'd be gauche . . ." at the same time my mind was re-creating the gown. I could hem it to the knee, dye it (plum? light blue?), and accessorize with strappy heels and dangly earrings.

He paused, letting me mentally restructure for a moment. "And if you're a designer, you're in the right neighborhood." I must have looked puzzled, because he pointed at the restaurant's front door. "Melrose Avenue is right around the corner. Where are you visiting from?"

"Arizona."

He nodded. "Big fashion scene out there?"

I downed half my champagne in one gulp. "Not really. But I do work in the design business. Kind of. I'm a sales assistant in a boutique. And the owner said she might start selling some of my designs. Maybe next season." I sighed, omitting the fact that the owner had been saying this—and failing to follow through—since my first day on the job. Mostly, she wanted me to make coffee and clean lipstick stains off tops discarded in the dressing room.

"Hey, everybody's got to start somewhere, right? I used to work construction in Denver, and now all this is mine."

My eyes widened. "It is?"

"Well, it used to be seventy-five percent mine, but I recently bought out my business partner." He nodded at

Andrew. "Seems he had a fancy five-star wedding to finance."

"You must really love the restaurant business to put up with all the long hours and the snotty clientele like myself."

"Oh, I don't come in every day. I hire the best managers I can find and let them do their job."

"So what do you do with the rest of your time?"

"I have stakes in a couple of different businesses out here. A little of this, a little of that."

"Probably a good idea." I nodded. "I hear the restaurant business is pretty risky."

"I love a challenge." He grinned. "And I'm not really a nine-to-five kind of guy—I like to have a few irons in the fire. A drastic career change every now and then is good for the soul. Keeps life interesting." He watched my face closely. "You know, if you're really serious about clothing design, you should move out here. Here or New York."

"That's what they tell me." I finished off the rest of my champagne, slapped on a cheery smile, and prepared to make my way back to the Carolina Herrera fan club in the next room. "But I'm only out here for two more days, and then it's back to Phoenix, hotbed of haute couture."

"You must be a good designer if she was willing to let you make her gown." He glanced at Claire, who was now barking orders into her cell phone. All I could hear over the din of the crowd was the word "tulips" repeated over and over.

"Oh, I'm not good enough for Melrose yet," I assured him.

"How do you know until you try?"

I shrugged.

"Life is short," he said. "I actually need a replacement for one of my hostesses. She's heading back to London for a month and you could sub for her. Just dip your toe in. Send a few samples out, shop them around during the day, see if you get any nibbles. You'll never know if you don't try."

"But . . ." I automatically started to refuse, even as I envisioned all the possibilities. All those stylists buying all those outfits for their red-carpet clients. "Why would you do that for me?"

"Why?" He paused for a moment, then put both hands in his pockets. "Because I know your brother-in-law-to-be? Because I remember what it's like to start out in this city?"

I gave him a long, assessing look. "Uh-huh."

He laughed at my expression. "Don't worry. I'm completely up to date on all sexual harassment laws. You and your fiancé have nothing to worry about on that score."

I tapped my fingernail against my glass. "That doesn't change the fact that I don't know how to be a hostess."

"Can you smile, answer a phone, and pander endlessly to self-important egomaniacs?"

"Did I mention I work in retail?"

He grinned. "Thirty days. Give yourself a chance."

And then he excused himself, leaving me alone with an empty glass and a heady rush of potential.

6

I broke off my engagement during a Friday night airing of *Gladiator* on cable a week after Claire's wedding.

Bad timing, true, but I'd already bought tickets for a Southwest Airlines flight leaving for LAX on Saturday morning, and every time I tried to discuss the state of our union, Kevin tuned me out or changed the subject. It was as if he knew, like a Jedi sensing a disturbance in the force, what was coming and vowed to restore the natural balance of things with benign chitchat about the weather. When I finally called him the day I got back from L.A., he acted as if nothing untoward had ever happened. Wedding plans, olive trees, and lifelong romantic commitments suddenly vanished from our conversational horizons.

"Kevin," I began, giving up any pretense that I could focus on Russell Crowe's blood-soaked battles. "We need to talk."

He frowned at the TV screen. "You know, actually, in ancient Rome, when the emperor gave the 'thumbs-up' signal, it meant 'kill him', not 'spare him.'"

"Uh-huh." This was a big thing with him—pointing out all historical inaccuracies and implausible plot points in films and TV shows. Most of the time I found this clever and endearing, but lately it had started to wear a bit thin. "Listen. I'm going to Los Angeles tomorrow. And I'm going to be out there for a while."

He crammed popcorn into his mouth and crunched furiously.

I sighed. "Please don't ignore me. This is hard for me, too."

"When are you coming back?"

"I don't know. Maybe a month. Maybe longer; depending on what happens."

"Well, you must have given Alexa a time frame," he insisted. Alexa was my boss at the boutique.

"I didn't. In fact, I quit my job at the boutique."

This got his attention. "You *quit*? Becca, how could you do that?"

"Oh, come on, it was a bullshit job." I started twisting my ring around and around my finger, easing it over my knuckle and all the way up to the nail bed. "Practically minimum wage, crappy benefits, no opportunity for advancement . . ."

"But you—where are you going to work?"

I stared at my hands. "I told you. Los Angeles. I've got a job as a hostess in a restaurant near Melrose Avenue. I'll sew and try to market my samples during the day, then work at night."

"You said you were just going to visit Claire." His tone had taken on a distinctly accusatory edge.

"Kevin, I know you're unhappy about this. But you have to be fair. I did try to explain what I'll be doing out there."

"You . . . Becca." He fell back into his usual fatherly, analytical mode. "Be reasonable. You cannot quit your job."

"Too late." I winced. "I already did."

"This is insane. You know that?" He shook his head. "You quit your job, you go to California on impulse . . .what's wrong with you lately? You never showed any interest in restaurant work before. And your sister just got back from her honeymoon. Doesn't she want some time alone with Andrew?"

"They had to cancel their honeymoon because Andrew's having some sort of crisis at the studio. Claire begged me to come out because he's working twenty-four/seven and she's lonely in her gigantic new mansion. Try to put yourself in my shoes for just one minute, okay? I don't want to go from my parents' house to my husband's house and never take a risk, never put myself out there to see what I can do."

"This is Claire's doing," he decided. "She's always encouraged these flighty, frivolous impulses."

"I know you have very specific ideas of how our life together should be," I said, feeling the weight of these words in the pit of my stomach. "But I don't see this trip as flighty or frivolous. It's something I've wanted to do for a long time and I just . . . I feel like I'll never be happy if I don't try."

"So I don't make you happy?" he demanded, stung. "Well, life isn't about being happy. You have to consider other people's needs, not just your own." His face reddened as he broke out the big guns. "If you go to Los Angeles, there will be consequences. I don't have to let you walk all over me."

"You're right," I agreed. "You don't."

"If you go to Los Angeles, then we . . ." He took a deep breath. "We're finished! You have to choose: me or this trip."

"Kevin, please—"

"This doesn't fit in with our ten-year plan!"

I kept my tone steady as I said, "Well, maybe we need to make some adjustments to the plan."

He finally turned off the TV. All the sword slashes and battle cries and visceral grunts of pain gave way to silence. "What kind of adjustments? Is this about the stupid red door?"

"No." I collapsed back into the couch cushions. "Forget it. Forget I said anything."

"Fine. I'll forget you said any of this because you're being ridiculous." He took off his glasses and rubbed his forehead.

"Can't you try to support me in this? Or at least pretend to support me?"

"No." He turned back to the blank TV screen.

"I support your dreams and decisions, even though I don't always agree with them."

"Yeah, well, that's because my dreams and decisions aren't completely selfish and unrealistic." He crossed his arms over his chest. "This is your last warning, Becca. If you get on that plane tomorrow, we're through."

Years of living with Gayle had taught me how to gently verbalize feelings and fight fair. "I don't like being threatened with ultimatums."

"And I don't like giving them, but you leave me no choice."

I considered this for a minute, then plunged ahead. "I can't control what you do, but I'm going to the airport tomorrow. I have to."

He didn't say anything. Wouldn't even look at me.

I wriggled the diamond ring off and pressed it into his hand. "Should I leave this here?"

We sat on opposite sides of the couch, staring straight ahead and barely breathing.

Finally, he thrust the ring into his pocket, then turned to me and said, "Oh, don't be so dramatic. I'll drive you to the airport tomorrow. What time is your flight?"

He didn't give the ring back. More significantly, he didn't give me a security checkpoint wave or an in-flight book note, which meant that the ring was the least of our problems.

When we first started dating back in college, Kevin and I had perfected an airport drop-off routine that had attained the precision of a military drill as we saw each other off on family vacations (mine), job interviews (his), and business trips (also his). The dropper-off would always park in the short-term lot and accompany the taker-off to check in and snake through the security line. When the airline workers demanded boarding pass and ID, the dropper-off would step aside, watch the taker-off progress through the metal detector, and wave at regular intervals until the taker-off was out of sight. When I was the taker-off, Kevin would clandestinely tuck a little note in whatever novel or magazine that happened to be in my carry-on. Nothing sappy or grandiose, just *See you soon*s or *I love you*s scrawled on Post-its. Something to keep me smiling until landing.

So today, when he stopped his car by the curb under the DEPARTURES sign and said, "Bye. See you in a month," I was somewhat bewildered.

"Aren't you going to come in with me?"

He made a big show of checking his watch. "I have to go. Drew has an extra ticket to the Coyotes game and I'm supposed to meet him in twenty minutes."

I was 99.9 percent certain this was a lie, as neither he nor his friend Drew had any interest in professional sports outside of mastering Madden NFL 2006 on PlayStation. "So . . . does this mean we're officially breaking up?"

"No, it means I need time to think about what's best for us."

I forced myself to smile. "You get to decide all by yourself?"

"You already made your decision. I still have to make mine." He practically shoved me out of the car. I barely had time to lug my suitcases out of the trunk before he peeled away from the crosswalk.

"Bye." I lifted one hand as the car sped off toward the airport exit.

What the hell? Seriously. There were lots of questions bouncing around between us and no answers. I wasn't sure what it all meant, I wasn't sure if I had a boyfriend anymore, or even if that was what I truly wanted—to be Kevinless. All I knew for sure was that I suddenly felt impossibly, deliciously free. My hands shook with anticipation as I dragged my bags to the ticket counter and prepared to start the life I'd been dreaming about for the past five years.

7

The freeways were terrifying at first. All the brand-new cars—some of which cost nearly as much as the house Kevin had picked out in Phoenix—weaving in and out of the car pool lane with kamikaze speed. Everyone had places to go and people to see and traffic safety be damned.

"Are you kidding?" Claire, who had selected a very short black dress for airport pickup detail, laughed and swished her blond hair against the leather seat cover of her Mercedes SUV. Her massive diamond rings glinted in the afternoon sun. "This is nothing. Wait until rush hour. *Then* you'll see some carnage."

"I'll pass." I braced my hands against the dashboard as she

slammed on the brakes, stopping millimeters away from the bumper of the convertible in front of us. "Listen, is there any way I could take a bus to work or something?"

"A *bus*? Stop, please, you're killing me. Becks, this is L.A. There is no bus. There is no sidewalk. There is only freeway. Don't worry—you can borrow my Jetta while you're out here. I don't use it anymore since Andrew upgraded my wheels."

"I'll have to remember to wear nice underpants every day so as not to offend the ER orderlies when they examine my mangled corpse."

"Or quit wearing panties altogether," she suggested. "Give those poor exhausted residents a thrill."

"I hope you have lots of insurance coverage on that Jetta."

"Connor's restaurant is all the way over in West Hollywood; if you think I am driving your timid ass down Coldwater Canyon every day, you are sadly mistaken. Welcome to the real world, Grasshopper."

The next day, after some sisterly encouragement and several cups of the calming herbal tea Claire's yogi recommended for stress relief, I braved the highways and walked unscathed through the doors of the Rhapsody restaurant and bar. "Becca Davis, reporting for active duty."

Connor looked up from a pile of papers, obviously stressed and distracted, and ran one hand through his thick brown hair. "Hi. Listen, you didn't happen to bring a map to work, did you?"

"No. Was I supposed to—"

"'Cause I just got lost in your eyes." His mask of impatience dissolved into a laugh. "Now *that,* my friend, is a bad pickup line."

I grimaced. "I'm in physical pain."

"And I've got a million more where that one came from. I've been collecting them, just for you."

"Suddenly that job at Burger King doesn't sound so bad." I adjusted the neckline of the pink patterned halter dress I'd whipped up for the hostessing gig.

"That's what they all say, until they see the tips." He ushered me over to the bar and dug through the little refrigerator for two bottles of spring water. "So your flight out was okay? And you have a place to stay?"

I nodded. "Claire and Andrew's guesthouse. I had no idea that guesthouses actually existed outside of the set of *The OC.*"

"What, they only have one?"

"It's pretty big. Big enough to fit a bed and all four of my sewing machines. And I went fabric shopping on Maple Street yesterday, so already my bedroom's so crammed with muslin and cloth it looks like a third-world sweatshop."

"*Four* sewing machines? You planning on starting a production line in your closet?"

"Not quite yet." Claire had dragged me through a series of upscale west Melrose boutiques that morning to give me an idea of what they were stocking. "I am way out of my league here. Seriously. Do you have any idea how much Betsey Johnson charges for clamdiggers?"

"The real question is, do I have any idea what clamdiggers are?" He handed me a bottle of water. "Don't panic. Sunday evenings are usually pretty quiet around here, so tonight shouldn't be too taxing."

I nodded glumly, daunted by the prospect of trying to placate customers like the rail-thin fashionistas I'd seen lacerating the boutique salesgirls that afternoon.

"It's only your first day pounding the pavement," he said gently. "You have to develop a thick hide out here. I'm sure that whatever old Betsey's charging for clamdiggers, you'll be doubling it soon. And I'll even give you some free, unsolicited advice."

I raised an eyebrow. "'Plastics?'"

He laughed. "No. Charge more than things are worth, and everyone'll think you're worth more than you are. Especially out here. Your product is high quality, your time is valuable, and your prices should reflect that."

I must have looked skeptical, because he gestured to the water bottle in my hand. "Do you know how much we'd charge the customers for that?"

"Two-fifty?"

"Nine dollars. You know what we pay our supplier? A buck twenty."

"Jeez."

"Exactly. And we charge eighteen dollars for what's basically a three-dollar martini. But people are happy to pay. It makes them feel wealthy and important. You know you've arrived when you spring for a round of eighteen-dollar martinis."

"You have the temerity to charge eighteen dollars for a bit of vodka and a splash of vermouth and your customers are gullible enough to pay for it?"

"Gullible? They demand it! These people wouldn't want the three-dollar martini. They *spit* on the three-dollar martini. Three-dollar martinis are for the C-listers. Same thinking applies to clamdiggers. If Betsey Johnson sold them at anywhere near cost, you think even one single trophy wife worth her credit line would be caught dead in them?"

"Well. No." Obviously, I should have taken some marketing classes along with all those arts and humanities seminars in college.

"Don't worry. You'll pick up the right attitude in no time. Just remember, they should be *thanking* you for condescending to accept their filthy lucre."

He grinned. I grinned back.

Then my cell phone rang, jolting me back to reality, where I was a bad, until-very-recently-engaged girlfriend flirting hussily with a man I barely knew.

I dug the phone out of my bag and glanced at the caller ID: my mom, no doubt wondering if I'd survived another two hours without her. "Oh, I should take this."

"Boyfriend checking in?" He nodded. "No problem. Take your time. Ask for the manager when you're done—he'll introduce you to Aimee. See you later."

"Oh no, it's not my boyfriend," I called after him. "In fact, I'm not even sure I *have* a boyfriend anymore. We took a step back over the weekend and . . ."

But he had rounded the corner and headed off to oversee more important matters.

He didn't care whether I had a boyfriend or not, or what the status of our relationship was. Just like everyone else out here, he had places to go and people to see.

How professional. How appropriate. How disheartening.

"There are three types of important guests you have to be able to pick out." Aimee Chenard flipped her long, white-blond hair (topped with just enough dark root to give her an air of bad-girl rebellion) and dug a fresh cigarette out of what appeared to be a genuine Chanel bag. "Studio executives, radio people, and super-agents. They should be getting the best tables and the best service, but you're not going to be able to recognize them like celebrities."

"Then how will I know who's who?" I asked, drowning in the sea of information. Table numbers and phone systems and reservation policies . . .

"Most of them are regulars. You'll get to know them after a week or two."

"But what about tonight?" Dinner service was slated to start in half an hour, and at this point, I could barely remember my own name.

She took a long drag on her Marlboro Light. "I'll be helping you. Have no fear. You'll get used to life as a hyphen."

"Life as a what?"

"A hyphen. You know. Like I'm an actress-slash-model-slash-hostess. Which is why I can spot all the superagents at fifty paces." She whipped a stack of head shots out of her bag. "I hear you're a designer."

"I want to be. Progress has definitely been slow."

She laughed. "Didn't you just get here, like, yesterday?"

"Yes, but—"

"Then, cookie, the rejection rodeo has only begun. You'll get used to it—you just need to learn to speak the Language of No. Like 'I love your work' translates to 'You make me retch.' 'Fabulous' means 'Only slightly better than a sharp stick in the eye.' 'I'll call you' means 'When Puerto Vallarta freezes over.' 'You're so beautiful' means 'You didn't get the job, but I do want to sleep with you.' When in doubt, assume 'yes' means 'no.' "

"Then what does 'no' mean?"

"No. That's why we all have day jobs on the side, and this is a great place to meet contacts. Fred Segal comes in all the time. Let's see . . . what else do you need to know?" She glanced around the restaurant's main dining room, which was starting to fill up with servers, expediters, and bartenders. "I should give you a heads-up on Connor."

My eyes widened. "What about him?"

"Don't bother falling for him. All the new girls do, and it always ends the same."

"How?"

"Tears, heartache, your basic Shangri-Las song. You're only setting yourself up for disappointment."

"Well. I'm sort of already in a relationship—emphasis on the sort of—so that won't be a problem for me," I said, twisting my hands together.

She shook her head. "That's what I said, too, when the previous hostess gave me this same lecture."

"And now?"

"Let's just say I'm very impressed with his ability to resist curvaceous blondes. He doesn't date employees. Well, actually, he doesn't date *anyone,* as far as I know, but I'll keep working on him. He can't hold out forever."

I cast a surreptitious glance back toward Connor's office. "Why doesn't he date? Is he gay?"

She gave me a look. "Does he seem gay to you?"

"No, but—"

"Trust me, he ain't gay. But I've been working here for six months now, and as far as I know, he hasn't been involved with anyone since he broke up with Meena, the world's pit-iest pita."

"Pita?"

"Pain in the ass. She'd show up here at eight o'clock on a Friday night, no warning, with like ten of her very bestest friends and demand a corner booth. So then I'd ask her to wait a few minutes since weekends are always booked solid with people who actually *make* reservations and she'd have a hissy fit. 'Does Connor know you're treating me like this? You better get us a table right now, I don't care if George Clooney is still finishing his coffee.' And then she'd undertip." She took two more quick puffs on her cigarette, then stubbed it out in a glass ashtray tucked underneath the bar. "I have got to quit smoking. I just spent a fortune whitening my teeth and they'll be all dingy again by next week. Anyway, come on, I'll show you where we keep the menus."

I couldn't help myself. "So what finally happened with Meena and Connor?"

She shrugged one shoulder. "I guess he got tired of living with Mood Swing Barbie. And she got tired of all the rock climbing and skydiving and mountain biking."

"He's into rock climbing and skydiving?"

She laughed. "If you can break your spine doing it, he's into it. A one-man version of the X Games."

"Really?" Apparently, he hadn't been lying when he said he enjoyed taking risks in all areas of his life.

"Oh yeah. Half the time he comes in here, he's covered in mud and testosterone from some suicidal excuse for a sport. He even had a shower installed in the employee bathroom so he can get cleaned up before he goes out into the dining room." She rolled her eyes. "I don't know if Meena broke up with him because of all the cliff diving and whatever. All I know is, they had a big argument one night at the bar and when he got home after work that night, she'd moved out and taken all his stuff. The dishes, the flat-screen TV, the furniture, everything that wasn't nailed down."

"Did he ever get any of it back?"

"Nope. I think he just chalked it up to experience."

I raised my eyebrows. "He chalked a flat-screen TV up to experience?"

"Believe me, it was worth some high-end electronics and a leather sofa or two to be rid of that chick. They were doomed from the beginning—she kept demanding a ring and he's Mr. Restless Adventurer."

"Not the type to settle down?"

"Not unless you count jumping out of airplanes as settling down."

I couldn't suppress my smile. A man without a ten-year plan? Who didn't want to settle down? Be still my heart.

8

Five hours later, I had given up on sincere cordiality and settled for twisting my lips into a panicky permasmile. A public relations exec glared at me and demanded, "Where's the regular hostess?" A glassy-eyed former sitcom star screamed at me because the ladies' room was out of toilet paper. I spent the entire shift wringing my hands over how to recognize the appropriate people and how to react "appropriately"— friendly and impressed without being obsequious. As Aimee explained, "A-listers want to know that you know who they are, but they don't want you making a big deal out of it. So they get the best table and free drinks, but no autograph requests. If they wanted to be hounded and interrupted all night, they'd go to Planet Hollywood."

At eleven o'clock, my on-the-job mentor abandoned me to go eat dinner in the kitchen where, I suspected, she also wanted to flirt with the new expediter, a swarthy, aspiring action hero with biceps as big as volleyballs. I bent over to adjust the sandal strap digging into my ankle when an overdose of musky cologne inundated the hostess stand.

A shiny Italian loafer appeared next to my shoe.

"So . . . are we near LAX, or is that just my heart taking off?"

I made a face. "Connor, I thought you were—" I started, snapping back into an upright position. But the man leering at me from a scant four inches away wasn't Connor.

Short, squat, and bald, wearing a suit jacket cut way too wide for his shoulders, this man reeked of entitlement and Acqua di Giò.

"Hi." I took a quick step backward, almost tripping over my own feet. "Welcome to Rhapsody. How many in your party tonight?"

"You must be new here." He closed in on me, practically licking his chops. "Don't you know who I am?"

The rough stucco of the wall grated against my bare shoulders. I had no more room to retreat. Where the hell was Aimee? "Excuse me, sir, could you hang on for one moment?"

Lex Luther's doppelgänger reached out and poked one finger into the shallow divot between my collarbones. He slid his hand up my neck and traced my jawline. "A pretty girl like you shouldn't have to work all night. Why don't you join me at the bar?" This was a command, not a request.

"I'm really not allowed to drink at work."

He smirked. "Then let's go somewhere else."

"I don't think that'd be a good idea. I'm flattered, truly I am—"

"Don't bother playing hard to get," he barked. "Girls like you are a dime a dozen. I know everyone here and if I decide I want you fired, you'll be gone like that." He snapped his stubby fingers two inches from my face.

And then, just as I resigned myself to getting canned on my first day for refusing to prostitute myself to a guest, Connor materialized at my side.

He leaned over, ostensibly to check a listing in the reservations book, and wedged his body between me and the lothario. Then, with a smile and handshake, he said, "Hey, Mr. Jamieson. It's good to see you. I see you've met Becca, our new hostess. She's Andrew King's sister-in-law."

"Really. I didn't know." Mr. Jamieson backed off.

"We've got your usual table ready, of course. Follow me." And with that, Connor steered him toward the dining room.

The next morning, over green tea and egg-white omelets, Claire reaffirmed everything Aimee had said about Connor.

"He's a little, shall we say, eccentric." She jabbed her fork in the air with every word. "Doesn't smoke, hardly drinks, loves to vacation in far-flung places like Bhutan and Belize. Into backpacking, sleeping outdoors, the whole gung-ho wilderness nightmare."

"Not your type?"

"Why backpack when you can have room service and fluffy down pillows at the Four Seasons?" She shook her head. "*No hablo* L.L.Bean. Anyway, he's only had one serious relationship in the whole time Andrew's known him. And that fizzled out a few months ago."

"Meena. I heard all about it." I sipped my coffee and feigned nonchalance.

"Well, then, I'm only going to say this once. Watch yourself." She folded back the sleeves of her pink cashmere robe. "Don't get all infatuated with him. He's unlandable."

I choked on my coffee. "Who said anything about *landing* him?"

She gave me a pointed look. "I know you and Kevin are scrapping and you think you're on some magic L.A. adventure straight out of the Disney animation studios, but I'm warning you, if you're going to rebound, don't rebound in his direction."

"Okay, first of all, I don't even know what's going on with Kevin right now. I gave the ring back, we agreed we need to take a few steps back, but I'm not entirely sure we're broken up."

"Well, doesn't that seem like the kind of thing you *should* be entirely sure about?"

"Yeah, but he won't take any of my calls, so . . ."

She rolled her eyes. "Gee, Becca, let's puzzle this out. Do you *want* to be broken up?"

"Do I have to sit through another lecture on how you're a hard-headed realist and I'm a deluded romantic if I say yes?"

"No, I've given up on trying to talk sense into you." She paused for a bite of omelet. "Besides, it sounds like *he's* already broken up with *you*. Thank God your name isn't on that mortgage."

"Then why would he insist on driving me to the airport?"

"Who knows? Why do men do anything?"

I mulled this over for a moment. "Well, if he wants to break up, then—"

"No. Becca. We're not talking about him. We're talking about *you*. What do *you* want? Life is too short to be pussy-footing around like this. You think you have all the time in the world, but you're . . . wait, how old are you now?"

Lying about her age all these years must have permanently skewed her chronology. I smiled sweetly. "Well, I'm almost six years younger than you, so I guess that makes me twenty-four, right?"

She scowled. "You only have a few years left to find the right kind of guy, so if you're going to dump Kevin, you'd better get the lead out. Don't waste your time on a guy like Connor. You should start hanging around the UCLA Medical Center or something, find yourself a cute cardiologist. That car-wreck-with-no-panties scenario might not be a bad idea."

Glancing down at my white-on-white breakfast, I asked, "Can I have some toast and jam or something?"

"Sure, if you don't mind all those carbs." She started toward the state-of-the-art Sub-Zero refrigerator, pausing by the bay window to blow kisses to Andrew, who was backing out of the driveway in a low-slung, streamlined European sports car.

He waved, then screeched away.

"You know, I adore being married," she mused, popping two slices of 7-grain whole wheat into the toaster. "I'm happy. Really happy." She glanced down at the massive diamond on her finger. "Turns out, it's easy to be happy when you have a negative edge pool and a guesthouse."

"Claire." I laughed. "It's okay to admit you love your own husband. That doesn't make you a deluded romantic."

"Fine. I love him. But don't tell Gayle—I have a reputation to uphold." She got a dreamy, wistful look in her eyes that I'd never seen before. "I love getting up with him and making his coffee. I love being introduced as Mrs. King. I love sleeping in the same bed with him every night. Of course, I also love my new house and my Benz, but luckily, it's all a package deal. And guess what?" She sat back down and motioned me in, checking to make sure neither of the newly hired housekeepers were listening in. "We've decided to have a baby."

"Already?"

"Yeah. We started trying a few weeks before the wedding— for all I know, I might be knocked up right now." She beamed down at her minuscule waistline.

"But don't you want to spend some time alone, just the two of you? To bond as a couple?"

"I think we're as bonded as we're gonna get." She shrugged. "We both want children, and let's face it, I'm not getting any younger. I can't wait to decorate the nursery. We're going to redo the guest room down the hall from the master suite—I'm thinking white and green, with a bunny theme. There's this great Italian artist in Santa Monica who specializes in murals for kids' rooms; I was thinking we could paint a whole wall with scenes from *Peter Rabbit* . . ."

My eyes glazed over while she yammered on about Beatrix Potter and trompe l'oeil. Finally, when she started in on the merits of half-day preschool versus a European au pair, I interrupted.

"So *anyway*—"

". . . And that's why it's great to have the resources we do, you see? Our child can get bumped up the waiting list at Crossroads. All it takes is a phone call. Well, a phone call from Kate Hudson, but I'm actually pretty sure that one of my yoga buddies has a class with her, so—"

"Great. Back to Connor. How long has he been living out here?"

It took her a minute to snap out of her maternal reverie, but after a few sips of tea, she was once again ready for boy talk. "I'm not sure. He grew up in Colorado, I think. One of the ski resort towns—Aspen or Steamboat Springs or something."

"He mentioned he used to work construction in Denver."

Claire wrinkled her nose. "That doesn't surprise me at all. He has a do-it-yourself streak a mile wide. The man has no middle ground—he's either wearing an Armani suit and cufflinks or a sweat-soaked grimy T-shirt."

I grinned. "I think that's kind of sexy."

"Hey. What did I just say about steering clear of him?"

"But—"

"He's the opposite of Kevin Bradley, I grant you that. But do you really want to spend your prime dating years wandering through snake-infested canyons, courting death on white-water raft expeditions and remodeling roach-infested old houses?" She nodded. "Oh yes. That's what he does for fun. That and take heart-stopping risks with his stock portfolio."

"Well, it seems to be working out for him."

"Sure, he's stocked up on Armani suits today, but he could lose it all tomorrow, and then he'd be"—she shuddered—"poor."

"A fate worse than death," I said dryly.

"Hey, at least if I die I've got some fabulous black Valentino to wear at my funeral." She tucked her hair behind her ear and propped her freshly pedicured toes up on the empty chair next to us. "I keep telling you, you have to look at the bottom line: financial security. Especially if you're going to be a total professional washout like me and need someone else to carry you through the rest of your life."

"Hey." I touched her arm. "You are not a washout."

She flipped up the collar of her robe and stared at the sunlight pouring in through the window. "There's no point in denying it."

"How can you say that? Look at everything you've done."

"Everything my husband's done," she corrected. "I don't even pretend to have a real job anymore."

The toaster dinged, breaking the long silence.

"Thank God I found Andrew." She got up and stacked the toast on a translucent white china plate.

"Claire—"

She silenced me with a wave of her hand. "Listen. You did the right thing coming out here. Don't give up on your design stuff. You're very talented. And I'm . . ." She turned away from me and grabbed a jar of strawberry preserves. "I'm sorry about the wedding gown."

I shrugged. "A month sleeping in your guesthouse, driving your car ought to make up for it."

"No, it was horrible, what I did." She rubbed her forehead with her palm. "I *had* to have the name-brand dress to go with the name-brand ring and the name-brand groom. Total bridal psychosis, what can I say?"

"You could do a lot worse than Carolina Herrera," I conceded.

She turned around to meet my gaze. "No, Becca, yours was better. Yours was perfect."

This was the first time that anyone except Connor had said anything remotely encouraging about my prospects as a designer.

"Well I spent part of last week redoing the hem and changing the color from ivory to plum," I confessed. "If you still want it . . ."

"Of course!" She presented me with my customary, calorie-laden breakfast of toast and jam. "It'll be perfect for the charity dinner we're going to next month."

"But you damn well better wear it this time," I warned her.

"I will."

"And if anybody asks who designed it, you'd better drop my name like a slippery bowling ball."

"I will," she vowed. "I'm all about keeping my promises these days. Wait and see."

After I finished my first Friday night shift at Rhapsody, I felt the way I imagine new mothers must feel after they give birth to triplets—drained, sweaty, in desperate need of pharmaceutical intervention. (Though in my case, the agony was localized in my toes and ankles.) Curse that Aimee and her so-called foolproof formula for success: "Wear your hair down and the highest heels you have, then watch the tips roll in."

"But won't that permanently disfigure my feet?" I'd asked.

"Don't worry. Plastic surgery's come a long way." She'd pointed down at her own French-pedicured toes which, if I wasn't very much mistaken, were encased in sassy lime green Christian Louboutins. This season. She had quite a luxurious wardrobe for a restaurant hostess, but I was starting to figure out that an L.A. woman's income often had no bearing on her lifestyle choices. Rumor had it that Lily, one of the bartenders, had just bought a shiny new black Cadillac Escalade.

"She just lives for that car." Aimee had explained. "And *in* it. The payments cost as much as her rent, so she just sleeps in the backseat at night. Luckily, it's pretty roomy."

At Aimee's urging, I'd worn my highest-heeled sandals and mercifully lost all feeling in my toes by 9:30. I could only hope that the pitiful excuse for health insurance I'd COBRA'd over from the boutique would cover the inevitable amputation.

When I finally finished my shift, I collapsed on the luxurious new bedding in Claire's guesthouse and tried to rally enough energy to struggle out of my clothes and brush my teeth before turning out the lights.

My eyes fluttered closed. Personal hygiene was overrated.

The high-pitched chimes of my cell phone jerked me back into consciousness. I groaned, fumbling through my purse. Maybe I'd forgotten to punch out of the computer system at work. Maybe Lily the bartender needed somewhere to sleep.

"Hello?"

"Hi, Becca."

"Kevin?" I rubbed at my eyes with the heel of my hand. "It's . . . two-thirty."

"I know. But I need to talk to you."

"Okay. I'm listening." I struggled up into a sitting position. "I'm glad you're finally calling me back."

"Well, I had to wait until I was ready. I've had a lot to think about over the past few days."

"Okay."

Long pause, during which I almost fell asleep. Then he cleared his throat and announced, "I'm not giving the ring back."

My eyes popped open. "Okay."

"Not even if you beg."

"Okay."

"And as for the house, I'm going ahead with that whether you're on board or not."

"Okay."

"That's all you have to say?" he demanded. "'Okay'?"

"Well it sounds like you've made up your mind," I said carefully. "And I agree—we're not good for each other right now. Honestly, this breakup is—"

"Who said anything about breaking up?"

"You just did," I pointed out. "Not giving the ring back, building the house without me . . ."

"Yeah, but that doesn't mean we're breaking up. I'm just taking a few steps back until you reevaluate your life and get your priorities straight."

"Well, that's a very generous offer and I sure do appreciate it," I said, dishing out a double helping of sarcasm, "but I have my priorities straight."

"No, you don't. So I'll hold on to the ring and wait till you're ready."

"You don't get to make all the decisions." I bristled. "I like it out here. And I refuse to put everything on hold indefinitely. We're either in love or we're not."

He tsk-tsked. "Why do you always have to oversimplify everything?"

I gave myself over to all the aches and pains pulsing through me for a moment—my feet, my legs, my head, my heart—and then I said, "We're done. Someone has to call this breakup what it is. We're done."

"I understand you're upset right now, but—"

"You're right. I am upset. But I've been thinking about this too, and it's the right decision. You're not happy, I'm not happy. We need to make a clean break and move on."

"You don't mean that." His voice shook.

"I do. I'm sorry, Kevin, but I do."

For a moment, I felt sure he was going to break down and cry. Which would make *me* break down and cry because, no matter how different we had become, we'd shared five years of our lives and I couldn't bear to hear him mourn the end alone.

But he didn't cry. He took a deep breath and said, "Call me back when you're ready to discuss this rationally."

Mimicking his tone of supreme pragmatism, I said, "I am discussing this rationally."

"You'll change your mind. You always do."

"No. We're broken up."

"We are *not* broken up. Listen, I don't want to argue about this anymore. Call me tomorrow and we'll figure everything out."

My façade of rationality started to crumble. "Oh, no you don't! I don't need your permission! We are broken up! Do you hear me? *Broken up!*"

"No, you'll come to your senses—"

Mercifully, miraculously, call waiting beeped and cut out the middle of his sentence.

"—so call me as soon as you get your head straightened out," he finished.

"Okay. You know what? I have to go. Call waiting."

I clicked over to the other line, figuring that whatever was waiting for me on line two *had* to be less of a trainwreck than what I was dealing with on line one. "Hello?"

"Becca? It's Connor."

I sat up a little straighter. "Hi."

"I'm still at the restaurant, but I wanted to let you know— oh, damn, I just looked at the time. Did I wake you?"

"No." I smiled. Imagine. A man who could lose track of time, who wasn't afraid to start the day without every hour plotted out in advance. And who wasn't afraid to get his hands dirty doing *hot . . . sweaty . . . manual . . . labor . . . and then peel off his shirt, revealing chiseled six-pack abs . . .*

Connor interrupted my reverie, reminding me that this was a business call, not a 1-900 hotline.

"Good. Listen, I wanted to let you know that I found a

boutique owner who wants to look at your stuff. If you're interested."

"Oh my God. You're serious? Who?" All lingering thoughts of six-pack abs evaporated.

"Miriam Russo. I think her store's over on Robertson."

I made a mental note to ask Claire about the Robertson retail climate. "That's great! That's amazing! That's . . . how the hell did you do that?"

"Oh, you know."

"I don't know. Enlighten me."

"When you're in business out here, you make all kinds of contacts. And it turns out that one of my producer buddy's publicist's boyfriend's personal trainer used to work with Miriam."

"Ah."

"She was in for dinner tonight and I talked you up. She gave me her card and said you should call her after the weekend."

"Wow. What did you say to her?"

"Oh, you know, that you're a genius who's light-years ahead of your time, et cetera, et cetera. She said she'd be happy to give you ten minutes of her time. So what do you say?"

I took a flying leap off the bed and bounced around the room.

"Becca? You still there?"

"I'm here," I said, a little winded. "But wait. Not to look a gift horse in the mouth, but, well . . . you're taking an awfully big chance talking me up to a customer, aren't you? I mean, you barely know me . . . What if I'm unreliable? What if my designs are horrible enough to scar both Dolce and Gabbana for life?"

"Three days in L.A. and already a cynic?"

"I guess so." I took a few seconds to gather my nerve. Because I wanted to flirt with him, and here was my opening. Could I do it? I could. I should. As of two minutes ago, I was officially single. And the 1-900 fantasies were still fresh in my mind. That's the only possible explanation for what happened next. I, Becca Davis, eternal good girl and shrinking violet, somehow managed to convince myself to say, doing my best Kathleen Turner impression, "Unless, of course, you have *ulterior motives . . .*"

I held my breath through a few agonizing seconds of silence. Then:

"No!" he practically yelled. "Oh God, I'm so sorry you'd even *think* that I'm hitting on you . . ."

I curled up into a fetal position on the bed as he blathered, "I know you're engaged, I know you're an employee. Believe me, I would *never* suggest anything of a romantic nature. If I inadvertently gave you the idea I was attracted to you, I apologize, because believe me, I am *not!*"

I covered the phone's mouthpiece and started to whimper.

"Honestly, my interest in you is strictly professional and platonic. I never meant to imply I was attracted to you, God no, that couldn't be further from the truth . . ." He carried on along these lines for another full minute, after which point I couldn't believe I hadn't literally died of humiliation.

"Okay," I squeaked, when he finally stopped for air. "I have to go now. Thanks for everything. Bye."

And with that, I turned off my cell phone and settled in for a long night of festering mortification.

But in the "glass is half-full" department, I wasn't obsessing about Kevin anymore.

9

I stayed in bed as long as I possibly could on Saturday, toying with the idea of undergoing drastic facial reconstruction and moving to Orange County ("the dark side of the Orange Curtain," as Claire called it), where no one would ever find me. And then maybe, someday in the distant future, after years of intensive counseling and a lobotomy, I could put this whole flirting fiasco behind me.

In the meantime, I could always just kill myself. But then Kevin would insist on speaking at my funeral about how I'd always been prone to irrational fits of passion. Ugh. Forget it.

I was single now, and there were adventures to be had.

Not with Connor Sullivan, clearly, but adventures nonetheless. And I needed money to finance these adventures, along with groceries and gas. So I dragged myself to Rhapsody, where, to my immense relief, Connor wasn't expected until later that afternoon. Rumor had it he'd gone kayaking in Marina del Rey.

"What happened to you?" Aimee asked when I slouched in, clad in a black sweater, black pants, and black shoes. "You're an existential crisis in heels."

"Don't ask," I muttered, dropping my bag on the tile floor. "We expecting a big crowd tonight?"

"Booked solid, as usual." She put her hands on her hips and beamed. "But I have big news. News that is going to turn that frown upside down."

"Please tell me those words did not just come out of your mouth." I grimaced. "Next are you going to explain how 'assume' makes an 'ass' out of 'u' and 'me'?"

"I'm going to *kick* your ass if you don't wipe that puss off your face and stop killing my buzz."

"Okay." I braced both hands against the bar. "I'm ready. What's up? Did you get an audition callback?"

"Nope." She pursed her lips into a pouty moue. "All the casting people keep calling my agent and saying they like my auditions, but I'm just not right for the leading lady parts."

"Well, what do they think you're right for?"

"The woman casting the commercial I read for yesterday said I was more the 'slutty best friend' type. She said my boobs are too big for an ingenue. Can you believe that? Why didn't she just slap me in the face? Then she said you have to be flat to be a heroine. So I said, 'What about Angelina Jolie and Halle Berry?' and she said, 'What about Renee Zellweger and Kirsten Dunst?'"

"Sounds pretty arbitrary to me."

"Exactly. Anyway. On to my news." She flipped her hair over her shoulders, performed a little warm-up shimmy against the wall, then whipped off her jacket to reveal the corset I'd made for her. "Ta-da! Feast your eyes on the best advertisement you'll ever have!"

"Ha-cha!" I finally cracked a smile. "That was a Thursday afternoon well spent."

After the dinner rush on Wednesday night, Aimee had asked what kind of clothes I made, so I'd shown her a sketch of a new corset-top design I'd been working and reworking in my studio (a.k.a. my bedroom). She thought it was sexy and promised to wear it to "all the places I go to see and be seen" if I'd make one for her. So I'd spent Thursday afternoon hunched over my sewing machine, trying to get the boning lined up properly and the lacing grommets spaced for minimum bunching. Given her fair skin and blue eyes, I'd chosen layers of turquoise silk satin and chiffon, with a vanilla-colored ribbon threaded through in back.

She'd paired it with a dark denim microminiskirt and retro eighties pointy-toed pumps, sort of Anna Kournikova meets biker bar.

"It's laundry day, so I decided to trot out my new designer duds. What do you think?"

"I think I'm going to hire you to be the official Becca Davis fashion model when I scrape up enough cash to put a portfolio together."

"I L-U-V looove this corset. I can't believe you made it in . . . ?" She shot me a questioning look.

"Five hours. Well, I've been tinkering with the design for months, and corsets are easy because they're adjustable. Now, pants . . . those are hard. Especially for women."

"Because everyone's curves are different?"

"Particularly in the hip area."

"Is that why it's so frickin' impossible to find a pair of jeans that fit?"

"Yep. Anything fitted or tapered, with a zipper, is much trickier to make. It's actually quite mathematically complicated."

"So basically, it's my ass's fault I'll never be able to wear a pair of Sevens? I'm stuck with Levi's for the rest of my life?" She turned around to address her booty. "Did you hear that? It's all your fault!"

Without warning, Connor ambled into the midst of all this, looking disheveled in jeans and a navy pullover, his thick brown hair damp. He raised his eyebrows at Aimee's ensemble and said, "What, you couldn't afford the rest of the outfit?"

"Aren't you supposed to be kayaking?" she retorted.

"I'm back. What's with the *Pretty Woman* get-up?"

"Do you like it?" She batted her eyes at him.

I couldn't even look him in the face. So I stared up at the ceiling, trying to act casual and praying the roof would collapse on my head.

He ignored both the eye batting and the ample display of cleavage swelling out of Aimee's corset. "I'd like it better if you put a sweater over it. We do occasionally get minors in here."

She gave me a conspiratorial glance and informed him, "Becca made it. Isn't she talented? I'm her official spokesmodel."

"And it goes against the spokesmodel code of ethics to wear sweaters?" He winked at me.

I nodded stiffly and busied myself with stacking menus. The hell? How dare he wink? Did he think a paltry little *wink* could somehow erase the horror of last night and restore our rapport?

Well, it could *not*. There would be no more flirting of any kind. From now on, I was gonna be all business, all the time.

"And, hey, I've got a new one for you. Heard it last night at the bar." His dark eyes gleamed. "Your eyes are blue, like the ocean—"

"My eyes are brown," I pointed out.

"—and baby, I'm lost at sea."

I managed to keep my expression bland.

"No good?" He drummed his fingers on the counter. "Okay, how about: I believe it was Socrates who said, 'Know thyself.' Well, I already know myself, baby, how about I get to know you?"

Aimee looked horrified. "I don't think you're allowed to talk like that unless you're wearing a polyester leisure suit and gold medallions."

He smiled pityingly. "Don't be jealous of my *rico suave* finesse."

"Then don't hate me because I'm beautiful," she countered.

See? He bantered with everyone. How stupid was I to think he'd actually meant anything by it? I was turning into one of those pathetic narcissists who thought every guy who said "hi" wanted to take me to Paris for the weekend.

"Becca?" Connor was staring at me. As was Aimee. "You okay?"

"Yeah." I shook my head. "I'm fine."

"You look a little rattled," he said.

"She's crying inside because you won't let me wear the culmination of her life's work," Aimee said.

In the end, he let her wear the corset provided she changed into a longer skirt. And at precisely 8:30 P.M., my human advertisement paid off.

"Becca! *Becca!*" Aimee flagged me down from across the dining room, sprinting over to the hostess stand as fast as her pointy pumps would carry her.

I finished taking a reservation and hung up the phone. "What?"

"That woman who just left"—she pointed to the retreating

back of a woman with dark hair wearing well-cut jeans and a black leather jacket—"is a stylist. Rachelle Robinson's stylist!"

Rachelle Robinson was Tinseltown's red-carpet darling *du jour*. Tall, statuesque, and always impeccably dressed, she could have given Charlize Theron a lesson or two in glamour.

I watched the brunette escape out the door. "And I didn't even get her card. Dammit!"

"No, you don't understand. I got her card for you! She loved this corset and she wanted to know where I got it. Get ready: she wants you to make one for Rachelle Robinson."

I grabbed her forearm. "Get out."

"Oh, I'm out." She pressed a pale pink business card into my hand. "She wants you to call her next week. She said something about needing it for a movie premiere!"

I thought about all those press cameras taking all those pictures, which would then be reprinted in all those fan magazines. And the big, bold caption underneath the photos would read: "Rachelle Robinson dazzles in a corset by Becca Davis."

It took every last drop of self-control not to dial up the stylist this second and beg for a chance to lick her stiletto boots.

But then I remembered what Connor had said about placing a high value on my work. And how I should act like I was doing the fashion world a favor. So how to achieve the right balance of ambition, confidence, and gratitude?

I announced I was taking my break and headed back to the office to ask Mr. 1–900 himself.

*   *   *

"You look like a woman with exciting news," Connor observed when I poked my head into the back room.

"I am." I couldn't stop grinning.

"Well, then"—he closed his computer file and gestured to an empty metal chair next to the desk—"spill."

I took a seat and recapped my conversation with Aimee. "And so Rachelle Robinson might be photographed at a premiere wearing one of my pieces. I'd get my name in the papers and everything."

"Hang on a second." He held up both hands. "I reel in a boutique owner, and then Aimee comes up with an actual celebrity stylist? Damn! What trumps celebrity stylist? Magazine editor? Tommy Hilfiger himself?"

I laughed. "It's not a competition."

"Not a competition? Have you *met* Los Angeles men?"

"Sadly, I have. Where else would I get lines like, 'Dollface, if you were words on a page, you'd be what they call fine print'?"

He looked ill. "Someone actually said that to you?"

According to Aimee, witness to the linguistic offense, the perpetrator was a fairly well-known entertainment reporter. "I cannot incriminate the clientele. And, in his defense, I'm pretty sure he was plastered at the time."

"There's not enough tequila in all of Mexico to excuse that kind of effrontery."

"Says the man who resorted to 'Socrates says, "Know thyself"' not six hours ago."

"I was *kidding*."

"I know, I know. You've made that crystal clear."

"Good, because I wouldn't want you—you or your fiancé—to think that I would ever—"

"I get it." My smile evaporated. "*Anyway*. My question is, what do I say when I call up this stylist? I really want this job, but I don't want to sound too eager."

"Right. Good."

"And I don't have a huge résumé or a lot of room to negotiate, so I'm willing to give her the corset for cost. How do I convey that without sounding desperate?"

He started shaking his head. "You don't. Here's what you say—"

"Hang on. Let me write this down so I don't panic and cave when I'm actually having the conversation." I leaned over to grab a pen and sketch pad from my bag. The purse strap caught on the leg of Connor's chair, spilling glossy issues of *Vogue, InStyle*, and *Lucky* onto the floor.

"Whoa." He looked a little daunted. "No wonder you're always dragging around those huge purses. Did Claire assign you a style syllabus or something?"

I shook my head. "I read every fashion magazine I can get my grubby little hands on. Always have. To get ideas. Not to copy whole pieces, of course, but little details—lace trim, embroidery, the drape of a material—will grab my attention. I used to cover my entire bedroom wall in torn-out magazine pages. It drove my mom crazy, not to mention my ex-fiancé."

He tilted his head. "*Ex*-fiancé?"

"Yeah. He was kind of a neat freak." I waited to see if more questions would follow, but Connor just nodded thoughtfully.

So I supplied, "We broke up. Permanently."

"Okay." He shrugged. "No need to discuss it if it makes you uncomfortable."

"Okay. Fine." I uncapped my pen and prepared to record Connor's words of business wisdom. "Back to the stylist. I'm going to call her on Monday afternoon after I meet with the boutique owner."

"Show her you're interested and you can follow through," he agreed. And then the interoffice speaker blared: "Connor, call on line one."

"Sorry. Hang on," he said to me, then leaned toward the speaker. "Is it important?"

"It's Meena."

"Tell her I'll call her later." He turned back to me, his expression grim. "I apologize for the interruption. That was just . . ."

"Your ex-girlfriend."

He blinked. "How do you know her name?"

"Well . . ." My trusty women's intuition was whispering that *I pumped Claire and Aimee for information about your personal life and savored every juicy morsel they threw my way* was the wrong way to go with this. "She's kind of famous among the Rhapsody employees."

"Famous or infamous?"

"Depends on who you talk to."

He rolled his eyes. "Do you guys actually do any *work* at work, or just spread gossip and innuendo?"

"We spread gossip and innuendo *while* we work," I explained. "Think of it as esprit de corps."

"I can only imagine what unsavory rumors are circulating about me."

"I'll never tell." I settled back in my chair. "Now back to business: a plucky young lass like me, how much do you think five hours of my sewing expertise is worth?"

10

D o you want to hear something crazy?" I asked Claire on Sunday afternoon as we pored over paint colors at a tragi-cally hip home design shop in Brentwood. "Like, absolutely stark raving mad?"

"Sure. Hit me."

"You know how I have the appointment with the Miriam Russo boutique tomorrow morning? Well, Connor thinks I should charge nine hundred dollars for one of my corsets." I waited for the gales of laughter.

But she merely pored over the celadon paint chips. "Yeah, that sounds about right."

"Nine hundred dollars? Are you kidding me? No one's going to pay that!"

"Of course they are." She plucked at the cream cashmere sweater she'd thrown on over her jeans and James Perse T-shirt. "This sweater cost almost that much."

"You have nine hundred dollars to shell out on a sweater?"

She shrugged. "Andrew does. I keep telling you, Becks, it's just as easy to fall in love with a rich man as a poor one."

"Easy there, Ivana. Let's just stick to the corset."

"Fine. But you should listen to Connor when he says that Angelenos are into image. Cars, clothes, connections. It's not what you know . . . it's who you know, what you drive, what gym you belong to, and how many quasi-celebrities you can wrangle into showing up at your parties."

"Is that why Courteney and Jennifer were at your wedding?"

She ignored this. "Do you think most people you see in brand-new Boxsters on the 405 can actually afford their lifestyles? No. Most people are hopelessly in debt. I was, until I met Andrew. And, just between you and me, we had to take out some pretty hefty loans to afford the wedding and the house and the new cars. Because you need constant cash flow to maintain the image."

I thought about Aimee's Chanel bag and Lily the bartender's Escalade. "Ah, yes. The all-important image."

"If you want to be successful, you're going to have to be a lot more sympathetic to your target demographic," she said.

"And my target demographic is women with lots of money,

lots of time to shop, and a desire to impress other women with lots of money?"

"*Thin* women with lots of money," she corrected. "More precisely, thin women who want to *look* like they have lots of money. Which is why you'll be charging nine hundred dollars. If it's not hard to find and impossible for the average *E!* viewer to afford, nobody wants it."

"Except for all those *E!* viewers."

"That's right. And when they finally do get their hands on it, it becomes passé, like the whole pashmina phenomenon. If you want to play with the big girls, you have to do more than sketch and sew and fantasize about a world without polyester. You have to start thinking like a ruthless competitor. Women have to work twice as hard and be twice as smart as men to get ahead in the business world," declared the girl who'd never spent a single day in an office.

I managed, through Herculean effort, not to roll my eyes. "I'll bear that in mind."

"Good. Now, if we're done with today's Q & A session, I have other things to discuss. First up: How would you feel about doing the interior décor for the nursery? I'll knock a hundred bucks off your rent."

"You're not charging me any rent," I pointed out.

"Okay, then I won't throw you out in the streets."

"Tough but fair. But what happened to the world-famous Italian artiste in Santa Monica?"

"Eh. He's been done to death." She wrinkled her nose. "I

don't want the exact same nursery as every other mom on the A-list. I want something new and different. You know, cutting edge."

"I'm not sure 'cutting edge' and 'nursery' are terms we should really be putting together. Besides, I hate to be the one to point this out, but there is no actual baby to occupy this nursery."

She turned to me, cheeks flushed, eyes shining. "Until now."

I squealed so loudly, the shop clerk paused mid-phone conversation to shush us. "Are you serious?"

"Yep."

"When did you find out?"

"This morning. In the bathroom. I peed, the little line turned pink, I cried; it would have been a great commercial for First Response."

"I'm going to be an aunt!" We grabbed each other's hands and hopped up and down. The salesgirl upped the voltage on her death ray glare. "Does Andrew know?"

"I'm telling him tonight. After dinner." Her whole face glowed. "Somehow, it didn't seem like phone material."

"Yeah, I guess it's better to do it in person. And he seems pretty busy at work." This was a huge understatement—I'd barely seen the man since I'd moved into his backyard bungalow.

"Well, that's because he has, like, a whole department of people reporting to him." She sighed dreamily, then patted her cashmere-encased stomach. "He's very busy and important, you know."

"What do you think he'll say when you break the news?"

"He'll be thrilled, of course. At first I was afraid it was wedding stress making my period late, but nope, turns out I'm just incredibly fertile. We must have conceived one of the very first times we tried."

I squeezed her hand. "A wedding, a new house, a new baby—that's a lot of life changes all at once."

"But it's what I *want*." She laughed. "That's what I keep trying to tell you, Becks—you have to know what you want. And then, when you get it, you can really appreciate it." Her eyes misted up as she gazed at the massive diamond weighing down her left ring finger. "This baby is the last piece of the puzzle. I have everything I've ever wished for."

Her cell phone rang, breaking her reverie. She checked the incoming call screen—"It's Andrew. I can't talk to him now or I'll spill my guts and ruin the surprise"—then shut the phone off. "Now." She grabbed my elbow and steered me back toward the paint chips. "I know you'll do a great job planning my baby shower. I'm thinking finger sandwiches, petits fours, very country club kitsch. I'll give you the list of people to invite—don't you dare forget Courteney and Jennifer."

Aimee tagged along to the appointment at the Miriam Russo Boutique and insisted on wearing her prototype of my corset design, her argument being, "It'll look good on a mannequin, but it looks even better on me."

Immodest but true.

We hurried down Robertson together, me a bundle of nerves in what I hoped was a sufficiently stylish and professional black, V-neck wrap dress, she a head-turning sylph in azure chiffon and tight white pants.

We paused a block away from the boutique so I could straighten my hair, reapply lipstick, and think calm, confident thoughts.

"I'm gonna collapse," I announced, bracing a hand on a park bench to steady myself. "When the paramedics arrive, tell them I'm blood type O negative and allergic to sulfa drugs."

"*Chica.* You must chill." She tossed her head, whipped off her sunglasses, and checked out the driver of a passing BMW. "You're going to be great. Miriam will love you, she'll buy every single article of clothing you can put together, you'll quit your job at Rhapsody, sign me as the official face of Becca Davis designs, and finally give in and sleep with Connor and live happily ever after."

I stopped fretting about corsets and sulfa drugs for a second. "I'll *what*?"

"Don't play coy with me. There's enough chemistry between you two to keep DuPont labs going for a year. Everybody knows it."

"And who, may I ask, is 'everybody'?"

"The entire waitstaff at Rhapsody. Even though I wanted

him for myself, I forgive you. If I can't get him, at least he's going to someone I love."

I started sputtering outraged denials, but she just said, "Come on, we're going to be late," planted both hands on my shoulder blades, and propelled me toward the high priestess of high fashion.

"First of all, if you're going to work with me, you're going to have to change your name. Rebecca Davis? Blah." Miriam Russo crinkled her tan, freakishly small nose. Claire had warned me that Miriam had been the victim of a rhinoplasty gone horribly awry in the early nineties and I was not to call attention to it under any circumstances.

"But that's my name," I said meekly, focusing on everything except Miriam's lopsided nostrils: her platinum pageboy, the white silk wallcoverings, the bejeweled cuff bracelets displayed beneath the glass counter.

"Well, it doesn't work at all." She closed her leather glasses case with a snap. "You need a name that people will remember. But we'll get to all that in good time, if necessary. Let's see your samples. I have another appointment in twenty minutes, so make it snappy."

Before I could unwrap the perfectly seamed corset I'd packed in tissue and plastic, Aimee strutted into the fray and struck a pose, complete with vampy lips and jutting hips. "*Violà*," she announced, making love to a nonexistent camera. "The Becca Davis couture corset."

"Mm-hmm." Miriam's expression was that of a caffeine-deprived teenager in her fifth hour of traffic school.

"I do lots of other things, too," I hastened to add. "Dresses, tops, even wedding gowns. And I'm working on getting a website together, and a media portfolio . . ."

She waved these details away. "How much?"

"For the corset?"

"Yes, Rebecca Davis. How much would you suggest I charge for one of your little . . . creations?"

"Um." I blinked. Aimee flailed wildly in the background, jabbing upward with both thumbs. "Eight—no, nine hundred?"

"I see." She looked profoundly unimpressed.

"I could actually come in and do the measurements myself, if you want. I do custom fittings and alterations . . ."

One eyebrow shot up over that tiny crooked nose. "You do your own sewing?"

"Yes. Eventually, I'll hire some seamstresses, of course, but for now—"

"That explains why there's no zipper." She whipped her glasses back out of their case and put them on.

"No zipper? You mean, on the corset?"

"If one of my clients is going to pay nearly one thousand American dollars for a corset, she'll rightfully expect to be able to put it on without assistance."

"But . . ." I pointed to Aimee, who turned around to display her back like the dutiful spokesmodel she was. "There's lacing right there."

"Yes, but she can't possibly lace *herself* up, now can she?" Miriam demanded, her hawklike gaze zooming in on the criss-crossed ribbons cinching the garment closed. "Fashion is pointless without function."

I wanted to argue this point (because, really, what about feather boas, stiletto heels, and those horrible jelly shoes from the eighties?), but knew that forcing a debate would only hurt my cause. So I chose my next words carefully. "But *I've* managed to try these on without help from anyone else."

A polite, close-lipped smile flashed across her face. "How wonderful for you. But my clients won't be able to. They have delicate manicures, they have sore shoulders from going to the gym, and even if they manage to get it *on,* they'll have a perfect bitch of a time getting it *off* if they're drunk, in a hurry, or in the dark. You need to consider the needs of your clientele," she scolded, sounding eerily like Claire.

"So . . . you're passing?" I winced as soon as the words left my mouth.

The eyebrow went up again. "Add a zipper, give me fifty-five percent of the purchase price, and we might have a deal."

Aimee's jaw dropped at "fifty-five percent," but I had stopped listening long before that.

"You really want me to put in a zipper? On a chiffon corset?"

"Just tuck it in by a side seam. No one will notice."

"But it'll ruin the drape of the fabric."

"Then fix that. You're a *designer,* aren't you?"

"But I can't mix lightweight silk with a heavy metal fastener like a zipper. It'll just . . . well, don't you think it'll look odd?"

"Listen. Rebecca." My name sounded so horribly provincial when she said it. *Listen. Billie Jean. Sammy Jo. Misty Mae.*

I studied the plush beige carpet. "Yes?"

"I'm sure you're a very talented young lady, but I'm running a business here and I don't have time for stubborn artistic purists. Add a zipper and we'll talk. Otherwise"—she tapped her fingernails on the spotless glass counter—"it was lovely to meet you, and I'll give you a call if I ever need a piece for a costume gala."

And that was the end of that. I emerged from the whispery cool cocoon of elegance into the heat and the honking horns outside.

"I am such an idiot," I keened as the smell of smog and stale sweat smacked me in the face. "*Idiot!*"

"Are you kidding me?" Aimee darted out behind me, slinging one arm around my shoulder. "That was fantastic! You stuck to your guns, you refused to give up your vision and your principles. It was so David Bowie!"

"Yeah. Except *he's* a musical genius, and *I'm* a hack from Arizona. A stupid hack. Even Donna Karan probably had to suck it up and defer to the Man when she was getting started." I smote my forehead in time with my words. "Idiot! Idiot! *IDIOT!*"

"Oh, who cares? There's plenty more where she came from, and she was trying to fleece you anyway. Fifty-five percent."

She charged off toward the parking garage. "Why didn't she just stick a gun in your face? Outrageous. Although, I have to admit, she was probably spot-on about the name change."

"'Spot on'?" I snapped. "What, are you British now?"

"No, I'm internationally fabulous. And don't you get snarky with me just because Miriam Russo doesn't have the fashion sense God gave Britney Spears's Chihuahua." She dug through her purse for her cigarettes and a lighter. "Anyway, think about what you want your clothing labels to say. 'Cause 'Becca Davis' ain't working."

"At all?"

"Sweetie. David Bowie was born David Robert Jones. You see what I'm saying here?"

"The only thing I see is that I'm an *idiot*." I started whacking my forehead again.

"A very chic idiot who's got a celebrity stylist to call." She opened her car door and ushered me inside. "You've got customers pounding down your door. To hell with Miriam Russo. You're about to get your big break."

I spent the next hour nursing my rejection over a latte and an enormous slab of cake at the chichi bakery down the street from Rhapsody. After a few indelicately large mouthfuls of chocolate, life somehow seemed worth living again, and I decided to try my luck with Fiona Fitzgerald, stylist to the stars.

"Of *course* I remember you!" she trilled into the phone when I introduced myself. "Or at least, I remember that fantastic bustier you made for the hostess at Rhapsody. I simply must have one for Rachelle."

"Okay." I prepared to open price negotiations. "I use only the best materials and I make every piece by hand, so—"

"Of *course* you do, darling—that's what makes you so fabulous. Now. I'm at my office near the corner of Santa Monica and La Cienega. Where are you?"

"Right now, you mean?"

"Yes." Her laugh was light and tinkly. "Where are you this very instant?"

I licked a smear of chocolate frosting off my index finger. "I'm just leaving Sweet Lady Jane on Melrose, actually."

"Perfect! Do you have a few seconds to come by and chat?"

Ten minutes later I was trying—and failing—to look dignified in the giant pink overstuffed chair in her office, fidgeting as I stared at the lumpy garment bags draped over every available flat surface and hoping that I didn't have telltale traces of cake left on my cheeks.

"I'd be delighted to whip up a corset for Rachelle," I said, trying to keep my hands still in my lap. "What colors were you thinking?"

Fiona, a small and wiry woman in her mid-forties with tilted green eyes, a sleek black bob, and a stack of gold bangles snaking up her right arm, said, "Given her coloring? Red. Blood red."

I nodded. "Maybe a black ribbon lacing up the back?"

"I think black would be perfect. Sexy, very bold!" She got up from behind her desk and circled the perimeter of the room, coming to a halt directly in front of me. "I'll fax her measurements over this afternoon. But that's not why I called you here today."

"It isn't?" I stared up at her, acutely aware that we still hadn't touched on the issue of money.

"No. I called you here today because—now this is a huge secret, can you keep a secret and sign a legally binding confidentiality agreement if asked?"

"As long as it isn't about Jimmy Hoffa or the grassy knoll, I'm cool." I smiled.

She didn't smile back.

"Yes, I can keep a secret." Chastened, I turned my gaze down to the gleaming hardwood floor.

"All right then. Rachelle is known for her glamour and her unique sense of style. She's a red carpet icon and every girl in America wants to grow up and be just like her." She paused for dramatic effect. "So we're going to give them all a chance to have a little piece of her mystique. She's starting her own fashion label."

"Really? Good for her. I had no idea she was interested in design." Although I did vaguely recall reading in a magazine profile that she liked to knit on-set. "Is this something she's wanted to do for a long time?"

Fiona sat down in the matching chair next to mine and nodded conspiratorially. "It's something *I've* wanted to do for a long time. Along with her manager. We think this could be a huge market. She's world famous for her sex appeal, she's already won her Oscar so there's no risk of tarnishing her professional image with commercialization. Plus, I mean, let's just say it: she's not getting any younger."

"But Rachelle won't actually be doing any of the hands-on design herself?" I clarified.

She shook her head. "Rachelle will be, ahem, overseeing operations. In more of an advisory capacity. I'm in charge of finding a to-die-for team of designers and I want you on it."

I dug my fingers into the arms of the squishy pink chair. "Fiona, I can't even tell you how flattered I am! Honestly, I—"

She paused and held up a hand. "Maybe."

I tried not to look disappointed. "Maybe?"

"I like what I've seen so far, but I need more." She picked up a notepad and started scribbling her list of requirements. "I'll need the corset for Rachelle as soon as possible, to show the investors as a sample of your work. Then I'll need a series of sketches of other ideas you have for the line, plus the very best samples you can produce, plus a guarantee of exclusivity."

I raised my eyebrows. "Which means . . . ?"

"Which means that we have sole marketing rights to all the samples and patterns you create for us. It's for your benefit, really; you don't want a bunch of second-rate hacks knocking off all your best work once it hits the shelves, do you?"

"No, but—"

"And you are legally required to keep in strictest confidence any personal and professional information you may hear about Rachelle."

I tried to decode the hidden message here. "So you're saying I won't be able to take credit for my own work?"

"No, no, no, darling, don't be so paranoid! This arrangement is intended to protect *everyone's* best interests, but most of all yours."

When I opened my mouth again, she verbally steamrolled right over me.

"When we issue the press release announcing the line launch, we'll emphasize that Rachelle has a design team helping her to realize her unique vision of style. And of course you can tell people that you are an integral part of that design team. But . . ."

"But I need to keep my trap shut about all juicy gossip?"

"Now we understand each other." She got to her feet and strode back to her desk. "We have enough public relations problems without premenstrual employees running to the *Enquirer* with every little imagined slight."

"I would never—"

"Of course you wouldn't. Merely a legal formality, darling. Now, when you're working on the sketches, bear in mind that Rachelle is known for sleek, sexy sophistication. You want to bring that feel of international flair to pieces that a high school student could wear without getting grounded by her parents or a young midwestern soccer mom could wear to a play date."

"Flirty without being slutty?" I suggested.

"Yes. Our demographic is young women just like you: good girls. Good girls who'll experiment with their inner vamp for a night, but then go right back to being good girls. When can you have the corset ready?"

"I can have it for you day after tomorrow." My initial excitement started to return.

"Perfect. If I like it, Rachelle will wear it to the film premiere this weekend." She tilted her head, assessing my reaction. "Happy?"

"Very." I struggled out of the cavernous chair with as much dignity as possible. "So I'll do red and black. And for the price, I was thinking—"

"The price?" This time the laugh sounded fake and forced. "We don't pay you, darling; it's a sample, you see?"

"Well, yes, but I have to buy material and . . . and all the time . . ."

"Think of it as an audition. This is Hollywood—everyone pays their dues. Besides, do you know how many up-and-coming designers would *kill* to have Rachelle wear them on the red carpet? You should be paying *us* for the exposure. Send it over as soon as you're finished and we'll see how everything goes. Hopefully, next time we talk, we'll be discussing salary and benefit terms."

"But what about—"

Right on cue, her phone rang and she opened the office door. "I have to take this call, but it was great to meet you and I'm looking forward to working together. Thanks!"

The door literally hit me in the ass on the way out. But I ignored the impending bruises and danced a little samba on my way to the Jetta because, hey, I had a job! A real job! A job that would pay me to do the work I loved to do! In your face, Miriam Russo!

Maybe.

*   *   *

"So how'd it go with Miriam?" Connor asked when I clocked in at Rhapsody that evening.

"Oh, that." I adjusted the straps of my olive satin camisole. "Well, in a nutshell, I blew it."

"Come on. I'm sure you didn't blow it."

"*Au contraire.* I blew it. It's blown. She told me she'll call me if she ever needs a piece for a 'costume gala'. Her exact words. And I have only myself to blame." I summed up the zipper fiasco.

"Then why do you look so excited?"

"I thought you'd never ask." I grinned. "First of all, I'm excited because I actually stood up for myself. Miriam asked for a design change that I knew was one hundred percent wrong and instead of kowtowing, I stood my ground."

"And that's a big step for you?"

"Like Neil Armstrong."

"Well, you did the right thing."

"But wait! There's more!" I stepped back with a dramatic flourish. "You forgot to ask about the other reason I'm excited. I met with Rachelle Robinson's stylist today."

He leaned back against the bar. "Oh right, about that shirt."

"Corset, my friend, it's a corset."

"Corset. Got it. So how did that go?"

"Let me put it this way: remember how you said you don't date employees?"

"Yes."

"Well, with any luck, I will soon be an eligible bache-lorette." Wait. Did I just say that out loud? "*If* you were inter-ested in me that way, which I do understand you are *not*."

He started to say something, but I rushed ahead before he could launch into the litany of "no," "never," and "completely repulsed by you."

"I have a new job. A humdinger, in fact. A once-in-a-life-time opportunity." I paused. "Possibly."

"Possibly?"

"I'm sort of in the audition process." I described what had transpired in Fiona's office that afternoon. "So I'll drop off the corset the day after tomorrow and pray that I chose the right shade of red for her skin tone. Keep your fingers crossed."

"How much are they paying you?"

"Nothing, but it doesn't matter because—"

"Becca . . ."

"No, really, it's standard practice. Designers donate red car-pet ensembles to actors all the time. If it's good enough for Monique Lhuillier, it's good enough for me."

"Presumably, Monique has other sources of income," Con-nor pointed out.

"True, but I'm still getting my foot in the door. And if Fiona likes it, she'll hire me and then I'll have my income source."

"I don't know about this." He crossed his arms.

"What's to know?" I threw up my hands. "I have no power and no leverage in this negotiation."

"You have talent."

"Me and the eighty gazillion other aspiring designers living in a five-mile radius."

"But they want *you*. Remember, your time and expertise are worth a lot."

"So is free media coverage. If Rachelle Robinson wears my corset to an actual movie premiere, everyone will ask her who designed it and then . . ." I trailed off, awash in bliss at the thought of my name mentioned on *Entertainment Tonight* and the cover of *Women's Wear Daily* (hey, if you're gonna dream, dream big).

"Please tell me you haven't signed anything yet."

"I haven't. She said she has to look at the corset before she offers me a contract."

"Don't give her all the power here. And for God's sake, don't sign anything without hiring a lawyer to look it over."

"Hey, I thought you were all about taking chances. The Gambler? Sir Risk-a-Lot? What happened to all that?"

"When *I* do it, it's different." He looked sheepish and stubborn at the same time. "I have more experience."

I started to laugh. "Oh, so now I'm Little Red Riding Hood, heading into the big, scary forest with only my faux-chinchilla-trimmed Petro Zillia capelet to protect me?"

He shook his head. "It's a wonder Miriam Russo is still standing. You're a force to be reckoned with."

Still laughing, I said, "I don't think anyone's ever described me that way in my entire life."

"I find that very hard to believe. And listen, about the not-dating-employees thing . . ."

But before he could finish his sentence, Lily the bartender rushed in between us. "Becca, you have a phone call. It's your sister. I put her on hold, you can pick up the line in the back office."

I knew Claire wouldn't bother me at Rhapsody for anything less than a genuine catastrophe. She wasn't exactly the hardest-working woman in show business, but she had great respect for the effort that others put in. I hurried past the bar, through the kitchen noise of clanking metal and rapid-fire Spanish, and picked up the phone in the back office. "Claire?"

"Becks? When are you coming home?" She sounded faint and hoarse, like she'd just gotten her voice back after a long bout of laryngitis.

"Well, the bar closes at two, and then I still have the drive home, so not till late." I pressed the receiver against my ear. "Why? What's wrong? Did you tell Andrew about the baby?"

"Yes." She drew a deep, shaky breath. "He did a little jig and went around bragging to everyone in his office. And then he told me he lost his job today! The studio fired him. *Fired him.*"

"Oh my God. Why?"

"Because he's a *moron,* that's why! His boss was sexually harassing his secretary, right? Which, I mean, what else is fucking new? So what does my asinine husband, Mr. Moral Majority, decide to do? He convinces the secretary to complain to HR and *file suit*!"

"I want to say that was noble of him, but I'm guessing that's not the reaction you're looking for," I said.

"Hello? Sexual harassment suits are worse than death in Hollywood. He'd be better off embezzling money from the studio! At least then he could get another job. But now? Forget it. He's blacklisted! He will never work again in this town."

"Are you sure you're not overreacting just a little bit?"

"I can't . . . I can't even wrap my mind around this. And we just started making payments on the house, and all the furniture is on credit, and the wedding and the cars and the sailboat . . ."

"The sailboat? Since when do you guys have a sailboat?"

"We were going to entertain his bosses and their bitchy third wives!" She broke into sobs. "And now . . . God, I don't even know how we'll—"

"It'll be okay," I soothed, feeling awkward and fraudulent in the role of wise caregiver. She was the one who directed *me,* not the other way around. "He'll get another job. It'll be fine."

"Oh, don't be such a naïve little twit!" *Annnd* we were back to normal. "Do you have any idea what happens when you're blackballed in Hollywood? We won't be able to pay our cable bill, let alone afford a baby!"

12

At precisely 1:58 A.M., I locked the restaurant's front doors, scowled at the three boozy stragglers trying to finangle one last cocktail out of the bartender, collected my share of the night's tips from the servers, and headed for the parking lot.

As I passed the back office, I waved to Connor, who had stayed late to help the new manager master the accounting software. Despite his urgings to leave early and check on Claire, I'd chosen to stick out the shift. Andrew's job loss, while unfortunate, did not in my opinion constitute an actual emergency.

Claire begged to differ.

She'd left hourly updates on my voice mail (10:35: "I'm going to have to buy my maternity clothes at Kmart. I've never even been inside a Kmart. I heard it's like a scene from *Deliverance* in there." 11:23: "I called Mom and Dad and their big solution? They think we should come live with them in Phoenix. Like I'm really going to go from a four thousand-square-foot Tudor in Beverly Glen to my high school bedroom in a tract house in the fucking desert. If you hear me discussing this as a viable option, I want you to shoot me. Do you hear me? I want you to open the safe in Andrew's office, take out the handgun, and put me out of my misery." 12:30: "My baby's going to have to go to a daycare run by, like, Miss Hannigan. Call me back.").

Once out in the parking lot, I powered up my cell phone and braced myself for a torrent of fresh laments when Connor caught up with me. "Hey!"

"Sorry." I turned off the phone, noting with dismay that I still had three new messages. "I know I should have stayed to help clean up, but Claire is sounding more and more Sarah Bernhardt by the hour and I want to make sure she's not going to do anything drastic. I've heard that pregnancy hormones can really—" I clapped both hands over my mouth.

His eyes widened. "Claire's pregnant?"

"It's a secret. Dammit! Please don't tell Andrew you know." I sighed up at the smoggy black sky and the watery sodium light filtering over the parked cars. "I can't believe I just said that. She's going to kill me. Well, right after she kills Andrew for—" But I stopped myself in time.

He leaned forward. "For what?"

"*Nothing.* Listen, I gotta go."

He stood there, regarding me thoughtfully.

"Was there something you wanted?" I asked, jangling the keys to the Jetta that Claire would probably be reclaiming soon.

"I just wanted to make sure you got to your car okay."

"Oh. Well, that's very chivalrous of you."

He kept staring. "What's going on with Claire and Andrew?"

"I really can't talk about this with you." In the interest of self-preservation. "It's kind of a sensitive subject. But don't worry. It's nothing epic. Everything's fine, really."

"Nothing epic," he repeated.

I tried to smile. "You know what I mean."

"Listen, if you guys need help—" But then *his* cell phone rang, and when he glanced at the caller ID, his frown deepened. "Hold on. Sorry, I've got to take this."

I wasted no time escaping into my car, yelling, "See you tomorrow!" before slamming the door. And then I peeled out and headed for Andrew and Claire's house, checking my remaining voice mail messages while idling at a red light on Santa Monica Boulevard.

Even at two in the morning, the traffic here would be classified as "moderate to heavy" in the west Phoenix suburbs. And my fellow drivers weren't just shifty-eyed thugs or college kids out for a good time—some of these people were suited up in blazers and ties and had apparently just finished a very long day at the office.

"There's a saying in the entertainment industry," Andrew told my parents when he showed up late to the rehearsal dinner for his own wedding. "'If you don't come in to work on Saturday, then don't bother showing up on Sunday.'"

Which would explain why Claire had felt the need to fill up her days with visits to her personal trainer, visits to a past-life regression medium (which is how she'd discovered she'd been a French courtier in the days of Louis XIV), and me, camped out in her backyard to keep her company.

And her baby and all the designer accoutrements. And soon, unemployment checks.

I tried to focus on the positive. Perhaps Claire's baby, by foregoing designer diaper bags and brand-name private schools, would receive, in exchange, a father.

I gripped the steering wheel with both hands and braced myself for the three remaining voice mails.

But they weren't from Claire. She must have given up on me around midnight and taken her case to other members of the family. Who all, in turn, took her case right back to me.

Message #1 (my mother): "Becca, honey, Claire just called me with the bad news. She's so upset and she won't listen to Daddy and me. I tried to tell her that God would provide and that just made her cry harder. So listen, I know you're having fun out there, but you really should come home now. She and Andrew have enough to deal with; they can't be taking care of you on top of everything else. I've got fresh sheets on your bed and your room is just the way you left it. And if you want, I can call Kevin's mother and tell her when you'll be back. I'm sure she'll pass along the news to you-know-who!"

Message #2 (Gayle): "Just got off the phone with Claire—I think my eardrums are bleeding. She's in crisis mode, but remember, Becks, it's okay to have your *own* feelings about this. Mom said you're cutting your vacation short and coming back to Phoenix and I know you must be disappointed. But we have to think about what's best for Claire now, right? I've got a few book recommendations to help her and Andrew get through this. I want you to write these down and go pick them up for her. Ready, got a pen? Okay, first is *Marriage in Crisis . . .*"

I skipped ahead to Message #3 (Kevin): "Hey. Becca. I know you're off doing . . . whatever. But I just wanted to say hi. And ask if . . . you know. I'm still holding on to that ring for you, so when you're ready, call me."

And just like that, the undertow of guilt swept me into an eddy of confusion. I knew I'd done the right thing by finalizing the breakup, but suddenly I missed him. I missed the security we'd had and his confidence that he could maintain control in a universe of infinite chaos.

He was waiting for that ring to draw me back to my senses,

back to him like a lodestone. But with every passing day, I knew with greater certainty that I wasn't coming back. We both deserved more.

I turned off my phone and steeled myself for the onslaught of Hurricane Claire.

"He's not here," announced a weary voice when I tiptoed into my sister's dark kitchen.

I groped for the wall switch and flooded the room with fluorescent light. "You're still up?"

"I'm still up." Claire, wearing a plush black bathrobe over white silk pajamas, blinked and shaded her eyes against the sudden brightness.

"Then why is the whole place pitch black?"

She hunched into her chair. "I turned off the lights for two reasons. One, I kicked Andrew out and I don't want him cruising by, seeing a light in the window and trying to convince me to let his sorry ass back in. Two, electricity costs money and we don't have any."

Central air-conditioning also cost money, and theirs was cranked up full blast (Claire having long ago decreed that she could not be expected to sleep in a room even one degree above 69 Fahrenheit). But right now was not, as Gayle would say, "a teachable moment." Right now felt a lot more like a "shoot off your mouth, get your larynx torn out" kind of moment.

So I just cut to the chase. "You kicked Andrew out? Why?"

"Because." She stalked over to the stainless-steel refrigerator, snatched out a carton of blueberry soy yogurt, and retrieved a silver spoon from a drawer, which she then slammed hard enough to rattle the windows. "He's a lying, manipulative, gutless excuse for a man."

My eyes widened. "Tell me how you really feel."

"And have I mentioned that I hate him? *Hate* him?"

I boosted myself up to sit on the granite-topped island. "But why?"

"Because he lied to me, that's why."

"About . . ."

"Everything! *Everything*!" She shoveled a heaping spoonful of soy yogurt into her mouth and gagged. "Ugh. I hate this crap, but it's for the baby. Apparently, I'm supposed to be cramming calcium and folic acid down my throat like there's no tomorrow." She sank back down into the chair next to the table. "The bastard. He promised to love me, cherish me, take care of me. And look at me!"

She flung her arms out, a silk-swathed martyr in a state-of-the-art kitchen kept perpetually spotless by servants. "All this? Going, going, gone. The house, the cars, the furniture . . . we'll have to sell everything and we'll still be drowning in debt."

"You won't be in debt," I soothed, watching her devour her yogurt with a voracity that, for Claire, constituted bingeing. "You'll just have to cut back a little until he gets a new job."

She nearly spat out the soy in disdain. "Becca, sometimes you are so sheltered that I can't stand it. *Of course* we will be in debt. We'll probably have to file for bankruptcy. We haven't even made a dent in our mortgage—we owe more on the cars than they're worth, and the credit cards . . . just thinking about the credit cards makes my blood run cold." Her eyes narrowed to serpentine slits. "Don't you dare tell Mom and Dad about any of this."

"Oh." Understanding finally dawned. "So he lied to you about how much debt he had? Before you married him? That's why you kicked him out."

"No." She finished off the yogurt, stomped back to the fridge, and grabbed a big white bakery box. "I kicked him out because he got fired, thus breaking all his vows to take care of me. When we got engaged, he promised me all this—" her sweeping gesture encompassed the house and everything in it "—and he couldn't even hold on to it for a year. He knows how much I love this house! I picked it out myself, all the colors, all the furniture . . ."

"But you also love *him,* right?"

"That has nothing to do with anything!" She dabbed at her eyes with a paper napkin while snarfing down an éclair.

I tried not to stare, but I hadn't seen her touch processed sugar in at least five years. "But it's not like he asked to be fired."

The tears on her cheeks now mingled with smears of Bavarian cream. "I know, but he should have just shut up and let that stupid secretary deal with her own problems. Why did he have to do the right thing? The selfish ass!"

"Um." I tried to look as meek as possible. "I hate to say it, but—"

"But what? I should have known he would disappoint me as soon as we got married?"

"No. I was going to say . . ." I squeezed my eyes shut as I plunged ahead with what was surely a suicide mission. "It sounds like it might be partly—just a teeny, tiny bit—your fault you guys are in debt. He knew how much you wanted the top-of-the-line car and the top-of-the-line house in the top-of-the-line neighborhood, and he wanted to make you happy . . ."

Her porcelain complexion progressed from pink to crimson to maroon. "Oh, I see. I see how it is. *He's* the helpless victim and *I'm* the materialistic, conniving wife?"

"No, I'm just trying to—"

"Hey! I'm not through talking!" All those elocution classes had really paid off—her vocal projection and enunciation skills were unparalleled. "There are two people in this marriage. Two."

"That's all I'm saying," I murmured. "It's supposed to be a team effort. So it's not fair to put all the blame on him."

I fled down the dark hallway as she sprang out of her chair, presumably to seize the Japanese chef knives and fillet me.

She chased me into the master bedroom, where she switched on a lamp and continued to screech. "I can't believe

I'm getting a lecture on personal responsibility from you of all people!"

I turned my palms up in surrender. "Know what? You're right. It's none of my business. Let's just drop it."

But the time for dropping it had come and gone.

"You're happy to point the finger at everyone else, aren't you?" She twisted her face into an infantile pout and mocked me with a high-pitched whine. "'Oh, Gayle, stop treating me like a child!' 'Oh, Mom, stop putting my bras in the dryer when I'm twenty-five and still living at home and letting you do my laundry!' 'Oh, Kevin, stop trying to make me grow up and get my shit together!'"

"Claire—"

"Shut it! I don't want to hear another word out of you, you ungrateful little brat. Get out of my house."

"Claire—"

"*Get out!*"

So I did, slamming the front door behind me. By the time I made it down the front steps, she'd turned the master bedroom light off again.

Fine. Good. I didn't need no stinkin' guesthouse. I'd just sleep in my car like Lily the bartender.

Except, now that I thought about it, the car was yet another one of Claire's charitable donations.

So I'd sleep . . . somewhere else. Where did people go when they got locked out of their own homes in the middle of the night?

I whipped my cell phone out of my purse, dialed 411 for the number of a cab company, and slammed the gates that kept Claire ensconced in her soon-to-be-foreclosed paradise.

I hesitated just a moment before dialing up the one person in L.A. who might take me in.

13

W hoa," was all Aimee had to say when I arrived at her
doorstep thirty minutes later. "You look pissed."

"I am," I fumed, mincing into her tiny West Hollywood
apartment. (My self-righteous stride had morphed into a high-
heel-induced limp during the trek up the four flights of stairs
to her apartment.)

"You didn't have to take a cab. I would've come to pick
you up."

"No. The free rides are over, both literally and figuratively,"
I said firmly. "I'm going to rent a car tomorrow and hopefully,
I'll be able to find a place of my own in the next few days. In
the meantime, I'll chip in for your rent."

"Now you're just being ridiculous. You can stay here as long as you need, no charge. Us hyphens have to help each other out, you know. It's a tough town."

"No way. I'm an independent woman. I have to stand on my own two feet."

She shook a cigarette out of the Marlboro Lights pack. "Shall we put some Chaka Khan on the stereo to celebrate your emancipation? Maybe Donna Summer? Did Gloria Steinem ever do an album?"

"Stop making fun of me." I collapsed on her blue moleskin-slipcovered sofa. "I'm exhausted, I have no pajamas, and I reek of olive oil and garlic from Rhapsody."

"You'll feel better in the morning," she promised. "Go take a shower. You can borrow my shampoo and some pj's. And no, I do not accept payment for my Pantene."

"Thank you so much. This means a lot to me—Claire hates my guts, I don't know anyone here yet, and I didn't know who else to call."

"No problem whatsoever." She blew a series of perfect smoke rings. "When you make it big and spend all your time hobnobbing with the VIPs, I want you to remember who shared her shampoo with you when you were living on the street."

"I will," I promised.

"And then I want you to get her cast in a major motion picture."

"I'll try."

"And give her a whole wardrobe for free."

"Every season?"

"Every season." She picked up a stack of head shots from the coffee table and started stapling copies of her résumé to the back of each one. "Now keep your fingers crossed—I have a big audition tomorrow morning. I'm trying out for the role of a sexy young lawyer at a male-dominated firm. They want someone 'demure but aggressive,' whatever the hell that means."

"You'll do great."

"I even touched up my roots." She pointed to her hairline. "To prove that I'm a perfect leading lady. I, Aimee Chenard, am more than the slutty best friend. I even bought a boring black blazer to wear to the audition."

"Which you will be returning to the store as soon as you shake the casting agent's hand?" I guessed.

"Of course. I may be leading lady material, but I ain't made of money. Now get to bed, *chica*. You've got a red carpet outfit to whip up in the morning."

The next day, I headed back to Claire's house when I knew she'd be at her pre-natal yoga class, convinced her housekeeper to buzz me past the gate, and crammed all my sewing gear into my newly rented Pontiac like I was looting a Jo-Ann fabric store. Humiliating, yes, but a vastly more appealing option than round two of the Davis Sister Screamfest. I then spent forty-eight sleepless hours sewing, hostessing, and checking voice mail after I dropped off the corset with Fiona's assistant. But my message box remained stubbornly empty. And when I finally broke down and tried to get in touch with the stylist, I was frostily informed that she was "on the other line," which Aimee translated to "call here again and we'll have you shot."

"You just have to wait it out; she'll get back to you," Aimee assured me. "But not until she's damn good and ready."

"But what do you think it all means? Do you think Rachelle is going to wear the corset to the premiere this weekend or not?"

"Who knows? We'll just have to get the Sunday paper and find out for ourselves."

"Oh God, she hates my work," I moaned. "She must hate it or she would've called me back. I knew I should have gone with maroon instead of cerise silk!"

"You must chill. Everything is probably fine. Not returning phone calls is an art form out here. You think my agent's heard back about that lawyer girl audition? The one that I spent days prepping for, both physically and mentally? The one that could jump-start my acting career and prove that I haven't spent my entire adult life pursuing a dream that's never going to come true? *No*. It's a form of psychological torture."

"But even her receptionist was mean. That can't be a good sign."

"Are you kidding? The receptionists are the worst of all. Rumor has it they train them in Chinese prison camps."

I didn't hear from Claire, either, though I did get a call from Kevin (no message). By the time the weekend rolled around, I was little more than a bundle of frayed, twitching synapses.

"Ooh, here we go! Open it, open it, open it!" Aimee hopped up and down in her wife beater, plaid boxer shorts, and fluffy blue bunny slippers, splashing her cup of coffee all over the sidewalk.

"Hang on, I have to pay." I thrust a five-dollar bill at the newsstand clerk, my hands shaking so hard I nearly dropped the bulky newspaper.

"Okay! Okay, okay, let's look!"

I grabbed her elbow and sat down on the curb before the vendor had a chance to give me my change. Everyone who was anyone in West Hollywood was still sleeping it off at this ungodly hour on a Sunday morning, so we basically had the street to ourselves.

She plopped down next to me. "The suspense is killing me! Let's see."

I pawed through the sections, coating my thumb in ink. "All right. Faces and Places."

"It's in color and everything!"

"All the better for my portfolio, right?"

"I thought you didn't have a portfolio?"

"I will after today."

"Did they cover the premiere? What did she wear?"

An open-topped Jeep sped by, and as the pounding bass of Tupac Shakur pulsed through me, I saw it.

The full-color photo of Rachelle Robinson, absolutely gorgeous in my red corset and a tight black satin skirt.

"Holy shit!" Aimee squealed.

My excitement crested in a pure, thrilling fusion of hope and pride and teary disbelief . . .

. . . And then I read the tiny caption under the photo: "High-stepping starlet Rachelle Robinson dazzles in couture of her own making. 'I've always been interested in design,' the statuesque stunner tells us. 'In fact, I'm starting my own fashion line. This corset, for instance . . . [is] just a little something I whipped up between takes on the set of *Body Language*. Creativity is my passion—design comes naturally to me. I've been blessed with the gift to innovate beauty.'"

"I've never heard anyone swear like that," Aimee marveled once we were back in her apartment. "Did you used to be in the navy or something?"

I collapsed on the carpet and stared at the ceiling. "I *cannot* believe this."

"You know what always helps me after I have a crappy audition? French toast. There's this place down the street called The Griddle . . ." She took another look at my face and changed tactics. "Or you may just want to start drinking heavily. I've got vodka in the freezer and V8 in the fridge. Bloody Marys, anyone?"

"'I've been blessed with the gift to innovate beauty?' What a crock!"

"It's just some inane little sound bite her publicist fed her. Don't let it get to you."

"That's not what's getting to me!" I rolled my head to the side so I could address her directly. "What's getting to me is that she's taking credit for my design! Before I even got an official job offer!"

"Maybe it's just a misprint? Maybe?"

"'Just a little something I whipped up between takes on the set'? 'Design comes easily to me'?" I could feel the vein in my forehead pulsing. "How nice that she picks it up effortlessly via osmosis while everyone else has to spend years toiling over a sewing machine!"

"And you're positive Fiona never mentioned any of this to you?"

"She hasn't even returned my calls!" I pounded a fist on the floor. "But I know where she works and she *will* be hearing from me first thing tomorrow morning."

"If it makes you feel any better, my agent called yesterday. I didn't get the demure but agresssive lawyer girl part."

"That makes me feel worse."

"Me, too." She sighed and joined me on the threadbare beige carpet. "Obscurity totally sucks."

"You can say that again."

"So what do you want to do with the rest of the day?"

I groaned. "I have to go clean out the rest of my stuff from

Claire's guesthouse. I can only wear the same three outfits so many times. Which means I'm facing another histrionic rant about what a sheltered little halfwit I am. Not to mention ungrateful."

"You're *sure* you don't want to reconsider a twelve-hour bender?"

"Ask me again when I get back."

"I saw the paper today." This was how Claire, clad in rumpled yoga pants and one of Andrew's threadbare USC T-shirts, greeted me at her front door.

I avoided eye contact. "I'm here for my clothes. Don't want my ghetto rags cluttering up your rarefied guesthouse."

"I saw the picture of Rachelle Robinson at the *Body Language* premiere." She stepped aside, ushering me into the high-ceilinged foyer. Her feet were bare, her hair unwashed, her manicure chipped. "And I read how she quote-unquote 'whipped it up' herself. I know how you must feel."

"Can I please just go get my things?"

"You must feel the same way you did when I decided not to wear the wedding gown you made for me. Except ten times worse."

I inhaled deeply. "Well, now that you mention it, that *is* kind of how I feel."

"You were robbed. And Rachelle Robinson is a self-important hag on loan from the bowels of hell." She tugged a thread at the hem of her T-shirt. "And I'm sorry about throwing you out of the house. I don't really want you to move out. It's possible I was a little overwrought last night."

I nearly fell over dead. The Claire Davis apology, much like the Loch Ness Monster or the Yeti, was mythical in its scarcity and elusiveness.

"It's okay," I mumbled. "You've had a lot to deal with this week."

"I know, but according to Gayle, that's no excuse. She called me this morning and read me the riot act about 'letting other people into my marriage.' Apparently, I'm supposed to keep all conflict between me and Andrew private and sacred."

"Where is Andrew, by the way? Did you finally break down and call him after you talked to Gayle?"

"Nope." The phone started ringing. "Come on in, I'll make us some lunch. Empty carbs—that'll cure what ails you."

"Aren't you going to get that?" I asked, nodding toward the cordless phone on the hall table.

"No. I'm sure it's my so-called husband, calling to shove even more bad news down my throat. 'Sorry, angel, I lost my job.' 'Sorry, angel, we're going to have to sell the house.' 'Guess what, angel? I found a great apartment in"—she stopped, taking a moment to suppress her gag reflex—"Van Nuys, and our baby's going to be born into Dickensian squalor and you'll have to get a job.'"

"Did he find a new job yet?" I knew it had only been a few days, but my understanding was that executives bounced from studio to studio like tennis balls at Wimbledon.

"Be serious. Do you know what he said the last time I made the mistake of picking up the phone? He said he's interviewing for work as a PA."

"A what?"

"A production assistant."

I had no idea what that was, but interviewing had to be a good thing, right? "Well, that sounds encouraging."

"Becca. Going from his job to a production assistant would be like Diane von Furstenberg becoming a cashier at T.J. Maxx."

"Oh."

"You know what? I can't even discuss this without wanting to bawl my eyes out. Let's go make a whole stack of grilled cheese sandwiches." Our childhood comfort food. "That's the only upside of being pregnant, poor, and saddled with a deadbeat husband: I can eat whatever I want and not have to worry about what my nonexistent personal trainer will say."

The phone rang again as we started down the hall. She shook her head. "He's persistent, I'll give him that."

"Are you *ever* going to talk to him?" I leaned against the cool granite counter while the upper half of Claire's body disappeared into the refrigerator.

"Let's see . . . butter, bread, cheese . . . it's going to have to be heart-healthy fake cheese, but you can deal with that, can't you? And no, I'm not going to talk to him."

While she pulled out a frying pan and fired up the gas

stove, I tried to make myself useful, rummaging through the cherry cabinets for glasses. Even the kitchen shelves looked like a photograph from a Williams-Sonoma catalog—lots of big white plates and thick-walled tumblers, all lined up and dried by hand to prevent unsightly spots.

"But you'll *have* to talk to him, eventually. What about . . . you know?" I glanced pointedly at her stomach.

"What about it?" She snatched up a spatula. "It's not like he'll be able to support a child on a PA's salary. Marrying him was the biggest mistake of my life."

"You don't mean that."

"Yes, I do." Her eyes blazed. "See? This is what happens when you fall in love. You get your hopes built up, you settle in for happily ever after, and then *wham!* Just when you least expect it, the bottom drops out and you end up in the gutter."

"Claire—"

"I'm done with him! Done! Do you hear me?"

"So you're actually thinking divorce?"

"Divorce?" She stared at me. "I wish!"

"But you just said . . ."

"How can I possibly divorce him? I'm trapped; I *know* I'm trapped." She rested one hand on her belly. "I have no job, no professional skills—except slinking around in a swimsuit on the set of a beer commercial—which is not a viable career option for an aging pregnant chick who can't afford to get her roots bleached every two weeks at Fred Segal Beauty—no money of my own, and a pile of debt the size of Mount Everest. Who'd want me now? I had one chance to find security and I backed the wrong horse. Like it or not, I'm stuck with him."

As if on cue, the phone started ringing again. She continued fuming without missing a beat.

"Now I'll have to go live in some horrible apartment and we'll be just like everyone else. Bickering over stupid minutiae. Telling ourselves that 'love is all we need' and then worrying about how we're going to afford car insurance and still cover the electric bill. Decorating our tiny bedroom with those hideous wallpaper borders and bed-in-a-bag sets from Linens 'n' Things and thinking it's the height of fashion." She looked very tired and pale, two faint creases deepening across her forehead. "You know. Turning into Mom and Dad."

"Okay." I accepted the grilled cheese sandwich she offered up on a Limoges plate. "I grant you that the wallpaper border smacks slightly of quiet desperation. But the rest of it? I'm pretty sure that's what marriage is. I *know* that's what motherhood is."

"Pointless bickering and obsessive worrying?"

"Remember how much you hated Mom when you were in high school? How many arguments you guys had over whether you should be allowed to wear thongs under your jeans?"

"Yeah, but . . ."

"When you went to the senior prom and didn't come home until noon the next day and Dad called the police?"

"God, don't remind me." She pushed her hair back with both hands. "And they say *I* overdramatize things!"

"My point is, that's family for ya. Do you really think living in a huge house in a swanky neighborhood and driving a Mercedes will change any of that?"

"Of course." The creases in her forehead multiplied as she faced the prospect of motherhood without the Swiss au pair or play dates with children named Apple, Ryder, and Phinnaeus. "*My* child will be different."

"Hang on—I'm going to write this down so I can laugh my ass off in fifteen years."

"No, I mean . . . Mom and Dad have never been to Europe, they've never had oysters on the halfshell, they just plod through life, balancing checkbooks and clipping coupons and watching those endless Civil War documentaries together, day after mind-numbing day. Who wants to live like that?"

"They do." I bit into a grilled cheese, relishing the buttery goodness. "They're happy."

"But I want something more out of life. That's why I moved out here. I wanted to be one of the special ones."

"You are."

"Yeah, for about five more days. And when all this great stuff is gone, it'll just be me and Andrew, and let me tell you something: I'm not the type to watch Civil War documentaries."

"Is he?"

She paused. "I have no idea." And then she dissolved into

tears. "What are we going to do? I barely know him and now I'm destitute! And with child! I wish I were dead!"

"Everything will be fine. You'll see."

She blew her nose into a starched linen napkin. "But I'll have to get a job, and I'm qualified for nothing."

"You can always temp."

"Temping. Oh, the humanity." She flung herself down on a hand-carved mahogany chair by the kitchen table. "The only thing that's going to make today bearable is an enormous bottle of Ketel One—oh hell, I can't drink anymore, can I?"

"No, you can't. And you can't smoke or drive recklessly. Or ride Space Mountain at Disneyland," I added helpfully.

"And no sushi, no hot baths, no Crystal Light . . ."

"Crystal Light?"

"Pregnant women aren't supposed to have aspartame." She downed a monstrous multivitamin with her final bite of grilled cheese. "Or sorbitol, I forget which."

"Look who's been doing her prenatal research."

"Yeah, well, just because my life's a karmic shitstorm doesn't mean the kid should have to suffer. Which reminds me—come with me to my first prenatal appointment on Wednesday? I'm not quite eight weeks along yet, but I have to do it now, before Andrew's top-of-the-line health insurance runs out."

The phone started to ring again. There was a brief pause

while voice mail picked up, after which the ringing resumed.

"You sure there's not somebody else you should be bringing to that appointment?" I asked.

She smiled serenely, picked up the receiver midring, and slammed it back down. "Nope, nobody else."

Monday morning marked a new low point for both Davis sisters. While Claire slogged her sushi-deprived self into the Trailblazer Temp Agency for a typing test, I devoted the day to hunting down Fiona Fitzgerald, who proved a wily adversary in the game of phone tag.

Her assistant's upbeat tone never wavered as she rattled off the many reasons why Fiona was unreachable: she was in a meeting. She was en route to a photo shoot. She was laid up in a full body cast and couldn't possibly hold a phone to her ear.

"Sorry," she chirped. "But she'll return your call the minute she gets back to the office."

"That's what you said three hours ago," I pointed out.

"And I'm still saying it now." She started cracking her gum in my ear. "She'll call you back, I promise. I know she's eager to speak with you."

"Yeah, I'll bet she is," I muttered. "Don't think I'll get tired and go away—I've programmed this number into my speed dial."

"Okay! Have a great day!" She hung up with a lot more force than necessary.

Finally, *finally*, after hours of relentless telestalking, my cell phone rang.

"Darling! Hi!" Fiona sounded determinedly carefree. "I take it you saw the photos of the *Body Language* premiere."

"Yes, I did—"

"Isn't it exciting? Rachelle looked phenomenal. What a fantastic start to your career!"

I nearly dropped the phone. "*My* career?"

"Well, of course! We all adored the corset. We're going to manufacture it in a whole range of colors for our debut collection. We need you to finalize a manufacturing pattern as soon as possible."

Who in the what now?

"Fiona. I don't want to be difficult or anything, but did you happen to read any of the interview quotes from the red carpet?"

More girlish laughter. "Of course."

"Last week, you said I'd be credited as a designer, but Rachelle said that she made the corset all by herself."

"Oh, darling, you're upset about *that*? That quote was taken entirely out of context!"

Out of context? Wasn't that the hoariest old chestnut next to "don't call us, we'll call you"? I wanted to believe her, truly I did, but . . . "Come *on*."

"No, honestly, darling. Rachelle would *never* . . ." She sighed. "You work with the media long enough, you'll see how these things happen."

"I'm sure I will, but explain it to me anyway. For my own edification."

"I spoke with Rachelle this morning to clear the whole thing up—I was afraid you might misinterpret it. Well, turns out she *did* mention that one of her new design team members had whipped up the prototype for the corset, but did that idiot reporter include that in his story? No, of course not. He felt—correctly, if I may say so—that his readers want news and information about Rachelle, not her behind-the-scenes team."

"Yeah, but—"

"I understand what you're going through, Becca, believe me." She adopted a soothing tone that I imagined she used with Rachelle when some ignorant peon dared to put red roses in her trailer when her contract rider plainly stipulated *white orchids only*. "You work hard and you want credit for your work."

"That about sums it up."

"I promise you, Rachelle did mention your name. If you look at the part of the quote with ellipses and the brackets, the line that reads: 'This corset . . . [is] just a little something I whipped up between takes'? Well, those ellipses mean that part of Rachelle's sentence was cut out. And guess which part the reporter cut?"

"The part where *I* was actually sewing the corset?"

"Bingo. They wanted to break the news about the fashion line without using up too much text. So there you go."

Apparently, Fiona thought I was all bustier, no brain. "Uh-huh."

"Honestly. I wouldn't lie to you, darling," she vowed. "Hand to God. I can request the original interview transcript and fax it to you. It'll take a few days, but if that's what it'll take to prove to you—"

I finally relented. "No, that's okay. I was just—"

"Disappointed. I understand completely. But have no fear. Once we start doing line launches and runway shows, you'll get the acknowledgment and applause you deserve."

I started salivating like one of Pavlov's dogs. "Runway shows?"

"Oh yes—we're going to start with midpriced casualwear in the major department stores, but eventually we plan to move up to evening gowns, baby clothes, even a men's line. The sky's the limit! We like what we've seen, and we're hiring you on. You got the job! Congratulations!"

I stopped sulking about the news story long enough to imagine myself striding down a runway behind a passel of willowy, impeccably dressed models, all of them applauding me, and the crowd beneath the catwalk going wild . . . Rachelle Robinson herself stepping up to give me a congratulatory hug . . .

Back in the real world, Fiona was still yapping. "Drop by my office later this afternoon and we'll sign the contract."

I smiled, nonexistent clapping still ringing in my ears. "Well, I can pick the contract up today, but obviously I can't sign it until I find a lawyer to go over it with me."

Long pause. "You can't?"

"Is that a problem?"

"Well, I'm leaving for Australia with Rachelle tonight and I'll be gone for at least a week."

"Then I'll have it ready for you when you get back," I promised.

"No, no, that won't work. I need it signed before I go tonight. If you're going to work on our team, we need you to start working on your patterns and sizing charts immediately so we can start choosing fabrics, hiring seamstresses, scouting out factories . . ."

"But I don't have a lawyer yet."

"You can read, can't you? Either sign the contract this afternoon or we find someone else."

Holy split-second transformation from guppy to great white, Batman.

"Well?" she snapped. "What's it going to be? Do you want the job or do I call up one of the hundreds of other designers who have been begging us to look at their samples?"

Let's see. My options were this or Miriam Russo, Zipper Zealot. Talk about your tough calls.

"Becca? I'm giving you ten more seconds to get on board, or I'm moving on to the next name on our list."

"But—"

"Ten . . . nine . . . eight . . ."

"What's the pay?" I broke in, halfway to hyperventilation.

"We pay you a lump sum of five hundred dollars for every pattern you turn in and a variable commission for each piece we end up manufacturing."

"Okay . . ." Think, dammit, *think*! "Um . . ."

"Five . . . four . . . three . . ."

"All right, all right!" I finally folded. "I want the job, dammit! I'll take the job!"

"Fantastic." My sweet 'n' sunny fairy godmother was back. "See you before five."

I pounced on Connor the second he stepped through the restaurant's sleek glass doors that evening. "I have bad news and more bad news."

"Hmmm." He pretended to consider this. "I'll take the bad news first."

"Okay. The bad news is, I'm quitting my job here. The other bad news is"—I smiled hopefully—"I'm giving slightly less than two weeks' notice?"

"You got that job with the celebrity stylist?"

"Yep. I'm officially in the design business!" I announced,

striking a spokesmodel pose I'd picked up from Aimee. "Got the contract this afternoon!"

"Congratulations. Didn't I tell you everything would work out?"

"That you did."

"See? Life is about risks. You can't be afraid to take chances."

"You've taught me well, Obi Wan." I bowed.

"I'll give you the name of my attorney. Give him a call and he'll look over the contract for you."

My smile dimmed a few volts. "Oh. Um. About that . . ."

He narrowed his eyes. "What?"

Don't tell him! Don't tell him! Don't—"Actually, now that you mention it, I kind of already signed the papers."

"You didn't."

"I did."

"Why the hell would you do something like that? Didn't we just talk about the importance of—"

"Yes, but she said she's leaving for a business trip tonight and if I didn't sign this afternoon, she'd move on to the next desperate designer."

"And you fell for that?"

I drew myself up to my full height (5'7" in stilettos) and squared my shoulders. "Yes, I did."

"Becca." He started kneading his forehead. "She was bluffing."

"How do you know? She really does have a trip to Australia! She's going with Rachelle to—"

"Trust me. She was bluffing."

This possibility *had* occurred to me, but only after I'd signed everything in ink. "Well, I didn't want to take the chance. I need this job."

He shook his head. "You don't need them as much as they need you."

"If only that were true."

"It is," he insisted.

"Well, either way, I wanted a design job and now I have one." I crossed my arms. "It's a bit of a risk, but you just said—"

"I also said don't sign anything without a lawyer."

I threw up my hands. "I guess we all said a lot of things. But the bottom line is, I'm giving notice."

"Fair enough." He stopped treating his forehead like Play-Doh. "Have a glass of champagne to celebrate."

"Can't. I'm on the clock, remember?"

"I hereby give you permission to have a glass of champagne during your shift. What the hell, Aimee can have one, too."

"The good stuff?" Aimee, who had apparently been eavesdropping on the entire conversation, yelled over from the hostess stand.

"Hands off the Dom," he warned.

"Taittinger?" she pressed.

"Fine." He turned back to me as Aimee started bopping toward the bar, fingers snapping. "So. Becca."

I raised one eyebrow. "So. Connor."

"You're no longer a Rhapsody employee after tonight. Which brings me to my next point: What are you doing this weekend?"

I stared at him, trying to gauge his intent. Was . . . was he asking me out?

"We can ditch this hole-in-the-wall and go celebrate your new career." He looked at me expectantly.

He *was* asking me out. But . . .

"But you're not interested in me that way," I insisted.

"Not when you're engaged and working in my restaurant, no. But now that you're single and quitting, it's a whole other ball game. I was thinking we could hike Runyon Canyon . . ." He waited a few seconds while I considered this. "Or not."

Apparently, today was National Whiplash Karmic Reversal Day and no one had marked my calendar. "I'd love to."

"Great. Do you have hiking boots?"

"I have running shoes. Do those count?"

"Close enough."

"Hypothetical question: Did you ever sign a contract and then later wish you hadn't?" I asked Claire two days later as we slumped into the leather couches at a plush OB/GYN office suite at the UCLA Medical Center.

"Contracts I've regretted?" She balled up her fists. "Two words: marriage license."

"Claire, be serious."

"I'm dead serious," she vowed. "Do you know what time I

had to get up this morning in order to make coffee at the hell on earth that is Bullseye Business Solutions? And then I find out that it's inventory week. According to my boss, even though I'm in my first trimester, I should be on my feet for hours on end, counting boxes of legal pads."

"So you don't see this turning into your new career?"

"What I see myself doing is filing a grievance with the Department of Labor. Forcing a pregnant woman to do manual labor all day? It's inhuman."

"I'm not sure that counting boxes really qualifies as manual labor."

The receptionist behind the glass counter glanced over at us, then turned up the adult contemporary music on her deskside radio while the proud mother-to-be started working herself into a classic Claire Davis hissy fit.

"Let me explain something to you, Becca. I'm broke, none of my so-called friends will return my calls since Andrew got fired, and I'm putting on weight even though I've been puking my guts out every time I catch a whiff of anything food-related. Morning sickness is a bitch all day, and so am I."

"All righty then." I tried to move the conversation briskly along. "Do you think the baby's a boy or a girl?"

"I don't care what it is as long as it doesn't look like Andrew. Or talk like Andrew. Or punk out on me like Andrew."

"You still haven't returned his calls?"

"Even if I wanted to call him back, I couldn't. When I tried to use my cell phone this morning, guess what? That bastard called Sprint and canceled our service!"

I tried to accentuate the positive. "He's probably trying to cut down on unnecessary expenses?"

"You take his side, you die." Her lips thinned into a white line. "He didn't even run it by me before cutting off my lifeline to the rest of the world."

"How was he supposed to run it by you when you won't answer his calls?" I asked, raising my arms to ward off the torrent of physical blows that this question would surely elicit.

"That's it." She twisted in her chair, turning her back on me. "You're now number two on my shit list."

The receptionist turned up Celine Dion even louder.

Finally, a nurse called us into the office, where Claire was pelted with questions about her diet, exercise routines, pregnancy symptoms, and family health history.

And then, during the ultrasound, the physician asked the most important question of all:

"Do twins run in your family, Mrs. King? Because I think I see two heartbeats."

15

Okay. You know that scene toward the end of *Ferris Bueller's Day Off* where Cameron finds out the bad news about his dad's Ferrari and goes into, like, a catatonic trance? Well, that pretty much sums up Claire's response to the two heartbeats.

"*Get out!*" I yelled. "Twins! Are you sure?"

And Claire said . . . nothing.

"Well, I'm sure there are two heartbeats," the doctor confirmed. "Of course, at this early stage in the pregnancy, there is some risk of miscarrying one twin—there's a phenomenon known as 'vanishing twin syndrome'—but the chances of that happening after we see the heartbeats are extremely low."

And still, Claire said nothing.

"So she should call you guys if she has any bleeding, anything like that, right?" I asked.

"Of course. But don't worry too much." The doctor smiled. "Carrying multiples doesn't always mean a more difficult pregnancy, or even more weight gain, although a lot of mothers of twins report very severe morning sickness."

"Well, she's already having that," I said. "That and bizarre food cravings, like grilled cheese when she practically invented the South Beach Diet. Right, Claire?"

My sister's head lolled back against the crinkly white paper covering the exam table, her eyes closed, her brow beaded with sweat.

"Mrs. King? Are you all right?"

We all gathered around the table and peered down at her.

"I think she's in shock," I said. "She doesn't do well with surprises, and she's had a lot of them in the past few weeks."

"Mrs. King?" The doctor cleared his throat. "Do you need a few minutes alone?"

Her eyes cracked open a fraction of an inch. Her voice, when it finally came, was a strangled whisper. "I need . . ."

"What?" We crowded closer. "What do you need?"

Her eyes popped open as she lunged at the doctor, wrapping both hands around the sleeve of his white lab coat. *I need to know what the hell I'm supposed to do with two babies!*

The obstetrician attempted to free his sleeve, but resistance was futile. "I know it sounds overwhelming at first—"

"It's okay to be scared," the assistant soothed. "Lots of

women break down and cry when they find out they're having twins. And not tears of joy."

"I can recommend numerous resources for information and social support. Los Angeles has several Mothers of Multiples clubs . . ."

"You don't understand!" Her voice took on a shrill note of hysteria. "I don't have a job. I don't have a husband. I don't have a place to live. *I cannot have twins.*"

"You do have a husband, actually," I ventured. "And a job, sort of."

She released the doctor and fixed me with a venomous glare. "Shut up, Becca!"

"Sorry." I gulped and took a few steps back. "I was trying to make you feel better."

"You're making it worse!"

"But I only said—"

"La la la, I'm not listening!" She clamped her hands over her ears. "Everything you say sounds like Charlie Brown's teacher."

The doctor, the nurse, and the ultrasound technician exchanged glances. A scant ten minutes later, Claire was dressed, given some cursory advice about avoiding saunas and strenuous exercise, and booted out of the waiting room.

"I can't believe how rude you were to that doctor," she snapped as we headed down the hall to the building's parking lot.

"*Me?* You were the one who regressed to kindergarten."

She gasped.

"I'm sorry you're upset, but don't take it all out on me. You can't just use me as your punching bag every time you get mad at Andrew."

She whirled around to face me, her face puffy and red. "You have done a personality one-eighty since you broke up with Kevin and frankly, it's not an improvement. You used to be the cutest, sweetest little sister, but you are becoming a . . . you are just turning into a . . ."

"A woman with a spine?" I led the way to her SUV and waited for her to unlock it.

"No." She opened the car doors, climbed in, and slammed her side shut. "A pain in my ass."

"And you're a pain in mine. Unfortunately, we're blood kin, so we're stuck with each other."

"Don't remind me." She stroked her stomach. "And these poor kids'll be stuck with me, too." Then she fastened her seatbelt and burst into tears.

The waterworks subsided to a mere trickle by the time we reached her house, but the melodrama ratcheted right back up when we pulled into the driveway.

There was barely room to park behind the enormous U-Haul truck that Andrew, Connor, and a few other burly men were filling up with boxes, bulging green trash bags, and the art deco furniture Claire had so painstakingly selected from galleries and antique stores over the past six months.

Connor, who, I couldn't help noticing, looked good enough to do J.Crew print ads in his blue jeans and T-shirt, turned and waved at me.

Then he got a load of Claire's expression and his smile evaporated.

"What is the meaning of this?" She left the driver's side door open as she stomped over to the U-Haul.

"We have to move and you wouldn't call me back." Andrew seemed completely unfazed. "So I called my buddies to help us out."

"*Us?* There is no us!"

"Claire. This is neither the time nor the place to discuss this."

"Then where should we discuss it? In the cardboard box we'll be living in on the street corner?"

"I've rented us a very nice apartment in Van Nuys, and the landlord has generously agreed to let us move in before the first of next month. At least wait until you see it before you start hating it."

For a second, I was afraid she would pass out right there in the driveway. "You're really going to force the mother of your children to live in *Van Nuys?*"

"We've already discussed this." He paused to select a bottle of beer from the six-pack resting on the truck's back bumper. "I grew up in the Valley, and I turned out just fine."

"*That* is a matter of opinion."

Connor and the other moving buddies huddled by the

front of the van and feigned fascination with the hedges lining the house. I hastened to join them.

"Angry pregnant women scare the bejesus outta me," confided a guy in khaki shorts whom I recognized as a groomsman from Claire and Andrew's wedding.

"This is why I'm never getting married," whispered another guy in a Boston Red Sox cap. "Sounds just like my parents when I was a kid."

"Did your parents get through it?" asked Khaki Shorts guy.

"Nah. Ugly divorce, ugly custody battle, ugly new stepparents. But the good news is, my sisters and I paid for some shrink's summer house in Tahoe."

Halfway through Red Sox's hushed deconstruction of his lingering abandonment issues, Claire broke out the heavy artillery.

Andrew's patience seemed to be wearing thin. "Honey, you know I love you and I want to give you the best of everything. But right now, we're going to have to reevaluate and live within our means. So we have two choices: move into this apartment for the next few months or go live with my mom until the baby comes. Which is it going to be?"

During the long, loaded pause that followed, Connor, Khaki Shorts, Red Sox, and I exchanged terrified glances. What should we do if she started bludgeoning him with her deactivated cell phone?

She smiled icily. "Bab*ies*. I had my first ultrasound today."

"You did?" Andrew said. I winced at the raw hurt in his voice. "You went to the appointment without me?"

"That's right." She didn't sound the least bit contrite. "And guess what? There were two heartbeats. As in twins. As in double the work, double the sleep deprivation, double the financial crisis."

Dropped jaws, bugged-out eyes, and double takes all around on our side of the U-Haul.

"We're having twins! Did you hear that?" Andrew hollered over to his cowering moving team. "Twins. Who is the *man*?"

There was a loud smacking sound, which must have been him planting a big wet one on Claire, because she stopped lambasting him long enough to squeal girlishly. But then she got right back to business with, "So how are we going to support all these children your manly loins produced? Your sperm are writing checks your body can't cash."

"Oh, angel, come on, smile! Twins!" Andrew sounded like he was about to float away on a fluffy pink cloud. "This is great news! Money comes and goes, but family . . . that's forever."

"Okay, if I didn't already have morning sickness, I'd be puking my guts out from that line alone."

"Ooh." Red Sox flinched. "Flashbacks to fourth grade. I'm gonna have to get back into therapy. Good-bye, new Porsche."

"We should celebrate!" Andrew peered around the side of the van and waved to us. "You can stop hiding and pretending you're not hanging onto every word we say. Come on inside, I'll open a bottle of wine. And a bottle of apple juice for my beautiful bride."

But the innocent bystanders were not about to be suckered into another marital maelstrom. We were shocked, we were frazzled, and at least one of us was suffering from post-traumatic stress disorder.

"I gotta go, man." Red Sox practically sprinted for his car. "I can't handle this."

Connor touched my elbow and tilted his head toward his car. "Want to go find something less scary to do for the rest of the afternoon?"

"Like what? Enlist for active combat? Referee a street fight?"

He smiled. "Grab a bite to eat? Come marvel at the wreckage that is my new house?"

"Ah yes." I winked. "I believe I've heard about this house."

"So my reputation precedes me." He had a small dimple on one side when he smiled. How had I not noticed that before? "It's a thrashed old fixer-upper by the beach. It needs a little TLC, but it has lots of character. I'm doing most of the remodeling myself."

"When on earth do you have time to fix up a house?" I demanded. "With all the restaurant work, side businesses, sky diving, kayaking, slacklining, et cetera?"

"There's always time for a quick detour to Home Depot. So what do you say? Want to come check it out?"

"I see where this is going." I nodded knowingly. "We'll get to your place, you'll invite me up to see your etchings, next thing you know, I'm a fallen woman all alone in the harsh light of day and you have mascara smeared on your pillowcases." *If I was lucky.*

He seemed very intrigued by the picture I painted. "Tell you what. Come give a clueless bachelor some free decorating advice and I'll buy you dinner."

I pretended to think this over. "Well . . ."

"What if I told you that you must know kung-fu because, baby, your body kicks ass?"

"I'd say, how can I resist such chivalrous gallantry?"

"You can't. So let's away, shall we? My chariot awaits."

"I think I preferred the kung-fu line."

16

W ow," I breathed. "Color me covetous."

Connor had somehow gotten his hands on a cottage in Venice Beach, an oceanside community with bohemian ambiance and sky-high property prices. Venice was where people like Julia Roberts bought a house when they wanted to feel low-key and down-to-earth. Claire would've loved this neighborhood.

Aside from the occasional fetid stench wafting off the canal water when the wind changed, his house was a designer's dream. Lots of light, lots of warm-toned wood, lots of big windows and interesting angles. It didn't matter that some of the rooms had wires spilling out of walls, exposed studs, and a distinct lack of drywall—this place was bursting with potential. Add to that the soothing murmur of the ocean and the cool Pacific breezes and you had a recipe for raging domicile envy.

"Just as I suspected," I said as he ushered me into a living room featuring water-stained hardwood floors and a retro stone fireplace. "You lured me here to assist in some laborious Home Depot project, didn't you? Listen, I don't know nothing about installing no ceiling tiles. That's my story and I'm sticking to it."

He snapped his fingers, foiled again. "You're nothing but a tease."

"I'm an old-fashioned girl: 'Never renovate on the first date.' But, if you're a gentleman, I might deign to paint a baseboard or two at the end of the night."

"Ooh, that's hot." He turned his attention back to the ceiling. "I was thinking about doing pressed copper tiles up there. What do you think?"

"Interesting." I studied the gaping holes in the drywall. "What colors are you planning to use for the walls and the furniture?"

"No idea. That's why I'm trying to cadge free advice from you."

"Honesty. I like that in a man."

"I'll show you the rest of the house, such as it is. I'm open to any and all ideas."

He led me down the hall and paused with his hand on the last door on the left. "Brace yourself."

I nodded. "Braced."

The door swung open, and there it was . . . the bedroom. Connor's inner sanctum. Built-in bookshelves crammed with hardcovers, two bulky leather armchairs facing off over a blue Oriental rug, a huge window offering a breathtaking view of the ocean. But the space seemed to be missing something. Specifically, the *bed* seemed to be missing something.

The king-size bed with its brown leather headboard had only one pillow, and I couldn't help noticing that the gray comforter draped on the bed had been hacked in two, with one half inexplicably missing.

"Connor?"

"Yeah?"

"What happened here?"

"Meena happened."

"Wait. Aimee said that she went on some sort of rampage, but this is . . ." I stepped over to the bed and gathered up some frayed threads fringing the edge of the comforter. "Why did the Calvin Klein linens have to die?"

"I believe she was making a point." He looked like the traumatized witness to a twenty-car pileup whenever he discussed Meena, I'd noticed. "I let her move in a few weeks before we broke up, and I think she took that as a sign that an engagement ring was imminent. When I asked her to move out, she may have seen it as a symbolic divorce."

"Or she may just have a temper that would do Shannen Doherty proud."

"Another distinct possibility." He rocked back on his heels. "She left while I was at work one night, and she packed exactly half of the contents of the house. She took the salt shaker and left the pepper shaker. Took the lamps and left the shades. Swiped all the spoons and left the forks."

"Who got the knives?" I couldn't help myself.

"I got the butter knives, she made off with the fancy German steak jobs. Which means that she's out there somewhere, still armed with a whole drawerful of razor-sharp steel." He seemed haunted by the image.

"And she took half the quilt?"

"Sheets, towels, dishcloths . . . all massacred. As I said, she was making a point."

"And the point was . . . ?"

"I'm guessing it was, 'Fuck you, Connor Sullivan.'"

"But if you weren't married and you weren't engaged, why would she feel entitled to half of all your earthly possessions?"

He shrugged. "Rationality was never her strong suit."

"Okay. Now for the big question. Didn't you break up with her, like, *months* ago?"

He nodded.

"So why are you still living with a butchered comforter?"

"I guess I just haven't gotten around to replacing it."

I shook my head. "Not buying that. Try again."

"It's true," he protested. "I managed to replace the silverware and the towels and the TV so far."

I rolled my eyes. "Well, of *course* the TV."

"But somehow I keep forgetting to pick up some new sheets."

"Really." I leaned against the doorframe.

"Yep."

"You know, I suspect that something deeper than mere forgetfulness is going on here." I hesitated a few moments, trying to decide if I really wanted to hear the answer to my next question. "Is it because you still miss her?"

"No. God, no." He looked horrified. "I miss many things about my life before we broke up—my stereo speaker, my signed first edition of *Master and Commander,* having cufflinks that actually match—but Meena herself is not one of them."

"So? Why not head out and treat yourself to a new set of linens? Go crazy, buy a whole blanket all for yourself?"

He shoved both hands into his pockets. "Do we have to have this conversation?"

"Okay, pretend you're me for a second." I put my hands on his shoulders and steered him back to the bedroom doorway. "Look at what I'm looking at and tell me you wouldn't want an explanation from a potential boyfriend."

He looked alarmed. "'Potential boyfriend?'"

I brushed this off. "Okay, *so* not the point of this conversation."

"Hold on. Apparently, you've heard a lot of wild rumors flying around the restaurant, but some of them are true: I'm not the settling down type."

"Neither am I," I countered. "I just broke off my engagement and I have no plans to get sucked into another one any time soon. No one's looking to get serious." I sharpened my gaze. "I find it interesting, however, that someone who claims to love risking life, limb, and financial ruin won't take a chance and buy a new quilt."

He looked genuinely puzzled. "Buying a quilt isn't risky."

"I know. So why . . . ?"

He shrugged and crossed his arms. "I don't want to forget what happens when I make idiotic choices."

"So you spend week after week sleeping under a comforter that doesn't cover your feet?"

"Hey, I don't want to come home one day and find my pepper shaker gone, too." He pretended to wipe away a tear. "It's all I have left."

"I'm serious." I softened both my expression and my tone. "What are you afraid of?"

This had definitely been the wrong thing to say. He shut down faster than a post office at 5:00 P.M. before Labor Day weekend, closed the bedroom door, and refused to talk about anything except crown molding and copper plumbing for the next forty-five minutes.

When he dropped me off at Aimee's, I tried to apologize for overstepping my bounds, but he waved this away.

"You're right; it's ridiculous. I'll probably go to Target this weekend and buy some manly, flannel blanket," he said, obviously lying. "You still want to go hiking on Saturday?"

"Can't wait."

And before everything could get all high-strung and awkward, he leaned over and kissed me on the cheek. Which somehow progressed to kissing on the lips. He was a good kisser—warm and slow, with just the right amount of pressure. He was a gentleman about it, too, passionate without getting out of line. Not all of us could claim the same—it's possible I might have groped him a little. I hadn't felt this kind of searing physical desire in . . . well, *ever*, actually.

So the man didn't believe in overstocking the linen closet. So what? With chemistry like this, who needed comforters?

"So whatever happened with Rachelle Robinson and her corset-thieving stylist? I've fallen behind on the family news now that I spend all my time toiling in the supply closet and trying to gussy up our new apartment-slash-prison cell." Claire broke into a soulful rendition of Elvis Presley's "In the Ghetto."

I stopped changing the thread color in the sewing machine from black to gray long enough to make a face. "Van Nuys is hardly the ghetto."

"Ha." She collapsed onto Aimee's blue sofa and heaved her feet up onto the scratched, espresso-stained coffee table. The afternoon sunlight streamed through sliding glass doors to the balcony, making her platinum-blonde hair look even blonder. "Come on; give me some good gossip to get my mind off my nasty, brutish, and cockroach-riddled life."

"Cockroaches?" I shuddered.

"'Palmetto bugs.' That's what the landlord called them

when I demanded he call an exterminator." She shuddered. "'No need to be afraid of a few little bitty palmetto bugs.' Palmetto bugs, my ass. We are talking roaches the size of my SUV. Which, according to my so-called husband, we'll be giving back to the dealership this weekend before the repo man arrives . . ."

I could tell that she was just warming up, so I half-listened and got on with my threading. I'd spent all afternoon at Ninth and Maple, L.A.'s fashion district, where I'd loaded up on cloth, thread, lace, and buttons, courtesy of my brand-new expense account.

Since this new gig with Team Rachelle (as Fiona so nauseatingly insisted on calling it) might be my one and only shot to get my work out into the public, I was determined to create samples that were perfect in every way. (Not unlike Claire's wedding, though hopefully with a better long-term outcome.) I'd bought huge sheets of cardboard so I could make industrial patterns for my very best designs, the ones I'd been fine-tuning for years. Once I managed to produce patterns for the regulated clothing sizes Fiona had given me, I could figure out how big I wanted the stitches to be and perforate the cardboard appropriately so that factory sewing machines could reproduce my work.

Claire interrupted her philippic on marriage long enough to say, "Jeez, that's a lot of thread, Becks. You anticipating a strike at the Singer corporation?"

"No, I got a design job—"

She put down her glass of orange juice. "You did?"

"—so I need at least ten spools in each color, and different densities for working with cloth, Lycra, and leather."

"Oh my God, why didn't you tell me the minute I walked in here?"

I gave her a look. "I wanted to, but first we had to discuss the palmetto bug population in Van Nuys."

"This is so exciting! Soon you'll be rich and then you can hire me on to decorate your offices and I'll move back to Beverly Glen." Her eyes lit up. "Who are you working with?"

I flushed. "Remember Rachelle and her corset-thieving stylist?"

"Becca." Her feet came down from the coffee table. "You're *not*."

"Oh, but I am."

"But what about the interview in the paper?"

"Fiona explained everything on Monday. Rachelle's quote about doing everything herself was taken out of context."

"Out of context?" She threw back the rest of her OJ like a shot of baby-friendly tequila. "Are you kidding me? That's the oldest PR trick in the book. Page one: 'No comment.' Page two: 'Taken out of context.'"

I tried not to get defensive. "At the end of the day, it really doesn't matter what Rachelle did or didn't say. The point is, I have a job now, and my designs are going to be in major department stores across the U.S. And I'm getting paid."

"How much?" she demanded.

"A lot more than I expected. I won't see much until the line actually starts mass production, but in the meantime—"

"In the meantime, they're screwing you over and taking credit for your work!"

"This isn't about ego, it's about exposure," I informed her loftily.

"It's about desperation," she corrected. "But believe me, I've been there. Exhibit A: the beer commercial where I'm wearing a skimpy wet maillot, high heels, and lipstick."

"So?" I surveyed the fabric and sewing equipment strewn all over the living room. "Try to be happy for me. I know it's not my own boutique in Paris, but it's a start."

She sighed. "I know. This is a tough town and a girl's gotta get her foot in the door even if she gets frickin' hobbled in the process. I just don't want anybody taking advantage of my little sister."

"It'll be fine," I assured her, hoping with every last fiber of my being that this was true. "And I won't get hobbled. I read the contract very carefully." Although Fiona had been breathing down my neck the whole time, making pointed remarks about leaving for the airport.

Claire didn't say a word about my gross negligence in signing anything without a highly paid team of attorneys present. She just held out her glass for a refill and turned the subject back to herself. "Oh, and speaking of being hobbled? Andrew cancelled our basic cable. Not just HBO, which is grounds for divorce in and of itself, but basic cable. He says it's an unnecessary expenditure along with . . ." She closed her eyes against the horror of it all. "My Z. Bigatti moisturizer."

At a hundred and ten dollars an ounce, I had to agree with him on the Z. Bigatti, but nobody asked me.

"I had to use Neutrogena this morning. Bought it on sale at Walgreen's. I cried the whole time."

"Can't Amnesty International intervene?" I returned my focus to threading various needles, chiming in with "mm-hmm" or "an outrage!" at random intervals.

She had just started in on the humiliation of having to shop at Trader Joe's instead of Whole Foods when the doorbell rang. I buzzed up a delivery man, who arrived at the door bearing a green glass vase filled with purple irises.

He squinted down at his clipboard. "You Becca Davis?"

"That's me." I reached out to accept the pen he offered and signed where indicated while Claire grabbed the flowers. "Thanks."

By the time I closed the door behind him, Claire had snatched up the little white envelope taped to the rim of the vase. "Does my little Beck-Beck have an admirer?"

I turned up my palm. "Hand it over."

"I wish I could, but it's my duty as your L.A. chaperone to make sure you're not getting mixed up with the wrong crowd."

"Claire! Give it!"

Her smile gleamed with older-sibling sadism. "What if you're accepting gifts from, oh, say, Russell Crowe? How will Mom and Dad ever forgive me?"

"Russell Crowe is married!" I chased her around the display case, but she was surprisingly fleet of foot for a woman carrying twins.

"I know, that's what makes it so sordid! Or Tommy Lee, what if you were falling under *his* spell? No, we just can't risk it." She barricaded herself in the bathroom, slamming the white door in my face.

"Dammit!" I pounded on the door. "Tampering with the mail is a federal offense!"

"Luckily, I'm just tampering with FTD."

I heard the rustle of the envelope flap giving way, then a long pause.

"Dear God." She cleared her throat and prepared to orate. "'Becca—I've got a thirst, and baby, you smell like my Gatorade.'"

I collapsed in hysterical laughter.

"That is *disgusting*." She flung the door open, arms akimbo. "Seriously, how can you laugh? That's the most offensive thing I've ever heard!"

"Well, Tommy Lee reserves his very best material for me," I said, wiping tears from my eyes.

"It's signed 'Connor'." Her eyes narrowed. "Connor, as in Connor Sullivan?"

Oh boy. "Listen, I can explain . . ."

"You're dating your boss?"

"I quit last week, remember?"

"You're dating Connor Sullivan, even after I warned you

about him, and you let him talk to you like *this*? '*You smell like my Gatorade*?'"

"Lighten up—it's a joke. We have kind of a competition going . . ."

"Oh, Becca, where did we fail you?"

"You know, if you'd just give me one minute to explain, I think you'd see that you're way overreacting."

"Ha. You're too sweet and innocent to see that man for the . . . the rogue and the rake that he is—"

Evidently she'd been reading Regency romance novels again.

"—but I know for a fact that when a man starts comparing a woman to a sports drink, he's not after her for her sparkling personality." She stormed out of the bathroom, seized my cell phone, and commenced dialing. "Hello? Andrew? It's me. No, no, everything's fine with me, the problem is your sainted friend Connor. Would you like to know who he's treating like a Sunset Strip streetwalker?"

At least she was speaking to him again.

Hmm," Fiona Fitzgerald said, running her fingers over the samples I brought to her office on Friday afternoon. "Hmm."

A small but vocal part of me kept insisting that she looked *awfully* fresh-faced and well-rested for a woman who'd spent the last four days flying across the international date line and back, but the rest of me rationalized that, with enough makeup, Ambien, and first-class pampering, anything was possible. She *had* to have gone to Australia as she'd told me, because if she hadn't, that meant . . .

I swallowed loudly as she examined the seam of a silk camisole and let out another long "hmm . . ."

"Is 'hmm' good or bad?" I finally asked.

She retrieved a pair of black-rimmed glasses from her desk drawer and put them on. "You've certainly made some *interesting* choices with this piece."

Oh crap. "I guess silk isn't a very affordable material for a midpriced top? If you like, I can redo it with a cotton-rayon blend, maybe even—" I tried to be brave "—polyester."

She didn't look up from the camisole. "I see."

"And, of course, we can use any color fabric. I just used basic black for the sample because I was toying with the idea of doing some turquoise ribbon accents on the neckline."

She finally glanced up. "Were you?"

"Yes, but then I decided that I was better off keeping it simple so that the customer has the option of using it as a layer piece under the open-weave long-sleeved top." I pointed to the whisper-light black mesh shirt I'd been experimenting with for the last two years. Anything that soft and sheer, with that many natural irregularities in the fabric, was a total bitch to seam and standardize. But I thought I'd done a good job.

Apparently, I was alone in that opinion. "Try this again in a more practical fabric, and this time add the turquoise." She handed the camisole back to me.

"Yes, ma'am."

"As for this . . ." She tweezed up the mesh top between her thumb and forefinger and tossed it over to a table piled high with fashion magazines and office memos. "Eh."

"But . . ." I tamped down the urge to go after the shirt and embrace it like an orphaned puppy. "I already did a manufacturing pattern for the small, medium, and large sizes you wanted. I even did extra small!"

"I said 'eh,'" she snapped. "What else do you have?"

I handed over the denim jacket, drawstring "sweatpant" skirt I'd modeled after the one I'd worn on the fateful trip to Lilac Lakes with Kevin, plus a cotton sundress that I'd made by "remixing" the muslin panels of my sister's bridal gown.

She scrutinized these like a forensic scientist looking for traces of DNA evidence. "Eh, eh, and eh."

I tried to remain poker-faced.

One corner of her mouth twitched as she picked up on my disappointment and anxiety. "Leave the patterns, darling, but I don't think they'll make it into production."

"What's wrong with them?" I asked, determined to rally. "Tell me what you need and I swear I'll do better."

"You will? Are you sure?"

"Absolutely." Translation: absolutely not. These pieces represented my best, time-tested work.

"Well, I hope so. Because otherwise . . ." She let my imagination and abject fear of failure fill in the blanks.

Realizing that she probably thrived on designers' fear like a tiger shark on big bloody chunks of chum, I blustered ahead with, "Tell me exactly what your vision is and I'll make it happen."

"*My* vision?" Cue lilting laughter. "Darling, you're the designer. You're the one with the vision."

"Yes, but if you can be specific about what's wrong with these pieces, at least I'll have an idea of what *not* to do on the next go-round."

She exhaled, all loud and annoyed. "Fine. It's just . . . I can't see Rachelle wearing any of these pieces, can you?"

I blinked. "Maybe not—especially if I recut with polyester—but I thought we were marketing to midwestern moms?"

"We are, darling, but we still want the *feel* of Rachelle. Her sophistication, her iconoclastic glamour."

"But 'iconoclastic glamour' and 'rayon blend' don't go together."

Her tiny white teeth gleamed when she smiled. "They do if you're a good enough designer."

Medic!

"So just keep that in mind and come back next week with some fresh ideas." She rose to her feet, dismissing me. "Leave everything with me and I'll run it by our marketing people, but don't get your hopes up."

"Okay." I hung my head.

"And show me something really spectacular next time. I hired you because I know you can do better than this."

"Okay."

Her smile looked positively predatory by now. "And don't take any of this personally, darling—it's just business."

"So you decided to take it easy on me today?" I asked Connor the next day as we strolled toward the palm-dotted hills of the

Runyon Canyon hiking trail. "No cliff scaling? No bungee jumping?"

"Not yet, but if things go well, I'm thinking street lugeing, alligator wrestling, going over Victoria Falls in a rickety barrel . . . the whole works."

"Do I even want to know what 'street lugeing' is?"

He grabbed my hand as we navigated a tangled patch of rocks and roots. "Stick with me and you'll find out."

I batted my eyelashes. "Ah declare, ah may swoon."

"Hey, who needs candy and flowers when you can have a total adrenaline rush?"

"Along with broken bones and unsightly scars?"

"All the better for bragging rights."

"Gosh, you *do* know how to woo a girl."

"It's not for everyone," he agreed as we headed up the winding dirt trail, leaving the stress and traffic of Hollywood behind us. "Meena, for example, couldn't stand the outdoors. She was always nagging me to stop taking chances. But I say, life is short. You might as well get the most out of it. You can't be afraid to push the envelope and really go for what you want."

Except when it comes to dating, I thought, remembering the massacred half-comforter still draped across his bed.

"Well, I don't know how I feel about street lugeing yet, but I'm willing to try anything once."

"Then you're already a step ahead of most people." He recaptured my hand as we hit a smooth uphill incline. "Hell, just coming out to a new city was a gutsy move."

I took a deep breath of what passed for fresh air in L.A. "I guess."

"You left your family, your hometown, your fiancé . . . that takes courage."

I thought about Kevin, Trish, and the gaping hole in the ground at Lilac Lakes. "Not as much as you might think. In fact, now that I've left, I can't believe I lasted as long as I did with a boyfriend who was, for all intents and purposes, a Vulcan."

We passed a lithe blonde hiker in a discreet baseball cap who I was 99 percent sure was Naomi Watts, but he didn't seem to notice her. "A Vulcan? Really? Did he have pointy ears? Long, knobby fingers?"

"No." How best to put this? "He was just logical. Eminently logical."

"And you're the creative type."

"I know everyone says that opposites attract, but we were just plain opposite." I stopped for a swig from the water bottle he offered. "He was a good guy, basically. Maybe a *leetle* controlling." I handed the water bottle back to him. "What about you and Meena? It sounds like you guys weren't exactly a match made in heaven."

"Nah, we were doomed to failure. She wanted stability, I wanted adventure. And then she started in on the whole 'I will change you into my fantasy man' campaign . . ."

"And it didn't work?" I feigned surprise. "Women all over America will be shocked to hear that."

"I tried to tell her, but she kept hoping that I'd morph into some sensitive metrosexual who buffed his nails and couldn't sleep at night if he wore white socks with black shoes. She wanted me to give up all my fun weekend activities—"

"Cheating death and incurring concussions?"

"Exactly. The breakup was inevitable. I went my way and she went hers . . . along with the TV, steak knives, and most of the good furniture."

We hiked in companionable silence until we reached the summit, which offered sweeping views of the Hollywood Hills and the skyscrapers downtown.

"Beautiful." I gulped some more water, huffing and puffing noticeably more than Connor was. Mr. Action-Adventure had barely broken a sweat. "I had no idea Los Angeles could look so peaceful."

"Someday I'll take you to Bolsa Chica in Huntington Beach," he said. "It's right off the ocean and the views are incredible."

"How'd you get to be such the hiker? Did your parents used to take you backpacking up all those mountains in Colorado?"

"Nah." He shielded his eyes against the sun and stared off at the horizon. "My mom died when I was seven—cancer—and my dad and my brothers weren't much for hiking. Competitive skiing was more our thing."

"Oh God, I'm sorry." I touched his arm. "I didn't know."

"It was a long time ago." He shrugged. "I had three brothers and we were all on the ski team in high school, stupid, reckless, thought we were immortal, you know the drill. One day I hit a patch of ice at top speed and cracked a few vertebrae. I could've been paralyzed, but I wasn't. Then my dad got remarried to my stepmom, Brenda, and she tried to rechannel all that energy into more constructive outlets like Outward Bound."

"Hence, the hiking." My eyes were wide.

"Exactly. And there you have it: my life story." He turned and headed back toward the trail. "Probably more than you wanted to hear."

It was only the tip of the iceberg, but I knew it was time to change the subject. So I hurried to catch up. "Hey. Know where we should stop on the drive home?"

I didn't intend to sleep with him, truly I didn't, but we ended up in the bedding department at Bloomingdale's and who could really be expected to think straight, surrounded by all those intoxicatingly high thread counts?

"You run these through the dryer a few times before you use them, and you're never going to want to get out of bed again," I marveled, examining a deep-pocketed fitted sheet. Then I turned over the shrink-wrapped package to glance at the price. "*Ouch.*"

Connor was studying a display bed made up in gray pillows and darker gray blankets, accented with a pearl gray chenille throw. "Hey, what do you think of this?"

"It's a little Maoist, don't you think?"

He stepped over to the next display, a jumble of floral sheets and Pepto Bismol-colored shams. "I suppose you're going to try to fob this nightmare off on me?"

I flopped down on the puffy down comforter, then tossed a rose-strewn pillow his way. "I think it would be perfect for a single man living alone."

He sat down next to me. "Tell you what, grab some scissors and you can take your half right now."

"Sir, may I help you?" A no-nonsense blond saleswoman materialized in front of us. "Do you and your wife have any questions about our Vauxhall Garden collection here?"

I blushed and opened my mouth to correct her, but Connor said, "No, my wife and I are just fine, aren't we, lambikins?"

I hesitated just a second, then took my cue. "We sure are. I was remarking on how this comforter reminds me of the bed-and-breakfast where we honeymooned."

The saleswoman thawed a bit. "How sweet. Where did you honeymoon?"

I turned and passed the buck to Connor. "Where *did* we honeymoon, snookums? I can never remember the name of that island."

"Australia, pookie, remember? *Australia*." He broke out his most disarming grin for the clerk. "She's so forgetful. It's awfully cute." He patted my head.

"Well, aren't you two just precious?" The sale rep retreated to the cash registers, presumably to vomit into a wastebasket under the counter.

The moment she disappeared behind the towel displays, I whipped around and jabbed my index finger into his white T-shirt. "Australia? *That's* the best you could come up with?"

"Hey, if you don't want me answering the tough questions, answer them yourself."

"How stupid would I have to be to forget Australia? Come *on*."

"Don't worry, you're secretly very smart," he confided. "But you're my arm-candy trophy wife, so you *play* dumb to pump up my already overinflated ego. If anyone looks like a moron here, it's me."

"True." I laughed. "But I'm still kicking your ass all the way to Melbourne."

He grinned. "You know I can't resist you when you threaten me with bodily harm."

And then he shoved aside all the ruffles and chintz and kissed me. Right there in the middle of the bedding department. And good news: the raging chemistry we'd experienced last time our lips locked had been no fluke. I kissed him back, shocked and excited at my own daring. The old Becca Davis didn't believe in public displays of affection. The old Becca Davis couldn't understand why the tonsil hockey couldn't wait until the amorous couple got home.

But to hell with her.

The new Becca—the one into fun, casual dating—understood completely. Call her exhibitionist, call her immature and sex-crazed—she couldn't hear you anyway, because she was too busy smooching under the blinding department store lights. She had, in fact, lost her dignity to the point where she referred to herself in the third person.

And then my cell phone rang and yanked us back to Bloomingdale's.

We struggled to our feet, panting rather indelicately, and while Connor attempted to restore the Vauxhall bedding to some semblance of its former hospital-cornered order, I rummaged through my bag for my phone to see whose call I'd missed while attacking the new man in my life like a rabid wolverine.

Kevin Bradley.

It's always fucking *something*.

"Becca?" My dismay must have shown on my face, because Connor stopped fluffing pillows and stared at me. "Everything okay?"

"Yeah." I shook my head, wishing that the human memory worked along the same lines as an Etch A Sketch and that by doing this, I could expunge all traces of my former fiancé. "Everything's great. Really. So . . . want to go someplace a little more private?"

We made it all the way back to his house in Venice Beach—demonstrating incredible restraint on both our parts, thank you very much—before we recommenced pawing each other like freshmen under the gym bleachers.

"You sure you're ready for this?" he murmured, pressing me up against the front door while he fumbled for his house keys.

"Mm-hmm." I slipped both hands under his shirt. "Are you?"

The lock gave way and we tumbled through the door in a clumsy, fevered tangle of limbs and hormones. He slammed the door shut with his foot and peeled his shirt off. I yanked my sweater up over my head.

We left a trail of pants, socks, shoes, and underwear in our wake as we headed for the bedroom.

I didn't know what had gotten into me, but whatever it was, I wanted more. Rushing into, well, *anything* was so unlike me, but with Connor, I felt bold and playful and free. Just last week I'd barely been able to work up the nerve to do the Kathleen Turner imitation via phone, but today I shed most of my inhibitions along with my clothes. So this was what it was like to know what I wanted and just go for it. I was starting to appreciate the aphrodisiac of taking chances.

We laughed as we fell onto the half-comforter. No hesitation, no analytical discussion. Just skin on skin and his eyes meeting mine.

I shivered as he kissed my neck and by the time the afternoon sun set over the Pacific, I had discovered some unprecedented new pleasures along with my devil-may-care vixen alter ego.

I let him talk me into staying the night because I wanted to prolong the afterglow aura of intimacy. On some level, I realized that physical compatibility did not equal love, commitment, or emotional attachment, but I didn't want to ruin a perfect day by dwelling on all the things that could go wrong. Connor was right: life was short. So I took a quick shower, wriggled back into my clothes, and called Aimee to let her know I wouldn't be returning to her apartment until tomorrow.

"Oh my God, you did it," she crowed. "See, didn't I tell you? I told you—you looove him!"

"I barely know him," I corrected.

"Oh, I'd say you know him pretty well." She giggled. "So how was he? Was he great?"

Heat flooded my cheeks. "I'm not discussing this with you."

"Who initiated? You or him?"

"It was sort of mutual," I lied. "Listen, do me a favor and don't tell anyone at Rhapsody about this."

"Why not? It's not like you still work there."

"I know, but . . . just do me a favor and keep it to yourself."

"You are no fun. At all."

"That's not what *he* said," I retorted saucily, then hung up.

When I emerged from the bathroom, Connor was waiting to give me a kiss and a freshly washed strawberry. We couldn't stop grinning at each other.

"That was . . ." He gave me an exaggerated eye roll.

"I know." I tried to look all worldly and nonchalant, like I slept with men on the first date all the time.

"You want to go grab some dinner and . . . ?"

"And what?"

He offered up another strawberry. "You'll see."

The next morning I woke up to the smell of fresh coffee and the sound of Connor singing Queen's "I Want to Break Free," making up in volume what he lacked in pitch.

I clutched the jagged edges of the quilt around me in a sort of makeshift cape and padded down the hall to face the music. "Hey." I peeked into the kitchen. "Thanks for letting me hog the covers last night."

He broke off mid-chorus to kiss me. "No problem. I guess that comforter is too small for two people. I should probably buy a new one."

"Hey, now, let's not get crazy."

He looked relaxed and refreshed in his boxer shorts and stubble. "Cancel all your plans for today. I made a few calls this morning and I have a special surprise for you."

"Ooh, do tell." I was thinking roses, champagne, beachside picnics . . .

"My buddy Snake runs a skydiving school out by Riverside. We're going skydiving."

"We're what?"

He laughed at my expression, patted my rear, and turned back to the coffee grinder. "Hit the showers, señorita, this is your lucky day."

I had misgivings from the start. Maybe it was the six-hour class I had to sit through to prepare for my first jump. Maybe it was practicing the "drop and roll" maneuver I was supposed to exe-cute upon landing (assuming, of course, that I didn't get my parachute tangled up in a sparking set of power lines and/or my foot didn't shatter in five places the second I hit the ground). Maybe it was the series of videos we had to view, illustrating the endless variety of ways one could die both in and out of the drop plane. Connor held my hand and threw back a few cups of lukewarm coffee while the voice-overs described, in chilling detail, the potential for equipment failures and human errors and the ways in which one was supposed to correct these while hurtling toward certain death at heart-stopping speeds.

It did not help that Connor spent all the breaks introducing me to his skydiving buddies—including "Snake" Sampson, a former Army Ranger who owned the skydiving school and would be supervising my first jump—and engaging in a competitive discussion of who had had the worst sports-related injury.

"I once broke my collarbone mountain biking," Connor volunteered. "Busted the hell out of my bike, too. I had to carry that damn thing five miles back to the main road."

I gaped at him. "With a broken collarbone?"

"Uphill both ways," he assured me.

"I bet he cried the whole time," Snake scoffed. "Anyway, that's nothing. I went rock climbing in Cozumel one time and the belay slipped . . ."

The breaking point came when I signed the company's release form. Having learned my lesson about the importance of reading all fine print before signing any legal document, I went over each and every clause with a fine-tooth comb. And the news was not good: If I happened to end up maimed, dismembered, or dead as a result of this "adventure" . . . oh well.

"But none of that's going to happen," Connor assured me

when I pointed to the sentence stating that they'd be happy to scrape up and return my flattened corpse to my family, assuming they could find it.

"Then why is it in the contract?"

"They have to cover their ass, just in case. We're living in the land of the lawsuit."

"Yes, but look at all the things that can go wrong!" I jabbed my index finger at the two-page encyclopedia of Horrible Ways to Die.

"Again, none of that's going to happen to you." He leaned over to kiss my cheek. "Don't you trust me?"

I did a spit take into my coffee. "This has nothing to do with trusting you. This has to do with trusting my life to a man named Snake and a parachute, and I *don't*!"

"Well, that's why you have the emergency chute."

"And what if that fails, too?" I demanded, sounding eerily like Kevin Bradley.

"The odds of that happening are roughly the same as you scratching off the winning lottery ticket during your free fall and simultaneously getting hit by lightning."

"You say that now that we're on solid ground, but it could happen! What if some new guy was in charge of my gear? What if he was hungover while he was packing my chutes? What if the back of the plane hits me in the head as soon as I jump out? What if, I don't know, some kid's kite takes out an eye on my way down?"

"Becca." He smoothed a lock of hair back from my face.

"You don't have to jump if you don't want to. But I promise, you'll be fine. In fact, you'll feel better than you ever have. All the adrenaline, all the endorphins . . . it's such a high."

"Maybe I can just stay on the ground and drop Ecstasy?" I suggested.

He laughed. "I've done this hundreds of times. Believe me, you'll love it."

"Hundreds of times?"

He nodded. "High-altitude drops, low-altitude drops, you name it, I've done it."

"Just don't tell her about the base jumping," Snake muttered as he walked by.

My eyebrows shot up. "Base jumping? What's that?"

"Nothing," he said a little too quickly. "Anyway, stop worrying and start getting excited. Snake will take good care of you. And great news—since we're old buddies and you're obviously such a natural, he's agreed to let you do your first jump solo."

I blanched. "As in, all by myself? Without a handy, dandy instructor strapped to my back to make sure I don't freak out and forget to pull the rip cord?"

He seemed totally unconcerned. "You won't forget. I'm telling you, you're making this out to be much scarier than it is. The free fall is actually very quiet and peaceful."

Scenes from the *Your Parachute Won't Open . . . Now What?* video flashed through my mind. "I *want* to trust you."

"Then do. This is going to change your whole life. You

won't regret it—I swear." And he looked into my eyes, meeting my fear and self-doubt with such confidence and pride that I decided to show him that he was right to believe in me.

"Okay, what the hell." I grabbed the combat boots and red bodysuit I was supposed to wear on the jump. "Into the wild blue yonder."

Snake, blue-eyed, grizzled, and balding, grinned maniacally at me as the little propeller plane took off with me, Connor, and two other veteran jumpers in the cargo hold. We had to yell over the noise of the engines and the wind, which roared through the open side door.

"You look scared." Snake seemed highly amused by my pinched little face under my helmet.

I forced a smile, all the while thinking about small aircraft crash statistics.

"She looks scared!" he shouted over to Connor, who squeezed my hand and mouthed something to me I couldn't understand.

"What?" I mouthed back, but he just shook his head and grinned.

We reached our designated jumping altitude all too quickly.

"Keep your hands on the rip cords," Snake hollered at us.

Yeah. Like I'd forget. Like anything short of a crowbar could pry my fingers from their death grip on my only link to survival.

We'd been lined up in order of weight, heaviest to lightest, which meant that Connor went first and I went last, with two thrill-seeking frat boys between us.

The man who had, not twelve hours ago, explored every inch of my body with utmost patience and passion, hunkered down in the doorway and prepared to leap out into the void.

"One, two, three . . . GO!" Snake yelled.

Connor hurled himself out into the vast sea of blue and white without a second's hesitation. Though I couldn't watch his fall from the back of the line, I pictured him plummeting toward earth, glorying in the temporary escape from sound and time and gravity. He liked to think of himself as above the laws of nature, but when I visualized his body falling, a fragile bundle of heart and blood and bones picking up speed with every passing second . . .

"Oog," I moaned as Frat Boy #1 leapt into thin air.

"Urg," I added as Frat Boy #2 bailed out with a whoop.

I inched toward the doorway, making eye contact with Snake as I'd been taught in the prep session, trying not to look down. Or up. Or left. Or right. The wind whipped against my cheeks and plastered my helmet straps against my neck.

"Ready?" Snake gave me a thumbs-up.

That's when I looked down. If I had been snug in the window seat of a 747, I would've thought, *Oh, we're flying so low, we'll be landing any second,* but seeing as I was sans seatbelt, sans tray table, and sans window, my perspective was quite different. From here, the earth looked awfully hard, not to mention far away.

"You have to go now or we'll miss the drop zone," Snake cried. "Ready?"

No doubt about it. I was going to die.

I maintained eye contact with Snake and nodded.

"Great. One, two, three . . . GO!"

I was still making eye contact with Snake.

"GO!"

My hand refused to release the solid metal doorframe. It wasn't even optional—my nervous system had ceased operations.

"Last chance! GO!"

19

So you didn't jump?" Aimee poured me yet another glass of wine (Trader Joe's price tag still adorning the label). We had made ourselves comfy in her apartment's tiny living room, high heels and purses and other uncomfortable accoutrements cast aside as we ordered pizza and prepared for a girls' night in.

"Not 'didn't,'" I corrected. "*Couldn't*. I wanted to, but my survival instincts took over."

"But Connor jumped."

"Like he was escaping a burning building." I took a sip of the finest discount Chardonnay. "He thought he had enough enthusiasm for both of us, but he thought wrong. I practically kissed the runway when the plane finally landed."

"You realize, of course, that the odds of dying while skydiving are infinitesimal."

"So I'm told."

"I mean, it's a recreational hobby."

"For adrenaline junkies with a death wish." I shuddered at the mere memory. "Look, the bottom line is there are two kinds of people in this world: those who will voluntarily fling themselves out of an airplane and those who won't."

"Well, at least you'll never have to stay up nights wondering which type you are." She toasted me with her wineglass.

"That's the problem. I don't want to be an ultraconservative little priss like Meena. I want be the bright new future of his love life. I want to be the kind of girl who can match his appetite for adventure."

"So you keep the adventures on land, big deal." She perused the pizza place magnets on the fridge. "And anyway, why do you care so much what he thinks?"

"Maybe because I had sex with him less than twenty-four hours ago?"

"That's my point." She nodded. "*He* should be worrying about whether he's good enough for *you*."

I picked at the dish of chocolate-covered cranberries she'd brought out with the wine. "He was pretty quiet on the drive back from Riverside. I think he's disappointed in me."

"Now you're just being ridiculous."

"No, honestly. I think he's worried that I'm going to be like all the other ex-girlfriends who tried to change him and rein him in and blah blah blah."

"Men." She snorted in disgust. "They should all be broken down and reprogrammed at age eighteen."

"Who would do the reprogramming?" I wondered.

"Martha Stewart, Vera Wang, and that 'Hints from Heloise' chick," she decided. "So they could bake delicious blueberry muffins, get excited about getting married, *and* remove ink stains from our white shirts. Do you want mushrooms or sun-dried tomatoes on the pizza?"

"Tomatoes. I'll probably never hear from him again, and it's too bad because I really like him."

"But not enough to risk ending up a paratrooper pancake. I think he'll understand."

I slouched back into the sofa cushion. "I don't know. Maybe I'm just not ready to start dating again."

"Yeah, let the specter of your dorky ex-fiancé ruin the rest of your twenties. That's the spirit." She picked up the cordless phone and dialed. "Hi, I'd like to order a large pizza, please. Half sun-dried tomato, half anchovy."

"Anchovies?" I repeated after she hung up the phone. "I didn't see you as the anchovy type. Grilled zucchini and basil-almond pesto, maybe, but anchovies?"

"I hate them, actually. I hate most seafood, but I'm supposed to eat it for my new diet."

"Aimee," I said firmly. "We have discussed this. You are a

size-two shadow of a woman. No matter what any of those casting directors say, you do not need to lose weight."

"Oh, I know." But even as she said this, she reached for her ever-present pack of Marlboro "diet in a stick" Lights and lit up, waving smoke toward the direction of the open balcony doors. "It's not about weight, really, so much as nutrition. Energy. Looking younger."

"You're twenty-six."

"Exactly. Practically Diane Keaton territory. Only without all the Oscars and snazzy suits. And this diet is guaranteed to make me look and feel ten years younger after only eight weeks."

"So you're aiming for sixteen? You want to relive your junior year of high school?"

"Don't mock it till you've tried it. My acting coach raved about it. She's in week five and her skin is positively glowing."

"Let me guess: Atkins?"

"Oh, please." She seemed insulted. "Like I'd ever be so banal."

"Zone?"

"Zodiac."

"I beg your pardon?"

She scurried off to her bedroom, returning with a plastic-bound sheaf of paper that looked fresh off the Xerox machine at Kinko's. "The Zodiac Diet. It's so new and hip, it hasn't even officially hit bookstores yet. But my acting coach let me make a copy of her advance galley."

I thumbed through the manuscript—which had clearly been self-published, probably in a carport in the Valley—and tried not to scoff openly. "Give me the condensed version."

"Well, I mean, obviously the science is very complicated, but the gist of it is that all the signs in the Zodiac fall into one of four categories—earth, fire, water, and air—and by identifying your sign's element and eating accordingly, you're working *with* your body and spirit instead of *against* them. Like, I'm a Leo. That's a fire sign. So I need to eat things from the ocean to counterbalance my fiery tendencies."

"Like anchovies?"

"Bingo. Seafood, kelp, anything water-based, really. Lots of ice and soup. And I'm supposed to avoid stuff that fuels the fire—peppers, spices, that sort of thing."

"Got it," I said. "Well, I'm a Cancer . . ."

She consulted the manuscript. "That's a water sign. So you should be piling on the spice. Next time, get red peppers and pepperoni on your pizza."

"But I don't like red peppers or pepperoni."

"That's just years of bad nutritional conditioning talking. Your poor body." She puffed away on her cigarette. "Now. Back to the skydiving fiasco. What's your plan?"

"No plan." I shrugged one shoulder. "I'll just have to wait and see if he calls. And if he doesn't . . ."

"That's it? You're handing all the power over to him on a big silver platter?"

"No, but I'm not going to beg him to—"

"What happened to the gutsy femme fatale who called me from his bathroom yesterday?"

"She went AWOL right about the time my knees gave out at five thousand feet."

She assessed me with a cool, calculating stare. "You're just scared."

"Maybe I am. Maybe I'm also out of practice when it comes to dating."

"Oh, just call him and feel him out." She tossed the cordless phone over, hitting me square in the shin. "Don't be so stubborn. You know you can't live without his heinous pickup lines. Plus, he's good in bed. Plus, now you're addicted to life on the edge."

I nudged the phone back toward her with my toes. "I've got a better idea. As soon as we finish the pizza I'm going to grab a cab and go pick up someone who puts Connor to shame in the life-on-the-edge department."

"I'm glad you called," Claire said, cramming a french fry into her mouth. "But how sad that neither of us has anything better to do on a Sunday night."

"What could be more important than spending a little quality time with my sister?" Since we were now equally broke and declassé, we had agreed to meet for a late-night snack at a McDonald's in Studio City. (Claire's suggestion. Apparently, becoming pregnant had freed her from the di-

etary chains that had bound her to tofu and brown rice all
these years.)

"How's the job going?"

I thought about Fiona tossing my shirt sample into the corner. "Awful. How's your marriage?"

"Awful."

"L.A. really worked out well for us, huh?"

She glowered. "Here's the latest: Andrew King is a delusional sadist getting more delusional by the day. When he's not
lecturing me about how I should be delighted to eat red beans
and rice every single night, he's trying to convince our landlord
to accept a tiny down payment—I am talking, like, the price of
this Extra Value Meal—on our crappy new apartment. He said
we had to buy now before our credit rating is completely anni-
hilated. So we could be stuck making payments on that hell-
hole for the next *thirty years*."

"You can do this, Claire. I know you can. You grew up
middle class, remember? In Phoenix, for heaven's sake. If Paris
Hilton can survive backwoods Arkansas, you can hack Van
Nuys. Besides, I hear red beans and rice are really nutritious.
Between that and your prenatal vitamins, you're totally covered. Speaking of which, how are my nieces- or nephews-
to-be?"

"Starving." She helped herself to more fries. "Am I going to
hell if I get another order of these?"

"No. But good lord, woman—I can't remember ever seeing
you eat fries. I didn't even know you liked them."

"I don't. The *babies* like them. And I'm trying this new eating plan, the Zodiac Diet, and—"

"Oh no. You're doing that, too?"

"Of course. Everyone is. Anyway, I'm a Gemini, which is an air sign, so I'm supposed to eat lots of vegetables and tubers because—"

"Because they grow in the ground so it *grounds* you?"

"Bingo. And I've never felt better." She took a huge bite of her burger.

"And the Big Mac?"

She shrugged. "Cows eat grass. And grass grows in the ground."

"Please don't tell me you actually believe all that hooey?"

"Don't be so negative. All my friends from yoga started doing it."

"Do they look any different now?" I asked.

"I don't know." She attacked her fries with renewed vigor. "They don't return my calls anymore. Not since we were stigmatized with an eight-one-eight area code."

"No offense, but your friends are bitches."

"They're just practical." She looked strained and sallow under the bright fluorescent lights. The faint lines at the corners of her eyes had gotten noticeably deeper over the past few weeks. "I knew it would happen. And I have work to fill my day now, so I don't have time for all the lunches and shopping trips. I wouldn't want them to ever see me like this, anyway."

"Like what?"

"Exiled from Eden."

"Claire . . ."

"We have no savings. We have no AC. No washing machine, no long-distance carrier, no car insurance—which, yes, is illegal—and no reason to think that any of this is going to change anytime soon. All we have are two people and two more on the way crammed into the square footage of a shoebox."

"You'll rebuild." I tried to radiate confidence. "You and Andrew are a team now; you can build a new future . . ."

"I don't want to build." She put down her french fries, looking drained. "I want security."

"Money isn't the only source of security."

"It's the only kind that's going to furnish a nursery for my kids. When I asked Andrew where the babies were going to sleep, he said, and I quote, 'We'll just put some blankets in a drawer for the first few months.'"

I laughed. "Didn't Popeye's son have to sleep in a drawer? Swee'pea?"

"Swee'pea was his nephew, not his son," Claire corrected, and I caught a glimpse of the bossy, impatient older sister she'd been before the wedding. "And it's not funny. I don't know how we're going to manage. I couldn't have picked a worse time to get pregnant." She closed her eyes. "But now that I am . . ."

"You can't wait to have the babies," I finished softly.

"Exactly. Is that unforgivably selfish of me?" She reached across the table and gripped my hand so tightly I winced. "Am I a horrible mother if I keep them?"

"Hang on. Since when is keeping them even an *option*?"

"Since we lost all our money and our long-term health and dental coverage. I don't know what to do. My heart and my brain are pulling in different directions . . . can you keep a secret?"

I shook my head. "I don't think I want to know this secret."

"One of my friends adopted a baby girl last year and I got the name of her lawyer. I have an appointment to meet with him next week, and I want you to come with me."

After several seconds of silence, she let go of my hand and pulled away.

"An adoption lawyer? Are you serious?" I tried not to sound as shocked as I felt.

"Well, what else can I do? You tell me. I don't know how we're going to be able to take care of them once they get here. We can't afford daycare, but I won't be able to afford to stay home with them, our marriage is falling apart, and I just . . ." Her eyes teared up. "I know I won't be able to give them any of the things children should have. A happy family. A yard to play in. Summer camp, college, a basic sense of security."

"Hey." I tried for a stern, take-charge tone. "I don't know if this is depression or pregnancy hormones or what, but you have to stop this."

"I already love them so much," she continued as if I had never interrupted. "Is it horrible of me to want to keep them for myself when there are so many other families who could give them everything we can't?"

"Stop talking like that! These problems with Andrew? They're temporary. You guys will get back on your feet, and if things really get bad, you can go live with Mom and Dad for a while. You can stay in my old room."

She wolfed down another handful of fries. "You don't understand. Andrew and I hardly speak anymore. I'm disappointed in him, he's disappointed in me. Both of us are just so frustrated."

"But you can work it out," I urged. "They say the first year of marriage is the hardest."

"Who says that? People who get divorced?"

"Look. You love him, right?"

"Regrettably, yes." She glared out the plate glass window at the litter-strewn parking lot.

"And he loves you, too," I said firmly.

"Gee, all our problems are magically solved! Woo-hoo! It's a miracle!" She rolled her eyes. "Will you come with me to meet this attorney or not?"

Rather than answer this question, I chose to employ the Socratic method. Of avoidance. "Have you told Andrew about all this?"

"Of course not." She crammed the rest of her burger into her mouth.

"'Cause I don't think he's going to go for it."

"No kidding."

"And doesn't he have some legal rights to his own children?"

"Don't worry about *his* rights. We're just going to get some information about *mine*. Are you with me or not?"

20

Connor called on Monday evening, just as I was preparing to call him so that I could: a., determine if he and I were still dating and/or sleeping together and/or ever speaking to each other again; and b., beg him to rehire me at Rhapsody.

I'd faxed over some new sketches to Fiona that afternoon and, judging by her response, I might have been a wee bit hasty in quitting the hostessing gig.

"Yawn," she'd said, flipping through the pages.

I'd tried not to panic. "Did you see the denim skirt with the Swarovski crystals on the back pocket?"

"Yes, I did."

"And?"

"Tepid, at best."

"Well, what about the halter top with the keyhole neckline? She sniffed. "Blah."

I tried to view this as constructive criticism. "Well, what about the miniskirt with the kitschy fifties poodle motif? You have to admit, that's pretty—"

"Insipid? Yes, it is."

"You didn't like any of them?"

"Do I sound happy to you? Honestly, Becca, I'm disappointed. I really don't feel you're giving us your best."

So much for constructive criticism.

"Hello?" she snapped. "Are you still there?"

"I'm still here. I'm just—"

"Suck it up, darling. If you're going to survive in this business, you're going to have to learn to deal with negative feedback. Now. Are these the only sketches I'm going to get from you this week?"

What would Betsey Johnson do in this situation? Would she cry and whine and crawl into bed with a carton of Ben & Jerry's? No. She'd get right back in the game—that's why she was the queen of clamdiggers. "Give me a few days to come up with something else."

She clicked her tongue. "I've got to tell you, we're not having these problems with any of our other designers."

I hung my head. "Sorry."

"Sorry's not going to help me, now is it?" Her impatience

was palpable. "Go ahead and make up the patterns for these pieces this week—"

"The tepid, blah, and insipid pieces?"

"I have to show the rest of Team Rachelle *something*, don't I?"

"But—"

"And I don't have time to constantly be covering for your mistakes. If this truly is your best work, then maybe you should think about bowing out. Before we have to, you know . . ."

I knew. I also knew that I'd had given her every piece I had that could be easily standardized for mass production. Plus the couture corset.

No doubt about it, I was doomed. And the worst part was, I had only my own hubris to blame.

So by the time Connor called, I was in full panic mode.

"How are you doing?" he asked when I answered the phone.

"Hanging onto the edge of sanity with one raggedy fingernail. Listen, about the skydiving thing . . ."

He started to laugh. "Don't worry about it."

"I don't jump out of planes, okay? Never have, never will."

"And I'm fine with that."

His easy acceptance took me off guard. "Oh. Well, all right then."

"As long as you're fine with the fact that I *do* jump out of planes."

I took a moment to relive the paralyzing terror I'd felt while watching him hurl himself into the void.

"Becca?"

"I . . . am . . . fine with that," I said slowly.

"Very convincing."

"No, I mean it. You do your thing and I'll do mine and we'll just be happy as two clams in saltwater."

My fear and frustration must have come through because he asked, "Hey, are you okay?"

"Sort of." I closed my eyes. "Fiona called about the latest designs I gave her and let's just say I hope that other hostess hasn't come back from London yet."

"It can't be that bad."

"It's worse."

I heard glass breaking in the background and he swore under his breath.

"Crisis at the restaurant?"

"Kind of. Listen, let's have dinner tomorrow and we'll figure everything out. Skydiving, Fiona, peace in the Middle East . . ."

"Sounds like more of a business dinner than a date," I teased.

"Yeah, but with a lot of sexual harassment."

I finally cracked a smile. "I look forward to it."

Claire started to sweat visibly before we even got through the front door of the law office.

"Okay." She straightened her white blouse with shaking hands and wiped at the fine sheen of moisture glistening on her forehead. "I'm ready."

I stopped in the middle of the courtyard, impeding the progress of attorneys and investment analysts scurrying from one sleek skyscraper to another. "You sure? Because you don't look ready. You look like you just got caught robbing a bank."

"It's hot out here, that's all." She continued to dab at her brow with both sleeves.

"It's seventy-five degrees and breezy." I gazed up at the cerulean blue sky dotted with fluffy white clouds.

"Listen, when *you're* three months pregnant with twins, drowning in hormones and slogging an extra twenty pounds around, *then* you can tell me how and when to perspire. Until then, shut it."

"Spare me. You haven't gained anywhere near twenty pounds." Though it certainly hadn't been for lack of trying. After years of fasting like a Tibetan monk, the nutritional floodgates had been flung wide open. The McDonald's fries were a mere warm-up. She had developed an obsession with Cookie Crisp cereal and Pringles that bordered on the pathological. "You're just . . . retaining a little water, that's all."

"I'm ready. Right now." She squared her shoulders. "Let's go."

The waiting area of Cole, Goodman, Pierpont & McKeever was a study in chrome and sleek black leather. The receptionist looked like a secretarial pool's version of Uma Thurman—a blond chignon, razor sharp cheekbones, and black-rimmed spectacles.

"May I help you?" she purred.

I nudged Claire, who let out a barely audible squeak. I waited another long moment, then took the lead. "This is Claire King. She has an appointment with Howard Mercer." I turned to my sister to make sure I had the correct name. "Right?"

She nodded, still mute.

Uma scanned her day planner, then glanced back at my sister, who was rapidly dissolving into a reservoir of sweat. "Can I get you anything, Ms. King? A glass of water perhaps?"

She nodded mutely.

"Are you okay?" I demanded as Uma disappeared down the hall. "I don't want to be alarmist, but if we wrung you out, we could solve the L.A. water crisis single-handedly."

"I'm just a little nervous, okay? I'm allowed to be nervous."

"Do you want to leave? We can turn around right now and leave, no harm, no foul."

She took a deep breath. "No. We came all the way out here, let's hear what this guy has to say."

"Okay, but I'm not doing any of the talking in there. And I don't want my name dragged into this when Andrew finds out and turns into something straight out of *The Shining*. You got that?"

But before she could reply, Uma swept back into the reception area and handed Claire a tall glass of ice water.

"Okay." My sister chugged the whole glass in about twenty seconds. "Let's do this."

Uma escorted us to a corner office where we were formally introduced to Howard Mercer, a.k.a. the Man with a Giant Sucking Sound Where His Soul Should Be.

You know how on crime dramas and nightly news interviews, neighbors and coworkers of serial killers always say, "Something about him was always just a little . . . off. I don't know how to explain it, but the first time we met, my skin crawled"? Well, that was Howard Mercer, Esquire. He rose up from behind a mahogany desk, an Armani-suited monolith with graying black hair and intense blue eyes, and extended his hand. "Ms. King. It's a pleasure."

"It's . . . I . . . hi." Claire eased her hand into his, her expression that of someone waiting for the cyanide pill to take effect. I couldn't help but stare at her belly to check for signs that the twins were rioting within.

He turned his steely gaze on me. "And you must be . . . ?"

Involuntarily, I took a step back. "Becca Davis. I'm her sister."

"Have a seat, ladies." He nodded at two black leather armchairs facing his desk and made a big show of helping Claire get settled.

"Ms. King. I understand you're interested in finding an adoptive family through one of our agencies."

My sister was once again reduced to wordless nodding.

"And . . ." His chair squeaked as he leaned forward with the rapacious hunger of a panther. "You said on the phone you're having *twins*?"

She quit nodding and drew both knees up against her chest, an impressive feat for a woman who claimed her legs were so swollen she could barely put socks on.

"Well, I assure you, you've come to the right place." He all but licked his chops. "We can find a perfect home for your babies. You name it, we can get it for them: Ivy League-educated father, stay-at-home mother, big family reunions, world travel, private schooling, hefty trust funds. The best of everything."

"So she's allowed to screen potential adoptive parents?" I asked.

"Yes, of course. And all expenses will be taken care of. Physician, hospital stay, and of course, a very, very generous allotment for, heh heh, 'personal expenses.'" He started to turn back to Claire, but I wasn't finished.

"But isn't that kind of shady? I mean, I'm not a lawyer by any means, but I Googled 'adoption law in California' last night, and it said that a lot of super-selective, big-payout adoption isn't totally on the up-and-up. Isn't there a specific limit to how much expense money she can get?"

He didn't bat an eye. "I think you must have us confused with one of the cut-rate legal firms that has to advertise on late-night cable. Would we be able to charge six hundred dollars an hour and maintain an office environment like this if we were breaking the law?"

"That doesn't answer my question."

His smile vanished. "The legal channels are complex, shall we say, but don't worry your pretty little head about all the technicalities. That's *my* job. Once we get permission from the biological father and the documents are drawn up, I think you'll agree the children will be much better off. Think of the *children,* Ms. Davis . . ."

"I am, finally. And I can't do this." My sister braced her hands on her chair's armrest, hoisted herself to her feet, then raced out of the room as fast as her water-retaining feet could carry her.

"I can't do it," Claire sobbed when I caught up with her in the courtyard. "I just can't. Did you see his *eyes?* How can I trust him with my precious little babies?"

"I wouldn't trust him with my e-mail address, never mind my offspring." I dug through my purse until I found the travel pack of Kleenex I always carried with me, a habit my mother instilled in all three of us from the time we started school. *You never know when you're going to spill, slip, or sniffle, so it's best to be prepared.* That was our family. So practical. So full of foresight.

Not.

"And did you hear what he said about 'personal expenses'?" She snatched five tissues at once and blotted the mascara dripping down her cheeks. "He just threw in that bullshit about stay-at-home moms and Harvard educations to make me feel better about selling my kids to the highest bidder."

I led her over to a shaded wrought-iron bench and sat her down. "Okay, sit down. Deep breaths."

"And you agree with him, don't you?" she gasped. "You think I just wanted to find out how much money I could get?"

"What? Of course not."

But she had worked herself into a red-faced frenzy. "You really, truly, in your heart of hearts, believe I am the kind of person who would rather have a big fat check than her own children?"

"Claire. Simmer down. I do not think—"

"How the hell was I supposed to know 'adoption' was this guy's code for 'selling infants into yuppie slavery'?"

"You couldn't know, okay? Nobody's arguing with you. But . . ."

"But what?" She seethed at me with puffy, mascara-smeared eyes.

"I don't know, maybe you could've thought this through a little better. I mean, how do you think your Brentwood gym buddy managed to get her hands on a newborn with no waiting lists or red tape?"

"Well . . ." Her rage lapsed into bewilderment. "I just thought, you know, rich people would be considered better candidates. And it doesn't matter anyway, because in the immortal words of Madonna, 'I've made up my mind, I'm gonna keep my babies.'" She pointed both index fingers at me. "And if you ever breathe a word of this to anyone, especially Andrew, they'll never find your body. Do I make myself clear?"

"Don't worry."

"I'm not kidding, Becca. There's a lot of uninhabited desert between here and Palm Springs. Think about it."

"Believe me, I'm thinking about it."

"Good." She wadded the tissues into a tight little ball. "You know what all this means, of course."

"You're going to have to have two more sets of twins and put together a musical act, *à la* the Von Trapps?"

"Andrew and I are going to have to move back to Phoenix."

21

I hear Claire's hellbent on moving back to Arizona," Connor remarked from across the candle-lit, linen-draped table at One Pico, a posh beachside restaurant in Santa Monica.

"Yep." I paused for a bite of penne. "She'll do anything to escape Van Nuys, and you know how we Davis girls get once we set our mind to something."

"Boy, do I. I told Andrew he should start forwarding his mail right now. Probably just as well. He hates the PA job."

"They're going out there this weekend to scout out job opportunities. And somehow my mom guilted me into coming along. So I won't be available for any more Evel Knievel exploits until next weekend."

The corners of his eyes crinkled up. "I take it skydiving is out?"

"Correct. But now that you bring it up . . . about the sky-diving?"

He looked wary. "Do we really have to talk about this again?"

"Yes." I sat up a little straighter. "I've learned my lesson about bottling up tensions and avoiding conflict when it comes to dating."

"You have?"

I nodded and pointed to my conspicuously naked left ring finger. "There's no point in pretending a problem doesn't exist. Trust me; my sister's a therapist."

"If you insist. What about the skydiving?"

"To be honest, this is about more than just skydiving. It's about the cliff diving, the bungee jumping, the high-altitude slacklining, the base jumping—I still don't know what that even is, by the way . . ."

"You forgot street lugeing," he added.

"Ah, yes. The street lugeing. I mean, do you see any kind of pattern in all those activities?"

"They're all fun?"

"Not quite the word I would use."

He rubbed his chin. "They're all *exhilarating*?"

"How about, they're all dangerous?"

He appeared shocked by this assessment. "They are not."

"They are so."

"No. I would agree that they're mentally challenging and physically demanding, but that's not the same as dangerous."

I leveled my gaze. "Connor. Remember that story you told Snake about breaking your collarbone?"

"Yeah."

"And remember that story you told me about cracking your vertebrae?"

He shifted in his seat. "Yeah."

"How many other broken bone stories do you have?"

He sidestepped this question by saying, "Maybe I used to get a little crazy sometimes, but I've matured."

"I see. When did you break your collarbone?"

"Last year. *But*! That was a one-in-a-million piece of bad luck."

I folded my hands on the table. "And so is parachute failure when you're skydiving."

"What are you getting at here?"

"I know you aren't afraid to take risks. It's one of the things I like most about you."

"And you're open to new things," he returned. "That's one of the things I like about you."

"Thank you. But sometimes, you gotta know when to scale back. You don't have to take *constant* risks in every single arena of life."

"Yes, I do." He furrowed his brow. "There's no growth or opportunity without risk."

"Okay, but just because you take risks in business doesn't

mean you have to go out in the woods and cheat death every weekend."

"So you want me to treat life like a risk cafeteria? Pick and choose when to take chances?"

"Well . . . yeah."

"But life doesn't work that way! It's all or nothing."

"That's not true. I'm learning to take risks with my career, but that doesn't mean I have to be a regular in the ER"

He was shaking his head. "The way I look at it, I could get run over by a bus tomorrow while crossing the street—which is a lot more likely than dying while skydiving, by the way—but I'm going to live every day to the fullest while I'm here. No fear, no regrets, that's my motto. And I can't change that for anyone."

"Really."

"That's right." His tone dared me to challenge him.

As gently as possible, I said, "I think maybe you do have some fears and regrets."

"Oh?"

"They're draped across your bed."

He put down his fork. "I'm not having this discussion."

"Why not? I'm only trying to—"

"Let it go! It's just a piece of cloth! It doesn't mean anything!"

"Then why—"

"There is no secret, underlying symbolism!"

Right. That would explain all the rabid denials.

"I like my life the way it is and I'm not going to stop pushing the limits." And there it was: his proverbial line in the sand.

So I drew mine, too. "You do what you need to do, but you should know that I don't want to spend every Saturday and Sunday waiting for the coroner to call."

"Fine."

"Fine."

"*Fine.*"

"*Fine.*"

We both set our jaws and stared at each other.

"Well, this is shaping up to be a pleasant evening," he said.

I made a conscious effort to relax the muscles knotted in my shoulders. "I don't want to fight, but I needed to get that out."

"Well, it's out. Let's move on." He rubbed his hands together, his eyes suddenly glinting. "You haven't even heard my pickup line of the night yet. It's *great.*"

"I'm going to need a few drinks before I'm ready for that." I grabbed the wine list and scanned the list of reds. "I think I'll try a glass of the Pinot Noir."

He glanced at my plate. "With penne arrabiata? Try the Cabernet."

"The Cabernet does sound tempting, but I'll go with the Pinot."

"The arrabiata sauce here is really spicy. The Pinot won't be able to keep up with the flavor."

Why did this discussion feel all too familiar? My head snapped up and I stared him straight in the eye as I said, "Don't tell me what to order."

He scanned the wine list as if nothing were amiss. "I'm just saying, the Cabernet's a better choice considering—"

"Listen! I am not having the Cabernet!"

The couple seated at the table next to us stopped talking.

"But you won't even be able to taste the Pinot," Connor explained, all calm, cool, and supremely confident.

Just like Kevin.

At this point I might have overreacted a little bit. I admit that. But all my residual frothy-mouthed frustration churned up and I just snapped.

"I don't care! If I want to swill white Zinfandel out of a box, I will! Do you hear me? *You do not get to make all the decisions!*"

He stared at me like I'd just grown horns. "Whoa. Calm down. It's just wine."

"It is not just wine! I'm not going to sit here and let you walk all over me!"

"You know what?" He shoved his chair back, opened his wallet, and stacked several twenties on the table. "I think we're done. Let's go."

"Let's." I snatched up my purse and the cashmere cardigan I'd draped on the chair behind me, then stormed out to the valet station.

The ride home was quiet and tense. No words, no touching, and certainly no kiss before he dropped me off at Aimee's apartment building.

But that glass of Pinot was sounding better by the minute.

"I'm off for a delightful weekend of pointed questions about why I broke up with Kevin and when I'm moving back home," I said as Aimee pulled up to the curb at LAX. "Let the games begin."

"Oh, relax." She put the car into park and popped open the trunk. "Your sister'll take most of the heat, right? She's the one with all the big news. All you have to do is stay under the radar for forty-eight hours, then I'll pick you up at baggage claim and we'll go get a big frosty pitcher of sangria."

But by the time I met up with my traveling companions at the Southwest Airlines check-in line, I realized I had lost some of my talent for staying under the radar. Over these past few weeks, I had started to become the newest nervy, self-possessed member of the Davis family who couldn't quite keep her mouth shut.

Like we really needed another one.

"Well, well, well. Look who finally decided to show up." Claire, radiant with that slightly swollen pregnancy glow, had apparently given up on her size-four "fat clothes" and moved on to her husband's wardrobe. She was decked out in what appeared to be one of his short-sleeved golf shirts over black stretch pants and flat leather sandals. "Thanks to you, we're going to be in the last group to board, and no way will we get three seats together."

"Becca!" Andrew returned from checking in Claire's formidable pile of matched luggage and gave me a peck on the cheek. "Good to see you. How's the new job going?"

"Think hell meets The Gap."

"You know, I'm really going to need some maternity clothes," Claire interjected. "Rumor has it I'm only going to get fatter over the next six months."

"You're not fat," Andrew soothed. "Your body is just expanding a little to accommodate Frick and Frack."

"His little nickname for the twins," my sister explained. "Until we find out the sex. So what do you think, Becks? Can you whip up something black, chic, and open-waisted?"

'Cause our last collaboration had gone so well. "Yeah, I'll have to think about that."

"Come on! Look at what I'm dealing with here!" She tugged at the golf shirt. "From Blumarine to putting green in under two months. I'm in desperate need of a fashion intervention. I'll even help you sew."

My eyebrows shot up. "You will?"

She shrugged. "Sure. Cut a few pieces of cloth, run up a few seams on the old Singer, how hard could it be?"

"You know what, Claire?" I said coolly. "If it's so easy to cut a few pieces of cloth and run up a few seams, you shouldn't need my help. You can do it yourself."

"Oh my God. I'm offering to help you. Don't get all pissy about it."

"You're offering to help me do the favor you just *demanded*!"

"You know, that line at the security checkpoint isn't getting any shorter." Andrew jumped into the fray. (He'd grown up an only child and still cherished the sweet but misguided notion that it was possible to resolve sibling disputes with common sense and tantalizing distractions. Just wait until Frick and Frack arrived. Poor guy wouldn't know what hit him.) "We better grab our bags and get going." He positioned himself between Claire and me under the pretense of collecting her purse, wheeled suitcase, and white plastic grocery bag.

I didn't comment on the grocery sack, but Andrew caught me staring and smiled.

"Full of Pringles and caramel apples," he explained. "In case the twins get hungry on the flight."

I glanced at Claire. "Caramel apples? Isn't that a little state fair for you?"

"Hey, I don't want them, the babies do." She rearranged the voluminous polo shirt. "They also enjoy canned fruit and Cheetos. Apparently, I'm going to have hillbilly children. They'll probably be born with little mullets."

As predicted, we were among the last stragglers to board the plane, so I squeezed into a middle seat by the exit row while Claire and Andrew headed to the back. The last thing I heard before buckling my seat was Claire announcing, "So we're going to make a fresh start in Phoenix, honey, right? Well, that means a fresh start in our marriage, too, and I don't want us to have any secrets."

Oh no. I twisted around in my seat and started gesturing

wildly, pantomiming cutting my throat, anything I could do to save my sister from the ticking marital time bomb she was about to detonate.

She waved me off and turned back to Andrew. "I have something to tell you. Something bad. Something that I did that I'm not proud of, but I want us to be honest with each other."

Andrew said something I couldn't quite catch about loving Claire unconditionally while the flight attendant begged passengers to reshuffle so that the poor pregnant lady could sit with her husband (and, more importantly, the caramel apples).

And then . . . nothing. Their voices blended into the hubbub of preflight chatter and loudspeaker announcements. Which I took as a good sign. Maybe she'd decided not to tell him, after all. Or maybe she did tell him and he'd decided it was no big deal. Maybe I'd overestimated the impact such news would have on an already bruised male ego. If I'd learned anything from the past few months, it was that I didn't know jack about men.

Then Andrew spoke up. Though he was a good ten rows back, I could hear every syllable, as could my seatmates and probably the staff of the LAX control tower:

"*You went to a lawyer? Behind my back? And did what?!?*"

I couldn't decipher Claire's murmured response, but whatever she said didn't go a long way toward assuaging her husband. "You know, it's emasculating enough to lose my job, my house, and my entire family's respect without you trying to sell our unborn children to the highest bidder!"

This, of course, set Claire off. "How could you even suggest that? This isn't about money!" she screamed.

"Everything's about money with you!" he yelled back.

I winced as a flimsy airplane lavatory door slammed with hinge-cracking force.

"Sir, we're finished with preflight preparations."

I, along with every other passenger on flight 1339, craned my neck to catch a glimpse of the harried flight attendant pounding on the restroom door. "I'm going to have to ask you to take your seat."

Andrew stormed up the aisle and flung himself into an empty middle seat amid a group of startled Boy Scouts.

As we all securely stowed our baggage in the overhead compartment and ensured our seat backs were locked in the upright position, my sister jabbed her overhead call button and announced, "I want off this plane! Do you hear me? I'm not going anywhere!"

But it was too late. We were already taxiing down the runway, gathering speed with every passing second. For better or for worse, we were on our way.

22

"So? How was your trip, kids?" My dad turned down his beloved talk radio program and made a valiant attempt at conversation on the drive home from Sky Harbor Airport.

"I hope you're hungry; I have warm cherry cobbler waiting at home." My mother, relentlessly cheerful, refused to ask about or even acknowledge the tension crackling in the backseat of the Chevy Malibu. "And homemade vanilla ice cream. I've made up Claire's old room for you two, Andrew. It's nothing fancy, but—"

"It'll be fine, thanks," Andrew said, staring out the side window.

"Yeah, don't worry about him. He loves slumming it," my sister spat. "In fact, if you have any mutant roaches—"

"Maybe I'll just make this easier on everyone and stay in a hotel," Andrew said.

Caught in the crossfire, I leaned back into the seat and tried to make myself as inconspicuous as possible.

"You know we can't afford a hotel. Darling."

"We can if you auction off the children."

My parents exchanged a look in the front seat. A heavy, loaded silence enveloped the car. When we braked for a stoplight, I could hear a banjo-heavy country-western tune playing in the car next to us.

"So! Becca!" Dad tried again. "How's life in the fashion world?"

"It's interesting." I swallowed hard and pretended that this was just a normal family outing. With a normal family. I really had to stretch my imagination.

"Have you met any celebrities yet?"

"A couple." I launched into the gripping tale of my Naomi Watts sighting in Runyon Canyon. Everyone feigned great interest, as it gave them an excuse to avoid interacting with one another, until my mother interrupted with:

"Guess who I saw at the grocery store yesterday?" She turned in her seat, grinning like she was about to personally deliver the Publisher's Clearinghouse check. "Kevin Bradley! He just got promoted at work."

"Oh. Great." And before I could get back to my story, she

rushed ahead with, "He's such a nice boy. And so polite. In fact, he walked me out to the parking lot and carried all my groceries, so we got to catch up a bit."

I smelled treachery. "Exactly how long were you chatting up my ex-boyfriend?"

"Just a few minutes. Don't get so defensive. I had to ask how his mother was doing. You know . . ." She paused for effect. "I don't see her since you two went your separate ways."

Red alert! Red alert! This is not a drill! "Did you tell him I was coming this weekend?"

She turned back to face the windshield. "Look at all those clouds. They said we might have thunderstorms tonight."

"Mom!"

She readjusted the shoulder strap of her seat belt. "Did I mention I made cherry cobbler?"

"I can't believe this!"

"I couldn't help it, honey. He asked about you. What was I supposed to do?"

"You were supposed to lie, of course! Tell him I got mixed up with some track-marked trust fund babies at the Imitation of Christ show and you haven't heard from me since."

"Imitation of what, young lady?" my dad broke in.

"It's a design team, Dad. No need to wash my mouth out with soap."

My father glanced at all of us in the rearview mirror, shook his head, muttered something about Los Angeles and these kids today, then clicked the radio back on to *Car Talk*.

As we turned off the highway and headed toward home, my mother confessed the full extent of her betrayal.

"Anyway, I invited him over for dinner tonight, so I hope you haven't made other plans."

The title of Most Distressed Upon Crossing My Parents' Threshold went to . . . it was a tie, actually, between me and Andrew. I was aghast at the prospect of spending an entire evening with my ex; Andrew was absolutely apoplectic at the prospect of spending even one more minute with his spouse. Because I'd grown up in a house with two sisters and my sole serious love interest for the last five years had been Kevin, I'd forgotten exactly how angsty an angst-ridden man could be.

It wasn't pretty.

"Excuse me. I have to make a few calls," he announced in a tight, clipped voice as we pulled into the driveway. He was out of the car before it came to a complete stop, marching toward the side yard and whipping his new, cut rate cell phone out of his pocket.

I glanced at my sister. She avoided eye contact, keeping her beautiful face carefully neutral.

My parents exchanged another pointed look, but refrained from comment. This left the perfect opening to start round two with my mother.

"Mom, how could you do this to me?" I wailed as we opened the trunk and stared at Claire's tower of Louis Vuitton. "It's . . . he . . . you better call him right now and cancel."

"Don't be ridiculous; I can't do that. It's rude! What would I say?"

"Say I decided not to come at the last minute. Say I had to work. Say I missed my plane. Or, I know! Say I was so distraught after the breakup, I joined a nunnery and took a vow of silence. *And* I'm fasting. It's just tacky to chow down in front of a starving mute."

"Calm down, Rebecca. There's no need to get so worked up." She smiled and patted my arm. "It's just one dinner."

"If it's 'just one dinner,' it should be no problem to call him and cancel!"

"This is not up for further discussion." She reached into the trunk and pulled out a small valise. "I've already invited him and there's no reason to hurt his feelings more than they've already been hurt." She paused so the obvious implications could sink in. "No one's asking you to get re-engaged; it's just a nice chance to visit and catch up."

"But I notice you didn't invite his mother. If you really wanted to visit and catch up, you should've asked *her*."

She waved this away, but I thought I detected a slight blush in her cheeks. "When did you get so paranoid?"

"These girls," Dad muttered. "I'm telling ya . . ."

He and Claire staggered into the house with all the Louis they could carry. As soon as the door closed behind them, Mom turned back to me and pinned me with a no-nonsense frown.

"What is the matter with you? Making a fuss like this when

Claire and Andrew are already having problems? She's pregnant with twins, she's not supposed to be subjected to stress."

I rolled my eyes. "Believe me, Mom. This is appetizer drama compared to what she's used to. Spinach dip. Hot wings. You want the main course, go ask her why Andrew's stomping around our front yard."

"Ask not for whom the bell tolls." My dad chuckled as the doorbell echoed down the tiled hallways into the kitchen, where we were all helping my mom prepare dinner.

"Maybe it's just Girl Scouts hawking cookies," I said, grasping at straws.

Andrew gave me a pitying look. "It tolls for thee."

"Nuh-uh." I glanced at the clock. Still fifteen minutes before Kevin was due.

"Oh, Becca," my mother singsonged as she rushed to the foyer and flung open the front door. "Look who's he-eeere!"

He was early. But of course.

I wiped my wet hands on a dish towel, checked the jeans and white T-shirt I was wearing for visible food stains, and headed down the hall in my sassy new Rodolphe Menudier wedges.

"You're going to trip in those heels."

Those were the words with which Kevin greeted me after five years of dating, a formal engagement, a less formal disengagement, and several weeks of estrangement.

The words with which I greeted him? "I am not going to

trip. I wear shoes like this every day now." Thanks to Aimee and her invaluable insider's tips about the season-end clearance sales on Rodeo Drive.

I steeled myself for a filibuster about orthopedics and the research correlating high heels with the early onset of crippling arthritis, but he surprised me by letting the subject drop.

"It's nice to see you again," he said. "You look great."

My mother dashed back to the kitchen to spread the word that the engagement would be back on any day now.

"Yeah, you, too," I said vaguely, though I hadn't really noticed any changes in his appearance. I took a moment to look him over—sandy brown hair, blue eyes, immaculately ironed button-down shirt—then smiled back. "I heard you got railroaded into having dinner with us. Sorry about that."

"I always enjoy spending time with you and your family," he said gallantly. "It's no chore. And there's no point in pretending that we never knew each other just because we've been, you know, taking a break."

"You mean we've 'broken up,'" I corrected, leading him down the hall toward the kitchen.

"Well, let's say 'in negotiations,'" he replied.

I skidded to a stop in my controversial shoes. "No. Let's say '*broken up.*'"

I didn't turn around, but I heard his quick, irritated intake of breath. "Whatever. I'm not going to have an argument about semantics when the end result is the same. You left and I miss you."

At this, I did turn around. "But you're the one who issued the big ultimatum when I left for L.A."

He studied the floor tiles, suddenly looking young and vulnerable in the orange sunset glow pouring through the windows. "Yeah. Because I didn't think you'd really go. I miss you, Becks. Don't you miss me?"

I could hear cooking sounds down the hall—pot lids clanging, water running, oven timers dinging—but no one burst into the foyer to save me from having to answer this question.

He kept staring at the floor. "I think I deserve another chance."

I opened my mouth. Then closed it. Then opened it again. "Kevin. I'm sorry, but—"

He clenched his hands at his sides as if he'd been gearing up for this for weeks. "No, really. We can make this work. I know you were unhappy before, but you gave up on us too soon. Things can be different. I've changed."

I sagged against the wall. "Kevin, no—"

"You're skeptical. I understand." He paced around the perimeter of the foyer. "But I can prove it to you."

"There's something you should know. I'm seeing someone else."

He stopped pacing. "In Los Angeles?"

I nodded. Guilt washed over me.

"Is it serious?"

Nah, we're just sleeping together and having bitter quarrels over restaurant wine lists . . . you know, the usual . . .

"I don't know yet." I couldn't bring myself to meet his eyes. "But that's not the point. The point is, I've moved on. You need things I can't give you and we're just not—"

Incredibly, he appeared to be relishing the idea of a challenge. "You've only been out in California for a few weeks. We were together for five years. It can't be that serious."

"It doesn't matter how serious it is. I've moved on—"

"Because you weren't happy. But I've changed, Becca. I get it now. I really do." His eyebrows waggled. "I have proof."

My eyes narrowed. "What kind of proof?"

"You'll see. I have something to give you. Something big. After dinner."

All the blood rushed to my head as I scrutinized his pants pockets for jewelry box-size lumps.

"Becca?" He frowned. "Are you all right?"

I could barely discern his words through the haze of panic. A second marriage proposal, witnessed by my entire family this time around? My mother would cry (again). My father would shake Kevin's hand and welcome him to the family (again). And I . . .

I was going to dry heave. Again.

"Becca! Kevin!" my mother trilled down the hall. "Dinner's ready!"

He took a few steps forward, offering a hand. "Seriously. Are you okay? You look a little—"

"'Scuse me." I pushed past him, sprinting for the powder room.

As I slammed the bathroom door behind me, I heard Kevin's footsteps retreating down the hall and his cheery voice saying, "Everything smells delicious, Mrs. Davis! Thanks so much for inviting me."

"Oh, you're welcome," my mother responded. "And for the last time, call me Linda. After all, we're practically family."

Dinner was the culinary equivalent of sitting through a Hitchcock film festival: no way to predict what fresh horrors would leap out of the shadows at any given moment. I cowered in silence at my end of the table, terrified that every word, every glance, every pass of the bread basket might elicit Kevin's announcement, "As long as we're all here together . . ."

Hopefully, a little more time with Claire and Andrew would dissuade him from any further contemplation of matrimony. They devoted the entire meal to sneering at each other across the table, directing barbed pleasantries at the rest of us:

"Oh, Daddy, how nice of you to give me the last piece of bread. It's good to know that *someone* understands that pregnant women need special treatment."

"Why, thank you, Linda, I'd love another piece of salmon. *You're* always so aware of the needs of others."

Et cetera.

My parents tried to compensate for the undercurrents of hostility by asking Kevin all about his new job, but I couldn't tell if he even noticed anything was awry with my sister and her husband. He kept his gaze locked on me, leering like a serial killer whenever he managed to catch my eye.

You don't want to marry me! I wanted to scream. *Look at your prospective in-laws and run while you have the chance!*

Well. I'd just have to straighten him out after dessert. And if he decided to make his big move before then, I'd have to straighten him out in front of my entire family and my mom would have to fetch her smelling salts. Because, no matter what happened with Connor, I was not about to get ambushed into another promise I'd regret. Kevin and I were through and I wasn't buying his claims of newfound enlightenment and flexibility.

Men don't change. Everyone knew that. It was a fundamental life truth, along with "horizontal stripes make you look fat" and "turn off your cell phone in a movie theater."

And then Kevin put down his fork and reached under the table. Oh hell, what if he was going for his pocket?

There was only one thing to do: employ diversionary tactics.

"Claire," I said. "Why don't you tell Mom and Dad about the names you've picked out for the babies?"

This had the intended effect of throwing a freshly slain rabbit carcass into a hyena pack.

"You've already picked out names?" Mom's lower lip quivered. "And nobody told me?"

"We have a few suggestions, you know," my father said. "We thought a family name might be nice."

"The ones we're considering are family names," Andrew

hedged. "From my side of the family. Elise and Evelyn for girls . . ."

My mother continued as if he hadn't spoken. "What about Anastacia? That was my grandmother."

"What about Archibald?" my dad threw in.

"Archibald?" Claire made a face. "What self-respecting girl is ever going to go to the prom with an Archibald? Or worse, Archie?"

"He'll be beaten mercilessly on the playground," Andrew agreed, momentarily reuniting with his wife in a show of solidarity against bad baby names.

"All right, then, what about Gertrude? Trudie for short, isn't that adorable?"

Claire and Andrew shared another glance. "No."

"Herbert?"

"Come on."

"Dorcas?"

"Now you're just making stuff up."

The debate raged on all through dessert. Even Kevin offered up a suggestion: Isaac, as in Isaac Newton. Which I had to admit was sort of cute.

As we were preparing to uncork a bottle of wine and take the discussion out to the patio, the doorbell rang again.

"Finally!" Andrew consulted his watch. "Took him long enough."

"Who?" Claire demanded.

"Connor. He drove out from L.A. to pick me up."

23

Connor?" I croaked. "Connor as in Connor Sullivan?"

"What the hell is going on?" Claire demanded.

"I asked him to come out, pick me up, and drive me back to Los Angeles." His tone defied her to challenge him. "Called him before our plane took off. I can't stay here with you right now. And since we can't afford a hotel room and my credit card is too maxed to get a rental car . . ."

"Oh my God. *You're leaving me?*" She staggered backward into the kitchen counter. My mother rushed to her side.

"Hang on a second." I held up a hand. "You're telling me that Connor Sullivan is standing on our front porch, ringing our doorbell, right now?"

"Who's Connor Sullivan?" Kevin asked as my dad headed off to get the door.

"A buddy from Los Angeles." Andrew's glance caromed from me to Kevin, as if finally realizing that this might be more than a little awkward for me. "And no, Claire, I'm not leaving you. Yet. But I need to think about what you did, and I can't do that while I'm sleeping in your old bedroom at your parents' house. So I'm going back to L.A. for a little while. I'll pack up the apartment and drive back out here when the move is finished."

My mother rounded on Claire. "What did you do?"

"Nothing," Claire yelped. To which Andrew responded with a fantastically bitter, "Ha."

My mother brandished her spatula at both of them. "I will not have my grandchildren born into a broken home, do you hear me? So whatever little spat you two are having—"

"Hi." Connor stepped into the kitchen, followed by my dad, who looked like he would commit unspeakable crimes to be able to return to the safety and sanity of televised golf in the den.

Connor headed straight for me, threading through the drama unfolding by the counter to give me a kiss on the cheek. Which I interpreted to mean that he was calling truce on our Cabernet skirmish, or at least putting it on hold. Relief and gratitude washed through me; I would have kissed him back if my whole family hadn't been staring us down.

Along with my ex-fiancé.

"Hi," he said.

"Hi." I pulled away and made the introductions. "Mom, Dad, this is Connor Sullivan."

"I thought you were Andrew's friend?" my mother asked, bewildered.

"I am." Connor smiled his warm, easy smile. "But Becca and I have started—"

"So you're the competition." Kevin jostled his way through the crowd and offered up a handshake. "I'm Kevin Bradley."

Connor shot me a questioning look. I sighed. "Yeah, *that* Kevin."

The two men stood toe to toe, sizing each other up.

"We should get going." Andrew stepped in. "It's a long drive back to Los Angeles."

"No, *we* should get going," Kevin shot back. "Becca and I have places to go and things to do."

Connor didn't seem at all bothered by this. If anything, his smile got a little wider. "Is that a fact?"

"Yes, it is." Kevin hitched up his khakis. "That's what I kept trying to tell you at dinner, Becca. I have something to show you. Get your coat."

"It's seventy-five degrees out," I said.

"Then get your purse. We're leaving."

I tried to demure with, "I'm not sure this is a great idea . . ."

"Becca." My mother was still wielding the spatula. "Kevin has rearranged his schedule just to see you."

"But . . ." I groped for any excuse. "We have company who came all the way from California."

I could tell Connor was trying not to laugh. "Don't stay on my account," he said as Kevin marched toward the door. "It's rude enough that I show up uninvited and unannounced. I wouldn't dream of asking you to cancel your big date."

"Oh, believe me, it'd be my pleasure."

"Becca?" Kevin commanded from the front hall. "Let's go."

"Yeah, yeah, I'm coming." I grabbed my bag and trudged out the front door after my ex-fiancé.

"You kids have fun!" Mom yelled after us.

And, right before Kevin closed the door behind us, I heard my dad say, "Well, Connor, at least you don't seem like the jealous type."

"So that's the new man in your life," Kevin mused, setting the car's cruise control for precisely the speed limit as we headed north on the highway. "Interesting."

I crossed my arms. "Comments?"

"Nope. Except he seems a little old for you."

"I'll take that under advisement."

After another silent half mile, he said, "You know, Becca, people do change. When they want to. You can't change someone else, but you can change your own life. And that's what

I've done. It *is* possible—you have to admit that because you yourself have changed a lot over the last few months."

"Yes, okay, I admit it. Change is possible. But—"

"We put in five solid years together."

"You say that like it's serving prison time. Don't you think that speaks volumes about our relationship? Yes, we dated for a long time, but we probably stayed together a lot longer than we should have because we felt comfortable and we were scared to start over."

"I never felt that way."

I leaned my head against the window and welcomed the cool draft from the dashboard air conditioner.

"Would you still be with me if I hadn't taken back the ring?" he asked.

I tried to imagine how everything would have played out if he hadn't given me the ultimatum. If he hadn't insisted I give up all my dreams to fulfill his. I would have made the break by myself, eventually. It just would have taken me a bit longer to decide that my future was worth the risk.

"I don't think so," I said.

"I think you would." His expression got all grim and determined.

"But *I* think I *wouldn't.*"

"Yes, you would," he decided. "How about I give the ring back and we work things out?"

"No," I said firmly. "Do not give back the ring."

"You can't stop me," he warned.

My jaw dropped. "Yes, I can, actually."

He swerved off the freeway at the next exit, barreled down a bumpy side street, and pulled over into a deserted parking lot.

If my life were a miniseries, this would be the part where my seemingly mild-mannered ex-boyfriend's diabolical alter ego would emerge, his face half-obscured by shadow. He would reach for the glovebox, blathering that if he couldn't have me, nobody could, and too late I'd notice the cold glint of steel in the moonlight . . .

But this wasn't prime-time television. This was the Kevin Bradley show, and the contents of the glovebox were limited to road maps, flashlights, breath mints, and insurance forms. The man wouldn't even let people *eat* in his car, let alone bleed all over the front seat.

"Why are we stopping here?" I demanded. "Where are we?"

"Surprise." He unbuckled his seat belt, opened his door, and stepped into the parking lot.

"I'm not kidding around, Kevin. Where are we?" I'd been too busy debating the voluntary nature of engagement ring wearing to keep track of the exit signs on the highway.

"We're in Surprise. The city."

"Oh." Surprise is a fast-growing suburb on the west side of Phoenix. "What are we doing out here?"

"I wanted to show you this." He gestured toward the vacant storefront on the other side of the parking lot. "They're going to be building up this whole area soon. Lots of new residents, storefronts, even a mall or two. And this will be right in the middle of the action."

"Oh. Great." I tried to sound enthusiastic. "And why are you showing me this, again?"

"I put down an earnest deposit to hold the property. For you."

Perhaps I had not heard that correctly. "For me?"

He nodded. "So you can move back here and open a boutique."

Suddenly, that cold glint of steel under the moonlight wasn't sounding so bad.

"You're springing *another* piece of property on me? Without any warning?" I stared at him.

"It's a very sweet gesture," he informed me. "You should be touched. Most girlfriends would weep for joy."

But I was in no mood to cry on cue. "I am not your girlfriend, dammit!"

"You say that now—"

"And didn't you learn anything from the last stealth mortgage? What is the *matter* with you?"

"We'll start over. Just quit your job in L.A. and open up your own store here. I'll pay the lease, I'll buy the sewing equipment, cloth, whatever else you need."

I turned back toward the car. "I am going to go home now and when I wake up tomorrow, this whole debacle never happened. Got it?"

"You have to give me one more chance, Becca!"

"No." I enunciated clearly, since he seemed deaf to this particular word. "No."

"Yes," he insisted. "I already put down the deposit, so you have to move back and work here."

"*No!*" My mantra devolved into primal scream.

"Things will be different this time," he wheedled. "I've changed. I'm a new man."

"No." As I powered toward his Honda, my heel caught the edge of a jagged pothole and I stumbled forward, arms pinwheeling, catching myself just before my face flattened against the concrete.

"Ouch." I examined the fresh scrapes on my palms, then wiped the gravel off my jeans. "Let's go. Kevin?"

There ensued a long, agonized pause behind me. Finally, he could keep it in no longer:

"See? I *told* you those heels were too high."

I'd always considered Kevin too rational and efficient to sulk, but he proved me wrong on the drive back to my parents' house. He nursed a wordless but palpable pout for nearly half an hour, which was just as well, really, because what did we have left to say to each other?

"You don't have to pull over," I said as we approached our destination. "Just come to a rolling stop and I'll leap out."

"Don't be absurd." He checked the rearview mirror before smoothly braking exactly six inches parallel to the curb. "You'd break your neck in those shoes."

"I'd let that issue go, if I were you," I advised, reaching for the door handle.

"I already put down thousands of dollars in earnest money on the storefront, you know."

I sighed. "Well, I'm sorry about that. I am."

"And . . . ?"

"And nothing. It's not my fault you decided to railroad me back into the relationship with no warning."

"It's a gesture of love," he insisted.

"It's a gesture of control and manipulation."

"You'll change your mind when you calm down," he decreed, but he sounded a bit panicked. "And about the ring—"

"Good night." I opened the passenger side door, vaulted from the car, and—yes!—struck the landing, high heels and all. Perfect tens all around! Applause! Applause!

"Becca, wait—"

I closed the door on his justifications and demands and headed back to the comforting chaos of my family. Because he hadn't changed, but I had.

"So? What happened with Kevin?" My mom flung the door open the nanosecond my toe hit the welcome mat. "Uh-oh. You look unhappy. Did you break his heart again?" Her face filled with worry as she glanced over at the Civic. "Do you think he's all right to drive?"

Despite all the Sturm und Drang, Kevin refused to squeal away from the curb in a dramatic, James Dean departure. He waited for passing traffic and signaled before pulling out at a reasonable speed.

"He's fine. He's always fine, Mom. You know that."

She reached out to brush the hair off my face. "And how are you?"

"I'm fine, too." I gave her a condensed version of the real-estate bushwhack and kept-woman offer. To my surprise, she listened sympathetically and patted my shoulder.

"Well, you can't blame him for trying. The women in this family have always inspired grand gestures."

"But . . . even me?"

"Oh, honey. Especially you."

"So you don't think I'm making a huge mistake?"

"You're finally taking a risk. Big difference."

We smiled at each other for a moment before Claire appeared at the end of the hallway. "Back so soon? Have you heard anything from Andrew and Connor?"

"Not a word," I said. "I've had a few other, more pressing issues to deal with. Besides, shouldn't you be the one to talk to Andrew?"

She leaned against the doorframe and went back to skimming the issue of *People* in her right hand. "I'm busy." She pointed to a glossy photo layout labeled, "Stars Celebrate Motherhood in Style!" "I'm doing research on single parenthood. If Angelina Jolie can do it, so can I."

"Oh my goodness." My mother paled. "You don't really think Andrew's left for good? He has to forgive you. He *has* to!" She wrung her hands. "You're pregnant! Pregnancy is nine-tenths of the law in a marriage!"

"Mom. You don't even know why we're fighting," Claire said.

"It doesn't matter!"

"Um, in this case, it might," I said.

But Mom begged to differ. "This is unacceptable! I will not have it. Did you cheat on him?"

"No."

"Did you beat him up?"

"No."

"Did you threaten to keep him from his children?" Mom took the liberty of answering her own question here. "No. So I don't see what could be so bad that . . ." She trailed off as Claire and I exchanged a flurry of pointed looks. "What?"

Claire adjusted the collar of Andrew's golf shirt. "Nothing."

"Claire Louisa Davis King, what did you do?"

"I'm going to bed." I scooted for the staircase.

"Call Connor!" my sister yelled after me, right before our mother broke out the master interrogation techniques I remembered from high school. Miss a curfew, come home with a whiff of wine cooler on your breath, and she made the KGB look like the PTA.

When I dialed Connor's number, it went straight to voice mail; there weren't many cell phone towers in the middle of the desert. Claire would just have to wait until tomorrow to plead her case.

I washed my face, brushed my teeth, and crawled into bed, where I fell asleep in record time. I dreamed about white, slim-legged pants with delicate crisscrosses of satin ribbon across the knees, almost as if the wearer had fallen during a snit with a crazy ex and then patched herself up with red and blue silk. Parking lot pants, I would call them.

Connor called me back early the next morning. I wriggled across the bed, tangled in sheets and blankets, and tried to sound alert when I answered the phone.

"Mph?" I managed.

"Morning, sunshine." He sounded disgustingly energetic.

I rolled over and snuggled back into the blankets. "You're awfully chipper. Shouldn't you be, I don't know, sleeping at this ungodly hour?"

"Just finished up on the golf course. Andrew and I thought we'd get in nine holes before breakfast."

"Are you back in L.A.?"

"We're on your front steps, actually, but we don't want to ring the doorbell and wake everyone up. Want to go get some pancakes?"

I smiled. "Does this mean you officially forgive me for the wine list meltdown?"

"Yes. And I've learned my lesson; you can order any pancake syrup you want—maple, blueberry, heck, even boysenberry—and I won't say a word."

"What a man."

He laughed. "I hope you still feel that way when you hear the rest of the day's agenda."

"Why?" I teased. "You going skydiving or something?"

Dead silence.

"You are?" I pressed.

"No, *we* are."

24

No! No! No, no, no, no!" I flung open the front door, clad in a pink chenille bathrobe, and tried to clarify my position on skydiving. "A thousand times no!"

Andrew and Connor stood grinning on the stoop, both of them suntanned and slightly sweaty.

"So . . . you're saying no?" Connor deadpanned.

"Yes! I'm saying no! And how can you think, after what happened last time, that I would *ever*—"

"Relax." He drew me in for a kiss. "When I said 'we,' I meant me and Andrew."

"Oh." My arm-flailing vehemence sputtered out. "Well, why didn't you just say that before?"

"Because I wanted to see you all cute and disheveled in your pj's?"

"You're sick, you know that? Sick."

"I'll drink to that." Andrew took a swig from the bottle of Gatorade he held in his right hand.

"How was your big date last night?" Connor wanted to know.

"Let's just say I'd rather be skydiving."

"What'd he do?" Andrew wanted to know.

"He tried to buy me a building."

My brother-in-law feigned outrage. "That bastard! How dare he? What's next? Giving you your own island?"

"No, it was a passive-aggressive control thing. So I'd owe him. So he could decide the who, what, and where about my career." I paused. "And my shoes. Which is really where I draw the line. It didn't end well."

"Well, *I* like your shoes," Connor said.

I had shoved my feet into a pair of red flip-flops, which clashed horribly with the robe. "You're just trying to butter me up."

"Is it working?"

"It'll work better after I've had some coffee. So what happened to you guys? Where did you end up last night?" I pulled the robe tighter around me as our next-door neighbor emerged to collect her newspaper.

"All shall be revealed on the way to the IHOP. They do have IHOPs around here, right?"

I squinted into the harsh morning sun. "Yeah, there's one

about fifteen minutes away. But I didn't figure you for an IHOP kind of guy. Aren't you supposed to be an upper-crust restaurateur?"

"He's a total food pleb," Andrew confided. "Greasy pizza, In-N-Out . . . he's the only person I know who will actually eat the nachos from 7-Eleven."

"In-N-Out?" I gasped. "What would Wolfgang Puck say?"

"I'm pretty sure I've seen him in line behind me at the drive-thru," Connor claimed.

"Hey," I said as if the idea had just now occurred to me. "You know who loves pancakes? Claire."

By the time Claire had completed her sacrosanct skin care ritual and we arrived at the restaurant, the breakfast rush was in full swing so we had to wait for a table.

But the potent combination of boredom and hunger had spurred a passionate reconciliation between the feuding newlyweds. Love at the IHOP is a beautiful thing.

"Well," Andrew announced, finally meeting Claire's eyes, "I forgive you."

"You do?" She choked up. "Oh sweetheart, I forgive you, too."

He frowned. "What do you mean, you forgive me, too? I didn't do anything."

"Excuse me? You humiliated me in front of my family and threatened to abandon me."

"*You* humiliated *me* in front of your family," Andrew countered. "And I wasn't going to abandon you; I was just going back to pack up the rest of our stuff and get the apartment rented out so we wouldn't be penalized for breaking the lease."

At this point, Claire took a deep breath and did something very out of character. She swallowed her pride and capitulated. "You know what? Let's not fight anymore. I made a big mistake, and I'm sorry."

But the competition wasn't over yet. "No, *I'm* sorry! I shouldn't have made you worry I was going to leave you forever."

"And I shouldn't have made you worry I was going to give up the babies." She hung her head. "Believe it or not, I was trying to make our relationship better. Honesty and communication and all that."

"I can see that now. And I know you're not yourself these days. In your delicate condition and all . . ."

"Sometimes it's just hard to think straight," she agreed. "All the hormones rampaging through me, and the constant headaches, the cravings . . ."

As predicted, playing the pregnancy trump card elicited the desired effect: scrunchy-faced noises of male sympathy and general mollycoddling. Score one for Mom.

"I know it's hard on you, darling. Let's get you off your feet." He led her over to a single empty chair by the front window. "Things are tough right now, but we're going to make it. You'll see. It's like Connor was telling me last night . . ."

"Jeez." I turned to Connor. "What did you say to spur this total turnaround?"

"When?"

"Last night. Andrew mentioned some pearl of wisdom you rolled his way when you guys did whatever it was you did instead of driving back to Los Angeles."

"Oh, that." He looked slightly embarrassed. "We just went out for pizza and watched the Dodgers game."

"And you solved all his marriage problems over nine innings and a couple of brewskis?"

"In man world, we call that 'multitasking.'"

"Well, apparently your multitasking saved their marriage." I tilted my head toward the sun-drenched lovebirds nestled by the door. "They'll live happily ever after, poor but happy."

"Oh, I don't know if they'll be so poor." He grinned. "You never know what Andrew might pull out of his bag of tricks."

I lunged into his personal space. "Really? Tell me everything!"

"Not so fast there, Hyper." He started rubbing my neck (a very effective distraction). "He and I just tossed around a few ideas. But it's all speculation at this point."

"Come on. Give me a hint!"

"It's not my news to tell."

I rummaged through my purse until I found my emery board, which I brandished like a samurai sword. "It is if you want to escape with your life."

"What, are you going to *sand* me until I talk?"

"Oh sure, you laugh now, but wait until I start in on your cuticles. And if *that* doesn't break you, I'll have no choice but to use the hot paraffin wax."

"Let's not get crazy here. I'm an American citizen, you know. I have rights."

"What are you guys doing?" Claire and Andrew stood two feet away, staring at the emery board with what could only be described as parental expressions of disapproval.

And the hostess was right behind them. "Your table is ready."

Connor grabbed my hand, disarmed me with a flick of his wrist, and led me to the corner booth the hostess indicated.

"You are *so* immature," Claire informed me as she slid into the vinyl seat.

"Better watch what you say," Connor advised her. "She shows no mercy with the hot paraffin wax."

"So." I turned to Andrew. "I hear you've come up with an ingenious new career plan."

"You have?" my sister squealed.

"Well, I was going to talk this over with *my wife* first . . ." he shot Connor a look ". . . but, yes, I might have a few contacts out here."

"What kind of contacts?" My sister bounced up and down in the booth.

"Industry contacts, actually."

"By which you mean show business?" I clarified.

"Of course," the three Angelenos chorused in unison.

"Did you know that they do a ton of location work out here? TV and film?" Andrew said.

My sister looked doubtful. "Are you sure? I spent most of my life here and I never heard that."

"With the new labor laws and the cost of doing business in Southern California, more and more projects are filming out of state."

"Which is why places like Toronto and Vancouver are suddenly so star-studded." I nodded. "But Phoenix?"

"Are you kidding me? Phoenix is perfect. It's a fifty-minute flight from L.A. and you've got golf courses, spas, and luxury shopping. So the talent agencies and production companies out here are growing exponentially, and they all need agents with connections."

"But, um . . ." Claire faltered. "Aren't you having a little trouble with your industry connections right now?"

"I may not be mogul material anymore, but I still know a few key people in casting and development. Some of whom still owe me a favor or two. We'll start fresh, without the L.A. politics, and I really think I can make a go of it." He paused. "There's only one problem."

"Uh-oh."

"We'll have to relocate to the Scottsdale area. We can't stay at your parents' indefinitely. The commute from here to Scottsdale would be too long to—"

"*Thank God*!" She threw her arms around him. "I love you!"

"So you're okay with not having your mom right down the street when we have the twins?"

"I love you, I love you, I love you!" She nearly suffocated him in her public display of affection.

"I'll take that as a yes."

Claire nodded. "And you know, maybe after I have the babies, I can try teaching an acting class. Not Shakespearean monologues or anything, but improv and tips on how to hack it in the business. Like how to flirt with casting directors or how to sound weak-kneed and breathless over the prospect of trying a new brand of deodorant."

"That's a great idea!" Andrew gushed. "Most people would kill for a national beer commercial, never mind two. You have the working actor's equivalent of a Ph.D."

Our waitress waited for the gratuitous smooching to taper off before asking, "Are you folks ready to order?"

"You should have eggs and bacon," Andrew suggested to Claire. "All that protein. That's good for the kids, right?"

"I'll have blueberry pancakes and a huge vat of maple syrup. Like a wading pool." She shrugged off our stares. "Maple syrup comes from trees, and trees grow in the ground. It's totally Zodiac approved."

"I don't think that the maple syrup they serve here is exactly fresh from a Vermont forest," Connor said.

"This from the guy who eats the 7-Eleven nachos?" I started

to heckle him, then realized I was in no position to judge. "I'll have the chocolate chip pancakes, please. Extra butter."

"Well done." Claire nodded her approval. "That'll be one of my acting class lessons—when you're doing a media interview at a restaurant, always order something substantial. That way, no one can accuse you of having an eating disorder. And you can hand them a load of crap about how you're blessed with a naturally fast metabolism."

"Well, I'm loading up on protein," Andrew said. "I'll need it this afternoon."

"What's going on this afternoon?" Claire asked.

"Skydiving." I turned to Connor. "Listen, about that—"

"I know it freaks you out, but this is a once-in-a-lifetime opportunity." His hand found mine under the table. "Snake told me about this guy who has a plane way out in the desert and the views at the drop zone are incredible."

"But we should go look for apartments in Scottsdale today," Claire reminded her husband.

"It'll only take a few hours," Andrew said. "We can look at apartments tomorrow."

"Let me get this straight. You have two children on the way and you'd rather spend the day jumping out of an airplane instead of finding a place for your family to live?"

"No, but . . ." He fell back on Connor's catchphrase. "Once-in-a-lifetime opportunity!"

"Yeah, to die young. You're not going."

Andrew turned to Connor and muttered, "I can't go."

I hoped that this might kill the whole plan, but Connor just nodded and said, "Okay. I'll give you a call when I'm done and we'll meet up later?"

I tried to keep my mouth shut, I really did. I reminded my-self that no one likes a nagger and look what happened to Meena, and did I really want to be the Kevin Bradley in this re-lationship. But I just couldn't quell my anxiety. "I wish you wouldn't do this."

"I'm picking up on that." He threaded his fingers through mine. "Becca, you don't have to worry. I know what I'm doing. I'll be fine."

"But . . . something bad could happen to you."

"I'll be *fine*," he repeated.

I tried to look reassured. "Promise?"

"I promise."

I got the call from the hospital at three o'clock that afternoon while whipping up a batch of Oreo brownies in my parents' kitchen and trying not to think about my new boyfriend's self-destructive hobbies.

"Becca?" Andrew sounded apprehensive. "Claire and I are at the Lockwood Memorial emergency room in Mesa, and you might want to get over here."

I sat down hard on a kitchen chair. "What's wrong with Claire? Are the babies okay?"

"Claire's fine," he assured me. "Couldn't be better. We're ac-tually here because—"

"It's Connor, isn't it? What happened?"

"Well, the good news is, he's alive. The bad news is . . ."

"What? He lost an eye? I *warned* him about those kites!"

"No, his parachute failed."

"Oh God."

Andrew cleared his throat. "And then there was a screwup with the emergency chute."

My heart stopped. "*What kind of screwup?*"

"I'm not sure. All I know is that he basically couldn't steer at all on the way down so he landed on somebody's roof. But at least he missed the highway."

I waved away all these details. "I need to know how badly he hurt himself. Right now."

"He snapped his ankle bone and got some nasty cuts. Oh, and he hit his head, but don't worry, he didn't pass out."

I made a frightened little noise, like *meep*.

"But that's nothing, really, when you think about what could have happened. The odds of walking away from something like this are like a million to one."

"He didn't walk away from it," I pointed out.

"Yeah, but you know Connor. He's built like a tank. This one time, we went snowboarding in Utah and there was a blizzard starting up . . ."

I held the phone away from my ear, unable to bear even one more of Connor's iron man exploits. What the hell was wrong with these guys? They were like the Black Knight in *Monty Python's Holy Grail*: "'Tis only a flesh wound . . ."

"So he's in the ER right now?" I asked when Andrew stopped chuckling over the gory snowboarding story.

"Yeah, we're waiting for the orthopedic resident to show up and it's taking forever."

"How long have you guys been there?"

"Connor called us before he left for the hospital so we drove down here from Scottsdale."

"How come he didn't call me?"

More nervous throat clearing. "I think he's a little embarrassed to talk to you. You know, 'cause you were so worried he might hurt himself."

"Clearly, all my fears were groundless."

"But I'm sure he wants to see you. It should take you about forty-five minutes to get here from your side of town. All you do is take the Ten—"

"Lockwood Memorial, right? I know how to get there." I grabbed my purse and the keys to Mom's car. "I just hope he's learned his lesson."

"I wouldn't count on it."

"You look awful," I said when the nurse pulled aside the curtain, revealing my battered boyfriend. Connor was stretched out on a gurney, his left pant leg shoved up to accommodate a mass of ice packs. He looked like he'd challenged a lawnmower to hand-to-hand combat; his left side was covered in bumps and scrapes and he had a deep gash on his forearm, which an exhausted physician in blue scrubs was stitching up.

"Hey!" He lifted his head and smiled at me. "You came! Andrew said he called you, but I wasn't sure if you'd want to see me after . . ."

I hurried over to squeeze his right hand. "Of course I came. What did you expect?"

"I don't know. I thought you might be mad."

"I'm not mad." I ran my fingers along his cheek. "Scared witless, but not mad. Let's just agree that you won't be jumping out of any more planes and move on with our lives."

He let his head fall back. "Um . . ."

"Connor. Seriously. Tell me you're not sitting here planning your next jump."

"Um . . ."

I stared at him. "Andrew said the odds of surviving something like this are a million to one!"

"I know. And the odds of it ever happening again are a *trillion* to one."

"Are you doped up on pain meds right now?"

"Nope," the resident stitching up his forearm chimed in. "Just local anesthetic."

"Then how can we even be having this argument? Your parachute failed, your emergency chute failed—"

"My emergency chute worked fine," he corrected. "The problem was, my regular parachute decided to inflate at the same moment the emergency chute did, which made it impossible to direct my landing. I tried to cut off the first chute, but I dropped my knife, and—"

"Whatever." Exasperation had rendered me a little rude. "Point is, by all rights you should have died. But instead of looking at this as a fresh start, you're plotting new ways to cheat death? Unbelievable."

"You're very 'the glass is half-empty' today." He tried to coax a smile out of me.

"You can follow your bliss without living in free fall," I insisted for what felt like the hundreth time.

He grinned. "But why would I want to?"

"You're serious?"

"I told you—I am who I am. You can't change me."

And we were back to the old "men don't change" refrain.

"I'm not going to stop living my life just because you're scared," he said.

"Look at you! I think I have a right to be scared."

"You told me you could deal with this part of me."

"I guess I lied."

Our eyes met in a wordless clash of wills. The resident ducked his head and just kept stitching.

"Well, I'm not giving up skydiving. I'm not giving up any of the things I love."

I weighed my next words for a moment. "Then you're giving up me."

"Oh come on, you're just—"

"I can't live like this! I can't! I wish I could be different from all your other overprotective, nagging girlfriends, but I'm not! You're too scared to risk your heart and I'm too scared to risk your life, so . . ." I folded my arms and focused on the wall behind him. "I guess we're breaking up."

The resident paused mid-stitch.

Connor's expression was stony. "I guess we are."

I don't know what I'd expected from him, but that terse, nonchalant agreement was not it.

"So . . . okay," I finished lamely. "Bye."

"Bye."

I marched back into the waiting room, past Claire and Andrew, into my car and out of his life.

Sunday night, I boarded my second lonely flight to L.A. that month. I was depressed for different reasons this time; instead of mourning a relationship that had long passed its prime, I was mourning one that hadn't had a chance to reach its potential.

My mind could accept the fact that Connor wouldn't change his ways and nothing I could say or do would sway him, but my heart was throwing a tantrum and it wanted some answers, pronto. *Why* didn't he want me more than he wanted the thrill of free fall and the agony of the ER? *Why* did we have to have all that chemistry if we were doomed from the start? And most importantly, *why* did I have sex with him? If we hadn't gotten so physical so quickly, I'd never have to know what I was missing.

When I turned on my cell phone upon landing, I had two new messages. Neither were from Connor. The first one was from Aimee:

"Oh my God! . . . gonna be totally rich and famous . . . Jennifer Garner . . . Canada . . . get back here . . . oh my *God*!"

The second was from Fiona:

"Becca, darling, I talked to the other members of Team Rachelle this weekend and . . ." There was such a long pause that I thought her connection had cut out. Then: "I hate to deliver bad news over the phone, so do me a favor and come by my office tomorrow morning around ten. We need to talk."

25

"Guess who finally landed a role in a movie?" Aimee yelled through the open car window when she pulled up to the curb at LAX.

"You did?" I dropped my bags and ran around to the driver's side to engulf her in a hug. "That's amazing!"

"It's a *real* movie, too, not just some straight-to-video schlock. I have a totally juicy part: blond bimbo mob moll by day, undercover cop by night."

"A speaking role and everything! Next stop: world domination."

"Well, I mean . . ." She feigned girlish modesty to the best of her ability. "It's not the starring role or anything, but it's big enough that, if the Academy were feeling generous come Oscar season, I could be nominated for best supporting actress."

I laughed. "So in other words . . ."

"I'm the slutty best friend." She glanced down at her chest and shrugged. "All those casting directors were right. I have boobs; what do you want?"

"I want you to thank your humble waitstaff friends from Rhapsody when you win your Oscar."

"But of course. I'll thank you guys right after I thank my agent, my manager, my mom, and my wonderfully supportive husband, Michael Vartan, a.k.a. Special Agent Hotness."

"Michael Vartan?" I threw my bags in the backseat and clambered into the passenger seat. "But don't you think Jennifer Garner might have a problem with that seeing as she used to date him and they had a horrible, messy breakup and all?"

"Are you kidding me? Jen's a sweetie, everyone in the biz knows that. In fact, she'll probably give me his number herself."

"You realize you're only going to be her best friend *on camera*, right?"

She waved this away. "And of course, I'll be wearing a Becca Davis original to the red carpet premiere. There's only one catch."

"Isn't there always?"

"I have to go to Vancouver for the next five months."

I stopped celebrating. "Vancouver?"

"Yep. That's where they're filming. But don't worry—if

you want to sublet the apartment while I'm gone, it's all yours."

"But you can't go to Canada! You're my only friend in L.A.!"

She smiled slyly. "Not your *only* friend. There's always Connor."

"Yeah. About that. We broke up."

"Shut *up!*"

I nodded glumly.

"What? When? Where? *Why?*" She rattled off all the questions I'd been asking myself.

"Let's talk about it later." I found my sunglasses in my purse and put them on. "Right now we should be focusing on your new career on the big screen."

"But you—"

"I'm fine. I swear." I put on a sunny smile. "So when do you head off to the great frozen north?"

"I'm not sure yet; I just found out about casting today. But soon. Preproduction starts in a couple of weeks."

"What the hell is preproduction?"

She laughed. "I have no idea. It sounds impressive, though, doesn't it?"

"It does. Good for you," I said. "You deserve this."

"I couldn't agree more."

"Thanks for picking me up today. And for letting me stay at your place. And just, you know, for everything."

"Hey, what are slutty best friends for?"

*   *   *

Getting fired by Fiona Fitzgerald was like pulling my own teeth:

"Listen. Darling. I met with Team Rachelle this week and showed them all your samples."

I lifted my chin and squared my shoulders as if preparing to face a firing squad. "And?"

"And . . . well, the long and the short of it is, your pieces just aren't going to work for us."

"But I thought Rachelle liked the corset?"

"Yes, well. We appreciate your hard work, but this partnership just isn't working out."

I had to make this work. I *had* to. "Please don't give up on me yet. I swear I can do better. Give me a few more—"

"Let's not get pathetic, darling. It's nothing personal, it's just creative differences."

"But what about—"

"Now." She shuffled through the pile of papers on her desk until she found a copy of the contract I'd signed. "The question is, are you willing to resign or are you going to force us to terminate you?"

"What difference does it make?" I keened.

"Well, according to your contract, if you submit a letter of resignation, we have to pay you five hundred dollars for each sample you've turned in. I'll also be able to give you a letter of recommendation for your portfolio."

"And if you terminate me?"

She peered down at the contract. "If we terminate you, you get paid only for those patterns we choose to manufacture."

"Which will be . . . ?"

"None of them." She smiled cheerfully. "So it's your choice, darling. Entirely up to you."

"Some choice."

"Don't pout. You're a very talented girl, but you just don't share our vision."

Yeah. Their *vision* for craptastic polyester ponchos. Not that I was bitter.

"Fine," I muttered. "I'll fax over my letter of resignation this afternoon."

"Oh, don't bother with that, darling, you can just sign this one." She handed me a short, to-the-point form letter. I just had to print my name, sign, and date.

"You guys fire a lot of designers?" I guessed.

Her smile never wavered. "Not everyone shares our vision."

"No kidding." I scrawled my signature in the bottom corner and shoved the paper back at her.

"Expect your check and your letter of recommendation in the next few weeks. Make sure my assistant has your current mailing address on the way out, won't you?"

And just like that, I was back in the waiting room, forever banished from the chambers of Fiona Fitzgerald. I'd been so close . . .

But the stylist giveth, and the stylist taketh away.

I had officially hit rock bottom: no money, no career, no

prospects, and no confidence. My sister was moving back to Phoenix, my lone L.A. friend was heading to Canada, and my ertswhile boyfriend and potential employer had decided I was an acceptable loss, along with his fibula. As I slunk back to my rental car, I was horrified to realize that Claire and Kevin had been right all along: risks didn't pay off for people like me. I'd followed my dream and tried my hardest and look where it got me. I could pick myself up and try again, but what if I just couldn't hack the ruthless competition out here?

What if I had risked everything for nothing?

"Fiona Fitzgerald's office, how may I help you?" the receptionist intoned between smacks of gum.

"Yes, this is Becca Davis, I just had a meeting with Fiona." I was brisk, I was businesslike, I was not going to lose my cool.

"You again?" Smack, smack. "She's not available at the moment; she's—"

I went ahead and lost my cool. "Don't tell me she's busy. I don't want to hear about her starlet clientele or her video shoots or her imaginary flights to Australia. I want her on the phone, right now."

I expected the receptionist to hang up but she didn't. Her voice got high and tentative as she said, "Um, one moment please."

"Becca. What can I do for you? If this is about your check—"

"It isn't. You screwed me over, didn't you?"

"Darling!" She didn't sound the least bit surprised. "Whatever do you mean?"

"Why did you want me to quit instead of firing me? You don't care about me. You don't want to write me a letter of recommendation."

"Of course I do."

"Please. Don't embarrass us both. Just tell me what you're up to."

Sharp intake of breath. "You're a clever girl. I'm sure you can figure everything out."

Shit. "So you admit you are up to something?"

"I don't have to admit anything. I'm no longer affiliated with you in any way."

"Because you don't like my work."

"That's right."

"Then send back the samples and the patterns I made."

"I'm afraid I can't do that."

"Why not? If you guys don't want to manufacture them, then you might as well let me shop them around to—"

She started to laugh. Well, laugh was the wrong word. Cackle was more like it.

"Oh my God." I slammed my palm down on the car hood. "You're going to use them, aren't you?"

"We might," she trilled. "One never knows. They're ours now; we can mass-produce them at our discretion."

"But you still have to pay my commission if you do . . ." I winced. "Right?"

"Not exactly, darling. Not if you quit."

"But—"

"I don't have time to sit here all day discussing legal technicalities. I suggest you reread the contract you signed with us. And good luck with your future endeavors."

"But I gave you all my best work!" I howled.

"We appreciate that. And I'm sure Rachelle's many fans will appreciate it. Speaking of which, be advised that we own the rights to all patterns you submitted to us."

"So . . . I can't even sew my *own* designs anymore?"

"Not if you don't want to get sued. Good afternoon!" Click. Dial tone.

"You bitch!" I screamed at the phone. "You can't do this to me!"

But she already had. When I returned to Aimee's apartment, I broke out my copy of the contract and finally found the microscopic-fonted footnote stipulating that if they fired me, I was entitled to my full commission, but if I quit, they retained the rights to my work, they could do whatever they wanted with the patterns, and I was entitled to diddly squat.

"I'm ruined!" I wailed, burying my face in my hands. *"Ruined!"*

"But the upside is, at least you know you have real talent, right?" Aimee offered. "So much talent that people go out of their way to steal it."

"Wow. Validation from a lying, cheating, pattern-stealing sociopath. Suddenly life is worth living again."

She patted my shoulder. "All is not lost. I mean, I get that this sucks hugely, but just because they stole your designs doesn't mean they can monopolize your talent."

"I worked on some of those pieces for years! Do you know how long it'll take me to build a whole new portfolio?"

"Well, *chica*"—she dragged on her cigarette—"that's why God invented day jobs."

I started banging my head against the table. "I can't."

"You can."

"I can't."

"You must."

"Lowly grunt work here I come, right back where I started from . . ." I picked up the phone and made my second ego-crushing call of the day.

"Look who's come crawling back."

I dug the toe of my Rodolphe Menudier wedge into the plush white carpet at Miriam Russo's boutique. "Indeed I have."

Miriam's perfect platinum pageboy hardly moved when she nodded. "They all come back, and do you know why?"

Because they'd rather die than call Connor Sullivan and ask for their hostessing jobs back? "No."

"Because I know everything and everyone worth knowing."

I folded my hands in front of me, the very picture of penitence. "Then I'm very lucky you agreed to meet with me again."

"Yes, you are. Now . . ." She paused to savor her moment of ultimate power. "Do you have anything you'd like to say to me?"

I sighed. "I should have put the zipper in the corset."

She arched one eyebrow. "You're saying it, but you don't mean it."

"Oh, I mean it." I gritted my teeth. "But it's a moot point anyway since I can't even make the damn things anymore."

She stopped tormenting me and got serious. "And why not?"

"Because I got mixed up with the stylist from hell and now—"

"Fiona Fitzgerald?"

My head snapped up. "How did you know?"

"*Everyone* knows about Fiona. Tell me you didn't sign anything."

"Um."

"Oh no. What did she get?"

"The corset, all my best shirts and skirts, my sister's wedding gown . . ."

"So essentially, you're coming to me with no new designs?"

"Actually . . ." I whipped out the sketch I'd worked on all night. "I'm working on a new piece, Parking Lot Pants, I'm calling them. I haven't had time to whip up a sample yet—"

"But you don't have anything approaching a collection?"

"Not anymore, no."

She slid her glasses down her tiny misshapen nose. "Then why are you here?"

"I need a job. I'll do anything. Steam the stock, clean the carpets, make coffee—"

"Fine."

"Really?"

"Why not? I like a woman who can admit it when she's made a mistake. Besides, my last assistant just quit in a huff. None of them last long."

"I can't imagine why."

"Don't get uppity on your first day," she warned, but I could see a hint of a smile on her lips. "Very well, you're hired. As of right now, I'm your new mentor. I'm brusque, I'm demanding, and I'm going to hurt your feelings all day every day. But at least I won't steal your designs. Are we agreed?"

"Yes." I threw in a salute for good measure.

"You can start by getting me a cup of coffee. I like it strong, black, and scalding hot. McDonald's lawsuit hot. Once you master the coffee machine, I *might* trust you to steam the new Nanette Lepore shipment. Until then, watch and learn from the very best—me."

26

Over the next two weeks, I learned many great truths. Firstly, that I was broke. And not just by Los Angeles standards—none of that "I can't pay the electric bill because I just *had* to have the new Rene Caovilla slingbacks" claptrap—but by middle-class Phoenix standards. By shantytown standards, okay? At this point, Old Navy flip-flops were beyond my reach, forget Rene Caovilla. But, if I was very lucky and very economical and very willing to eat ramen and mac and cheese, I might be able to scrape together next month's rent.

The second great truth was that I missed Connor. A lot. I wondered how his broken ankle was healing, if the gash on his forearm would leave a permanent scar. I wondered if he was wondering about me. Countless times I dialed the first few digits of his phone number, only to abort the call. What could we say to each other that hadn't already been said?

Most of my great truths, however, came straight from Miriam Russo, Fount of Fashion Wisdom.

"Here is the secret to running a design business in this city: Los Angeles women are some of the most tragic fashion victims. Bear that in mind, and the clientele will come in and come back in droves."

"Fashion victims?" I cast my mind back to all the gorgeous models and actresses who'd swept through Rhapsody in the latest designs from Narciso Rodriguez, Catherine Malandrino, and Tracy Reese.

"You don't believe me?"

"Oh, I am not disagreeing with you. *Definitely* not."

"Good. Then I'll let you live."

"But most of the women I've seen here look pretty fabulous. I mean, if you want to see fashion victims for real, go to Arizona sometime. I myself have assembled an entire wardrobe from thrift stores and the clearance rack at Macy's, so I'm in no position to criticize anyone else."

"Arizona," she scoffed. "Macy's. Please. You're missing my point. The women you know in Phoenix, are they married to fantastically wealthy movie producers and plastic surgeons?"

"No."

"Is their primary goal in life to fit into Chanel's sample size and make other women writhe with envy?"

"No."

"Well, then, how could they possibly be expected to compete with my clientele? Women in the real world are too busy trying to pay the bills and raise their children to spend all day accessorizing. Take you, for example. It's all too apparent that you have a banal, suburban background to go with your banal, suburban name, but you still manage to pull together something with a little panache."

I looked down at my black peasant skirt and white, off-the-shoulder, Sophia-Loren-circa-1965 top. "Thank you. Got the whole outfit for under twenty bucks at a flea market in Paradise Valley."

"There you go. It's not about money, it's about fashion sense. You'll see," she promised. "You'll see when women start asking to buy the dress along with the matching shoes and the matching handbag and the color-coordinated jewelry. Lately, it's like lemmings throwing themselves off the cliff of Von Dutch."

"Or the Ugg abyss?"

"Exactly. The Aussies will never forgive us for that one. If you want your label to last, you can't oversell your product. Oversaturate the market and you're through. Call it the Burberry Effect."

By Friday, I had mastered the latte, the cappuccino, and the grainy hypercaffeinated sludge that Miriam needed twelve times per day "in order to behave in anything approaching a civilized manner." On Saturday morning, I fluttered around like a geisha and made apologetic noises while a temperamental pop star berated me because the store didn't have the newest True Religion jeans in her size (okay, actually, we *did* have them in her size— a 28—but she insisted that she wore a 25 and no one dared contradict her). I let her scream herself hoarse, then sprinted down the block to the Coffee Bean & Tea Leaf to fetch her the special dulce de leche ice-blended coffee she demanded, an errand for which I was neither thanked nor paid back.

So by Sunday afternoon, I was relieved when Miriam announced that a very high-profile client was dropping by with her stylist for a private shopping session that afternoon.

"You're dismissed for the rest of the day," she informed me, yanking the sunshades down over the front windows. "We can't have you eavesdropping on her cell phone conversations and then tattling to the tabloids."

"I would never do that," I protested.

"You don't seem the type," she agreed, locking the doors. "But some celebrities want their privacy, and I give it to them." She paused to slug down yet another cup of coffee. "And until I know for a fact that you're not going to be running at the mouth at the first offer of money, I'm going to have to give you the boot. Now beat it. Rachelle Robinson and Fiona Fitzgerald are going to be here any minute."

I gaped at her. "You're going to work with them?"

"Don't bother with the righteous outrage routine. First rule of business in this town: If they have money, you work with them." Her eyes glittered. "Besides, how else am I going to find out all the dirty details of their new fashion line?"

*　　*　　*

"Here's the lowdown: it's going to be called Raggs by Rachelle—that's Raggs with two g's, I kid you not—and it's gonna crash and burn as soon as it hits stores," Miriam reported on Monday. "Be thankful your name's not attached anymore."

"Really?"

"Really. Bad fabric, poor cutting, horrendous execution. If they weren't such duplicitous harpies I'd actually feel sorry for them."

"You never feel sorry for anyone," I reminded her.

"I know. That tells you exactly how bad it is."

"I'd gloat, except . . . my corset."

"Your corset's gone over to the dark side, along with all your other best pieces. They're never coming back. Mourn them and move on. And get me a new cup of coffee while you're at it."

I rushed to do her bidding (it was in everyone's best interest to keep her on a steady IV drip of caffeine), then harassed her until she agreed to look at the Parking Lot Pants sample I'd whipped up. I'd tailored them to fit me, but when I put them on and paraded around, she looked unimpressed.

"I don't know." She started flipping through a fashion magazine that had just arrived with the mail.

"But look at the cute ribbon detailing on the knees," I pointed out. "These are perfect for summer parties!"

"They're not exactly slimming, though, are they?"

I flushed and sucked in my stomach. "Yeah, but that's only

because I have short legs. If someone like Nicole Kidman were to put these on—"

"Most of my customers aren't Nicole Kidman. We can't all be five-foot-ten redheads with zero-percent body fat. You need a piece that's different from all the mundane crap already out there. You need an eye-popping, attention-grabbing couture original that positively *demands* to be photographed and written up."

"I hate to quibble, but the last time I came up with a piece like that it ended up a POW of Team Rachelle."

"Then don't be in such a hurry next time. Don't hand your most valuable designs over to someone you barely know." She turned back to her magazine. "Go home tonight, get to work on something really fresh and fun, sew the hell out of it, get it on a red carpet, and then we'll talk."

"Get it on the red carpet," I scoffed. "Right. Like it's so easy."

"It *is* easy if you know how to network," she replied. "Especially with awards season coming up. But don't waste your time worrying about that right now. First, you need to create something really spectacular."

And wham, inspiration struck like a skillet to the skull. "Spectacular? I can do that. As for networking, well, let's just hope Jennifer Garner looks good in gray."

27

I stayed late at the boutique the next Sunday, baggy-eyed from sleep deprivation but charged with the creative buzz that came with frenetic, all-night sewing sessions. My new piece was by far the best I'd ever done—better than Claire's wedding gown and Rachelle's corset put together. Though my energy had lagged as the day wore on (two shrill fashionistas nearly drew blood over the last coral pink Goldenbleu handbag and I'd had to intervene, nearly losing a finger in the process), my spirits were soaring. I was excited to be sewing again, excited to be pouring my passion into something new.

As I made sure all the displays were orderly and the clothes were lined up according to size, I allowed myself to linger over the lustrous new silks and feather-light cashmeres. Here I was, chasing the dream. I had desire, I had drive; in fact, the only thing that could improve this day was—

"You know what would look great here? A big pile of Becca Davis originals."

I turned around and there was Connor Sullivan with a grin on his face, a bulky cast on his left foot, and a bundle of shopping bags in each hand.

I froze. "What are you doing here?"

"You're still speaking to me." He nodded. "I'll consider that a sign of encouragement."

I continued to stare at him, dumbfounded.

"Don't worry, I'm not here to stalk you. No clandestine building leases, no flowery spiel about how I've seen the error of my ways and I'm a changed man."

"Then . . . why *are* you here?"

"I'm here because even though I'm the same stubborn guy I've always been, I've made a few improvements."

I was in pain just looking at the thick blue brace encasing his foot. "How's your ankle?"

"We'll get to that in a minute." He lifted the shopping bags. "First I have something to show you."

I peered inside the big brown bags and started to laugh.

"Is this supposed to be a joke?"

He shook his head, trying to look earnest. "The salesman said they're the best. Top of the line. The Rolls-Royce of bed sheets."

"Because obviously, you're so picky about your linens."

"You got that straight—give me a high thread count or give me death."

The sheets were a simple snowy white. And there were a *lot* of them. "You really stocked up, didn't you?"

"Oh yeah." He ticked off his purchases on his fingers. "Fitted sheets, top sheets, pillowcases, and something called a duvet. I'm not even sure what a duvet is, but the salesman assured me I can't live without it."

"Egyptian cotton?"

"I don't know what ethnicity they are, but I can tell you this: they're all whole."

I gave him a lopsided smile. "And somewhere out there, Meena is weeping."

He grabbed my hand. "This isn't about Meena. It's about you. I'm winning you back, you see."

"Oh really?"

"Yeah." He studied my face. "How's it going so far?"

"Surprisingly well, considering your big romantic gesture originated in the domestic department of Bloomingdale's."

"I was hoping to pick up a few bonus points in the sentimental category."

"Impressive," I acknowledged. "Very impressive."

"So look." He flung out his arms. "I'm growing. I'm changing. I have a duvet."

My heart pinballed around my chest. It would be so easy to just let him pull me back into his embrace and damn the consequences till tomorrow. But . . . "Connor, come on. I get the symbolism—*so* subtle, by the way—but how do a bunch of sheets really change anything?"

His grin widened. "The sheets are just supposed to melt the ice. *This* is what changes things: my parachute failed."

"I know."

"And then my emergency chute didn't work the way it was supposed to."

"I heard."

"Basically, I was sure I was going to die."

"I see."

"And while I was sure I was going to die, I got to thinking about you. How I'd feel if I never got to see you again. How I'd feel if *you* insisted on throwing yourself out of a tiny plane with a faulty parachute."

"And?"

He shifted uncomfortably. "I didn't like it."

"But what about all your ranting in the ER about how you're your own man and no woman will tame you?"

"Here's the thing about near-death experiences: there's a forty-eight-hour period after them where you feel invincible. Once I'd had a few days to come down off the high, I kind of saw your point."

"So why didn't you call me?"

"I just . . . I don't know. But then Claire told me to stop being so wussy about dating. She said if I can handle parachute failures, I can handle the risk of you rejecting me."

BETH KENDRICK

"She's a smart girl. And you'll notice I'm not rejecting you."

"Can we try this again? If I promise to stop doing some of the stuff that makes me a bad candidate for life insurance?"

"But I don't want you getting all angry and resentful in a few months. I don't want to be the controlling, killjoy girl-friend. Are you sure this is what you really want?"

"I'm sure. Becca, I want you more than I want to break a new bone every year."

"Aw." I went up on tiptoe to give him a kiss.

He kissed me back, then said, "Yeah, I figure I've already got enough stories to tell our grandchildren."

"Grandchildren?" I blanched. "Aren't you moving a little fast?"

"You know me, baby, I *live* fast."

"If that's the opening to another horrendous pickup line, I'm leaving," I warned.

"By all means." He picked up his bags and held the door for me. "I'll come with you."

We ambled off into the smoggy L.A. sunset, broken bones, baggage, and all. And the salesman had been telling the truth—those high-thread-count sheets were worth every penny.

28

Mute it!" Claire bellowed. "No one good is on the carpet yet, and I can't handle Joan Rivers with all these hormones racing through me."

I uncovered my ears as my sister, swathed in the pashminas she'd once derided, seized the remote control and clicked off the TV's sound.

"No need to yell; I'm right here." I perched on the edge of my parents' coffee table, trying to contain my manic knee jiggling.

"More grilled cheese, girls?" My mother emerged from the kitchen bearing a plate of sandwiches.

I shook my head. "I'm way too nervous to eat."

"That's okay; I'll have hers." Claire helped herself to two and dug in. The doctor had recommended she stay off her feet as much as possible, which she invoked as her excuse for lounging about, mainlining carbs, and issuing orders to the rest of the family. To be fair to Joan Rivers, nearly everything sent her over the edge these days: spilled soda, puppy food commercials, less-than-optimal weather reports . . .

"Don't be so self-centered. This is Becca's day and you're minimizing her achievements. You're even eating her dinner," Gayle lectured. But I noticed this didn't stop her from grabbing a sandwich for herself.

"It's fine," I assured my oldest sister. "I couldn't choke one of those things down if you paid me. I feel like I'm gonna hurl."

"That's my girl." Connor came up behind me and rubbed my neck. "Strong spirit, weak stomach."

"Besides," Andrew added, "the babies need calcium. Eat up, sweetheart."

"Okay," Claire mumbled through a mouthful of bread.

Connor and I had flown back to Phoenix for the weekend to watch the Golden Globes preshow coverage in my parents' living room. When my mother first invited us, I'd accepted without hesitation, imagining a series of soft-focus Hallmark moments. I'd surround myself with warm, loving supporters during the most nerve-wracking night of my life. Everyone would congratulate and fuss over me. I, little Becca, would be the pride of the Davis family for one brief, shining moment.

The reality was, of course, quite different. But at least we had grilled cheese, plus a bottle of champagne chilling in the refrigerator for the big moment.

"You know what would go great with this?" Claire finished off her first sandwich in record time. "M&M's."

"What kind?" Andrew had his car keys in hand before she'd finished her sentence. "Plain or peanut?"

"Peanut butter. Not the regular peanut ones, I need the ones in the orange bag."

"Orange bag, got it." He scurried off toward the garage.

"Hurry!" Claire yelled after him. "I love you!"

Gayle looked appalled. "Is that any way to treat your soul mate?"

"He doesn't mind. That's why he's my soul mate."

I glanced at the TV, which was still showing an endless stream of commercials, then said to Claire, "I take it his new job is going well?"

"Well enough to afford peanut butter M&M's."

"So, have you thought about any of my new name suggestions?" Mom was nothing if not persistent.

"Bruce is out," Claire decreed. "Think of the taunting that child would get. I'm not naming my kid anything that rhymes with 'abuse.'"

"So no Moose?" I teased.

"Or Goose?" Gayle threw in.

"Hey, you could do a lot worse than Goose," Connor said.

All four Davis women looked at him in bewilderment.

"*Top Gun*," he said. "Goose was Maverick's trusty sidekick."

"A second banana named after poultry. Yeah. That changes my mind." Claire rolled her eyes.

"Okay, it's back on!" I shushed everyone as the camera cut back to the parade of celebs working the red carpet.

I was dimly aware of Connor's strong, reassuring hands on my shoulders as we watched Drew Barrymore pose for the paparazzi. And then Rachelle Robinson swanned into the fray.

"Oh my God." Claire put down her grilled cheese.

"What is she *wearing*?" Gayle sounded shocked. "It's the visual equivalent of a seizure. Her stylist must have had a psychotic break."

And it did seem that Team Rachelle had cracked under pressure—Rachelle's floor-length gown was a chaotic jumble of red, yellow, green, and purple stripes. *Horizontal* stripes.

"I wonder if she'll take credit for designing that monstrosity?" I mused.

"She looks like a TV test pattern." Claire snorted. "And those earrings are so last season. I can't wait for Joan to eviscerate her."

"Suddenly you can stand Joan Rivers?" Mom asked.

"I adore her." Claire smiled angelically.

But Joan's interview with Rachelle was cut short as my own personal knight in shining armor stepped out of a limo.

"Jennifer Garner!" Claire squealed. "She looks breathtaking."

True to her word, Aimee had exploited her new Hollywood connections to the max, badgering her poor costar into considering my newest creation for the awards show. Jennifer had paired my gown with minimal makeup and dangly diamond earrings. She looked unusually luminous, even by starlet standards.

Gayle smiled as she recognized the dress. "That's the dress you got at the Paradise Valley flea market, right? The one you couldn't wear for your wedding?"

"It's similar to my dress, but better." I'd used the color and silhouette of the dove gray peignor for inspiration, mixing in metallic silver accents through the bodice, train, and hem and adding interest to the back with delicate mirrored beads.

"You really outdid yourself, honey." My mom started to choke up. "My little girl's going to be rich and famous."

"You can support us in our old age," my dad added from his armchair.

"Sshhh," Claire hissed. "They're going to talk about the dress!"

"Who are you wearing?" Joan wanted to know.

Ten seconds later, my cell phone started to ring.

I felt dizzy, like I'd already made serious inroads into that unopened bottle of champagne. Then Connor leaned over, squeezed my hand, and said softly, "I love you."

"Love you, too." On the precipice of a free fall into chaos and excitement and disbelief, I squeezed him back and found my footing.

Up Close and Personal With the Author

WHY DID BECCA STAY WITH KEVIN FOR FIVE YEARS WHEN HE WAS SO WRONG FOR HER?

When they first met in college, Kevin was perfect for Becca because she had no direction or confidence and he wanted someone to boss around (oh, sorry, I meant to say "guide and mentor"). But by the time the book opens, Becca is ready to stretch her wings and take risks and Kevin can't support her in that. They've been growing apart for years and, as mature adults, they're on completely different paths. After putting in so many years with a partner, it's very hard to make a clean break and to shake the feeling that you have to "justify" falling out of love.

I know a lot of women who had similar relationships in their early twenties—the guy was right for them at one point, but then they outgrew the relationship and didn't know how to extricate themselves without looking like a heartless wench. These women, like Becca, develop a deep-rooted phobia of diamond rings!

HOW DID YOU RESEARCH THE FASHION ASPECT OF THIS BOOK? DO YOU SEW?

I shop . . . does that count? As for sewing, I can reattach a shirt button that's come loose, but that's the full extent of my tailoring prowess.

Luckily, I lived in West Hollywood when I started writing this book, and I knew a few designers who were trying to break into the fashion business. Kelly Nishimoto patiently answered all my questions, like Where do you get new ideas?, How do you make a pattern?, How do you get your designs stocked in a boutique?, and the ever-popular Why do jeans never fit me? You can go to her website (www.kellynishimoto.com) if you want to see the couture corsets that inspired Becca's designs.

Turns out, fashion design is one of those occupations that *sounds* really glamorous and fun, but actually involves a lot of technical expertise, dogged persistence, and a sky-high threshold for criticism and rejection. Kind of like writing!

WHY DOES CLAIRE CONTEMPLATE GIVING UP HER CHILDREN? DO YOU THINK SHE'LL BE A GOOD MOTHER TO THE TWINS?

I think she'll be a very good mother and here's why: Claire thinks about giving up the twins not because she *doesn't* love them, but because she *does*. She wants her babies to attain what she sees as her ultimate goal: security. And she's willing to sacrifice to make that happen. But what she learns by the end of the book is that "security" does not necessarily equal "money."

There's security in love, both familial and romantic. There's security in learning to trust yourself to provide what you need. I think the healthiest relationships are those that encourage you to go beyond what you thought were your limits and, luckily, Andrew does that for Claire.

THIS BOOK FEATURES A YOUNGEST CHILD WITH TWO DOMINEERING OLDER SISTERS, WHILE YOUR FIRST BOOK, *MY FAVORITE MISTAKE,* IS ABOUT A RESPONSIBLE OLDEST SIBLING WITH A WILD YOUNGER SISTER. DO YOU HAVE SISTERS? ARE YOU THE OLDEST OR THE YOUNGEST?

I'm actually a middle child, and yes, I do have a sister. She's nothing at all like Claire (or like Skye from *My Favorite Mistake*); she's a very sweet, very stable physician. I have her home number on speed dial for when I need medical expertise for a scene. Or just have a sore throat. She loves it.

Like Becca and Claire, we used to act out scenes from *Annie* in our backyard, but I didn't always have to be Sandy the dog. Sometimes I got to be Molly, the sidekick orphan who's always getting dragged around by her ponytail.

WE CAN REALLY FEEL BECCA'S VISCERAL TERROR WHEN
SHE'S ABOUT TO JUMP OUT OF THE PLANE WITH
CONNOR. DID YOU GO SKYDIVING TO RESEARCH
THESE SCENES IN THE BOOK?

No. I am a total wuss, so I just interviewed my more daredevil
friends about their experiences. The freak accident that befalls
Connor in this book (double parachute failure) actually happened to my friend Wendy . . . on her very first jump. Needless
to say, there was no second jump. She was absolutely, 100 percent convinced that she was going to die, but she didn't. She
managed to get her emergency chute working and landed on
someone's roof. The homeowner was not amused.

Since I started asking around, I've heard about people
dying while hang gliding, body surfing, and cliff diving. So I'm
definitely not going skydiving now! I'll stick to my safe, earth-
bound hobbies of watching *Alias,* reading scary books about serial killers, and being a crazy dog lady.

Good girls go to heaven...

Naughty Girls go Downtown.

Introducing the Naughty Girls of Downtown Press!

Awaken Me Darkly
Gena Showalter
There's beauty in her strength—
and danger in her desires.

Lethal
Shari Shattuck
She has money to burn, looks to die for, and
other dangerous weapons.

The Givenchy Code
Julie Kenner
A million dollars will buy a lot of designer
couture—if she lives to wear it....

Dirty Little Secrets
Julie Leto
Love her, love her handcuffs.

Great storytelling just got a new attitude.

Visit the Naughty Girls at www.downtownpress.com.

A Division of Simon & Schuster
A VIACOM COMPANY

Naughty Girls

12919-2